SWING AND A MISS

AVEN ELLIS

Swing and a Miss

Copyright © 2018 Aven Ellis

Cover Design by Becky Monson

Formatting by AB Formatting

This book is a work of fiction. The names, characters, places, and incidents are the products of the author's imagination or are used fictitiously. Any resemblance to actual events, business establishments, locales, or persons, living or dead, is entirely coincidental.

CONNECT WITH AVEN

Amazon Author Page
Website
Facebook Page
Twitter
Facebook Reader Group

For Joanne
Thank you for your passion and willingness to take on any project I have. You made this book a better one.

ACKNOWLEDGMENTS

Thank you to Joanne Lui for her tremendous job editing this book. Your attention to detail is exactly what I need, and I love our collaborations. Thank you for taking on this project and putting your heart and soul into it.

Thank you Paula for the proofreading expertise. I adore you.

Thank you to Michelle and Gennifer, my Great Dane experts, for going above and beyond in answering questions, providing detailed information, and giving me all kinds of ideas for AJ and his dog crew. You were both a tremendous help!

Thank you to my Beta Baes. Thank you for always giving me what I need, and not just with the writing process. Thank you for reassurance, for reading, for being a part of my life every day. None of these books happen without you.

To Alexandra, my assistant. Thank you for being you on a daily basis and always being my calming center.

To the SJFC-thank you for reading, debating, and supporting every step I take. I love you girls to pieces!

Amanda and Claudia-Your love, friendship and support is always a given. I love you so much!

Alexa Aston, thank you for always providing your thoughts and your feedback. You are the best.

To my Twinnie, Holly Martin- Thank you for always reading my work, offering suggestions, helping me be a better author. But it is your friendship I value about all else. I love you.

Thank you to Jennifer, my sister of the heart, who runs the Aven Ellis reader group on Facebook (Kate, Skates, and Coffee Cakes.) You are always there for me no matter what. I couldn't do this without you!

The Aven Ellis ARC Team-thank you for wanting to read my words and review my books. I'm so lucky to have such an amazing group of readers with me, no matter what adventure we take!

A big huge thank you to Amy Barnes and Jenn Passero for the DC expertise. I value you both not only as my beta readers but as my friends even more so.

Finally, thank you to all my readers. None of this happens without your support. I'm truly blessed.

CHAPTER 1

Playlist Shuffle Song of the Day:
"Into You" by Ariana Grande

I wipe down the glass countertop at Scones and Such. It's been so slow on this Sunday evening. I have twenty minutes to go before we close.

It's a sticky June night, and everyone is apparently somewhere else rather than at the coffee house where I work here in Georgetown.

There's a guy reading a book in the oversized leather chair in the corner. Two women are chatting away over iced coffees.

That's it.

Slooooooooooooooooooooooooow.

I'd rather be busy than have nothing to do.

Wait. I take that back. Unless that means I have to help make coffee drinks, because I'm the worst barista at Scones and Such. Making coffee drinks stresses me out, and I always get some ratio wrong.

I swear if it weren't for my work ethic and positive attitude, my ass would have been canned when I started working here around classes at Georgetown University my junior year.

I continue to wipe the glass that I cleaned just an hour ago. It's spotless. I can see my reflection perfectly in it, and thanks to the humidity, my brown curls have gone all Mufasa again, like *The Lion King* character. I feel like I have a huge mane when the curls get springy.

I think I've killed another three minutes re-wiping the glass.

Michael, the barista whiz who is one of my co-workers tonight, has his phone out. I feel guilty looking at my phone while I'm working, so I don't. If I did have it out, I would be reading assignments from the law school boot camp prep webinar I'm taking.

But since Michael doesn't have such deep conflictions, I decide to ask him to check something for me.

"Michael, can you give me the final score of the Soaring Eagles game?"

I know they played a day game, and as a baseball addict, I need to find out if they won.

It's imperative to my baseball-obsessed soul.

Michael smirks at me. "Will the baseball score be sufficient? Or do you want to know what AJ's box score looks like? By the way, as someone who is entering law school this fall, you do understand stalking is an illegal activity, right?"

I feel a blush growing across my cheeks. AJ Williamson, the star outfielder for the Soaring Eagles, has been my celebrity crush since he was in the minor leagues.

I shoot Michael a mock glare. "I'm not stalking him. I *met* him because his best friend is dating my best friend, so I have an interest in both the final score and his at bats tonight, thank you very much."

Michael doesn't have to know I got so nervous meeting him that I fainted on him and became a babbling idiot, but who can blame me? I've followed AJ's career since he was drafted by the Soaring Eagles. A few months ago, my roommate, Hayley Carter, started dating the catcher for the Soaring Eagles. If she wasn't so sweet and adorable, and if she wasn't perfect for Brody Jensen, I'd be jealous of that fact.

Then I grin. Nah, I wouldn't.

Because Brody's not AJ.

I pause for a moment. Despite that fact, and even though AJ was super nice when I passed out on him and rambled a bunch of nonsense at him, there would be nothing but disappointment if I were—haha!—to go on a date with him. It would no doubt ruin everything. I mean, he's a celebrity crush. He can never be what I think he would be. More to the point, I have no idea who he is outside of his TV and social media interviews. Anybody can sound good in a sound bite, especially when they are dark-haired and green-eyed and have a dimple in their cheek when they smile. AJ throws up Instagram posts with his group of dude friends, things he's seen, or of his three Great Dane rescue dogs, but that's all I know of him.

I mean, these things are interesting. Make him attractive. Along with the fact that he plays the sport I have loved since my father took me to Soaring Eagles games as a little girl.

But I have no clue who he is.

The real AJ is bound to be very different than my crush AJ. Which would be so disappointing if I ever did go out with him.

Which is ridiculous, because after my intro, there's no way AJ would ever ask out an incoherent Mufasa lookalike.

Therefore, my fictional dating AJ crisis is completely resolved, I think as I repress a smile.

"Final score: Soaring Eagles five, Texas Rattlesnakes zero," Michael reads off. "AJ had four AB, two R, two H, zero BB, and three RBI."

I repress a giggle. Michael is totally into alternate world video games and could care less about sports. AJ had a stellar

3

night, with two runs, two base hits, zero base on balls and three runs batted in. Oh, I can't wait to watch it when I get home.

"Thank you," I say, taking inventory of what's left in the pastry case. If all goes well in the next two hours, I'll be able to take home a cinnamon roll. They're like the size of your head and have a super thick smear of frosting. While I hear a lot of customers say they are too big, I can easily plow through one by myself.

At times like this, I love my super-high metabolism.

A chair scrapes across the hardwood floor, and I glance up. The two women are getting up, both talking and laughing. They are in their forties, and I smile as I watch them. They have been here for a good two hours, and I know that will be Hayley and me in the future. We're like that now, and we've been that bonded since we met at Georgetown University. No matter where the future takes us, we'll always be the friends who can sit around for hours and find joy in simply having one of "our" conversations.

As they open the door to leave, I pick up my spray bottle and cloth and head over to their table. Yay! I can kill another thirty seconds with an activity.

I find working at the coffee shop strangely relaxing—as long as I don't have to make complicated coffee orders. I know that sounds weird, but I know law school is going to be incredibly hard and my mind is going to be overwhelmed, so I decided to work here this summer as a way to decompress before starting school in August.

It's funny. When I told my parents I was going to work at a coffee house, they were surprised. Mainly because they have always provided me with everything I need. My heart warms when I think about them. My parents are both successful, driven people, with Dad being a cardiologist and Mom working as a dietician. My sister, Meghan, and I have never wanted for anything—material or emotional. I grew up in one house, a colonial row house in this Georgetown neighborhood that has been in the family for more than a hundred years. A home filled with laughter and love.

Which is exactly why it was important that I started earning my own money. I wanted to work. My parents said they worked hard so Meghan and I could have "experiences" and not have to stress over studying and juggling a job, and I'm so appreciative of that. But I also wanted a job outside my comfort zone, i.e., not an office environment. I started going to Scones and Such when I was an undergrad, and the people working here were so nice. Elise, who owns Scones and Such, always took time to talk to her customers and did everything to make a cozy, lingering space for all who walked through her door. Finally, I simply asked if I could apply for a job, and after she sat down and had a cup of coffee with me, I was hired.

While I've done an internship at a well-known DC law firm the past few summers, I always kept a couple of hours a week at Scones and Such. I love talking to our regular customers and knowing their usual orders. I like quietly observing people. I've seen first dates. Old friends lingering over empty latte cups. People lost to their world on their laptops, and I can't help but wonder what they are doing. Working remote? Chatting with a friend on social media? Deciding to swipe left or right on Tinder? Writing a novel?

I've seen breakups. Interviews. Teens being silly.

I'm watching all aspects of life from my spot behind the counter.

It's fascinating. Beautiful. Sad. Hopeful. Lonely. Optimistic. Happy.

I'm participating, if only by observation, in the human experience.

And I feel lucky to be able to do so.

I walk back to the counter, where Elise has come out from her office. She opened Scones and Such after her divorce, and it is her baby. She's in her mid-forties, and having this coffee shop is something she had always dreamed of. She has made it her life passion. It shows, too. Elise has run this shop for several years now, while others have come and gone all around the neighborhood. She's a warm person who cares about her product and her customers, and she's rewarded with great reviews on Yelp and incredibly loyal patrons.

The music on the eclectic soundtrack moves to another folk song, and I inwardly sigh. I know it's perfect coffee house music, but I would love to hear something with a little more oomph.

"What's the sigh for?" Elise asks as she dumps a bag of coffee into the grinder.

What? Did that inward sigh escape?

"I was thinking I'd love to hear a song from my personal playlist right now," I admit sheepishly.

Elise smiles as she adjusts the grind setting. "And what would that be?"

"Beyoncé's 'Single Ladies,'" Michael teases.

"You're so funny," I say.

"Besides, we know that's my anthem," Elise chimes in.

"I wouldn't steal another woman's anthem," I say, grinning.

"So, what would be your song?"

I think of the first song that came up when I shuffled my Spotify this morning. It was Ariana Grande's "Into You," but oy, revealing that would give Michael ammunition to be annoying all summer long.

"'Dangerous Woman,'" I say, giving Michael a pointed look.

Elise grins. Michael cocks an eyebrow.

Once again, my on-the-spot-thinking skills come in handy. One of my gifts that will help me when I'm a trial lawyer in the future.

"Katie, would you mind grinding five of these bags? We

just received an online order for them. I've got the shipping label printed and the box ready, if you don't mind preparing the coffee."

Whew. As long as she isn't asking me to make five lavender-syrup infused soy milk lattes, I'm good with this task.

Of course, nobody asks me to make coffee drinks at Scones and Such. Even at peak hours, when the line is snaking toward the back of the door, I man the cash register and take orders.

I don't even think I'm allowed to stand near the espresso machine due to my bad coffee-making juju.

"Of course," I say, happy to have another clock-killing task.

"Thank you. All our Italian roast, all espresso grind," Elise says.

"Yes, ma'am."

Elise rolls her eyes, and I smile. She hates when I call her that, so I do it just to tease her.

She heads through the dark-wood swinging door and enters the back. I set about grinding the bags of coffee beans, inhaling the rich aroma of the darker roast. You think I'd be sick of this smell after working here for two years, but I'm not. There's something both seductive and comforting about the scent of coffee to me.

I finish the last bag and close it up, putting our signature Scones and Such seal on it, carefully smoothing the wrinkles out by lightly going over it with my thumb. Elise has drilled into us that presentation is everything. I agree with her. I look around the café, with its exposed brick walls, vintage floor lamps, and clubby leather chairs. The floors are a rustic hardwood, and there are large, arched windows that provide a view of the street. Chalkboards have the specials written out in beautiful lettering and pictures, thanks to Patrick, our barista who is studying art, and carefully selected historical drawings of iconic DC images are in vintage frames, hung around the walls of the small shop.

It has a cozy, dark, intimate vibe, one that says tuck your feet up under you in a chair, nibble on one of the goodies from the pastry case, and leisurely sip a big cup of tea or coffee.

"I'm going to run to the restroom," Michael says. "Do you want me to take those back for you?"

He inclines his head to the bags of coffee I have resting next to the grinder.

I glance at the sole customer, who is now standing up and closing his laptop.

"Don't worry, if anyone comes in I'll be right out," he teases.

"Oh, shut up," I say, grinning. "And thank you."

Michael grins back and scoops up the bags, disappearing through the swinging door.

The last customer leaves, heading out into the night. I busy myself by going over to clean his table. I glance out into the street, which is quiet this Sunday. The lampposts shine down on the cobblestone walk, illuminating it, and if I crane my neck just right, I can see the sliver of a crescent moon shining in the velvety-black sky.

I finish up and head back behind the counter. I take a moment to clean my hands, and once again, the lure of the pastry case beckons me. In addition to the fantastic smell of coffee, I love the smell of sweets. Of frosting and butter and glazes. I bend down lower, taking inspection of the bottom shelf. Yes. In addition to my cinnamon roll, there are two scones left: maple bacon and my favorite, double cherry with almond glaze.

Perfect. If all goes well, I'll be starting my morning with a cinnamon roll and a cherry scone.

I might be tall and rail thin with no curves, but I can eat both things and not gain an ounce.

I'll keep skinny and no boobs with a scone in one hand and a cinnamon roll in the other and claim victory is mine.

The chimes against the door jangle, signaling another customer.

I rise, armed with my smile and ready to give my "Welcome to Scones and Such," greeting.

But no words come out. None. In fact, I know my mouth has fallen open in shock.

Because the customer in the door is none other than AJ Williamson.

CHAPTER 2

I don't need a mirror to know my eyes are bulging out of my head like a ridiculous cartoon character. Or like Marty Feldman in the classic movie *Young Frankenstein*, if you care for a retro reference.

I don't know what to do. Diving under the counter isn't an option. Well, and the fact that our counters are glass make that the equivalent of hiding in a goldfish bowl.

My brain clicks to life as AJ approaches the counter. There's no way he'll remember me. We saw each other once. In April.

Of course, I fainted on him so that might be a bit of a memory keeper.

But he's AJ Williamson. Gorgeous, famous, professional athlete. He's distracted by beautiful women all the time, I'm sure, chasing from one to another the way Hayley's cat, Pissy, chases that dumb laser light toy that Brody uses. Oh! Sexy blonde! Wait, stunning brunette! Let's go there. He wouldn't remember a sweaty one with Mufasa hair.

Let's hope so.

AJ walks slowly across the café, and I'm becoming more of

a wreck with each step he takes across the creaky wooden floor.

How is he more gorgeous than I remember him being?

I take in his jet-black hair, swept back off his handsome face with some product. The vivid green eyes, ones that remind me of emeralds. The strong cheekbones. The way his shoulders are broad and how I can see his muscular biceps revealed by his gray T-shirt. The sexy veins running through his arms and… crap, I'm so screwed.

AJ stops at the counter, his eyes moving over our vast selection of drink options. I hold on to the cash register's sides for support.

If AJ remembered me, he'd greet me by now. He'd remember my name, or study me and say I seem familiar.

Crisis. Averted.

So now I'll just inhale the delicious cologne that is lingering on his tanned skin and sneak peeks at those amazing arms up close. They aren't tattooed like most athletes' are. I'll write his order on his cup, and Michael will come out and make his drink, and I'll laugh about this whole episode with Hayley later.

"Hmm," AJ says, his gaze continuing to move from drink description to drink description.

My brain gives me a shove. *He's a customer, dipshit. Treat him like one.*

"Welcome to Scones and Such," I blurt out as my brain pushes me into action. "May I help you?"

AJ slowly shifts his gaze back to me, and my breath catches in my throat the second those emerald green eyes connect with mine.

"That's a rather formal greeting considering you've had your head in my lap and advised me all food is served better in a helmet, *Katie*."

GAH!

The blood rushes to my head. I feel dizzy. Maybe I should pretend to faint, so I can escape this situation.

But AJ's so freaking nice he'd probably leap over the counter, scoop me up, and escort me to the hospital.

"You do remember me," I say, capitulating to the realization that this is what it is. AJ is here. He remembers me. Wait. Why is AJ here? Random chance? But he doesn't look surprised to see me, and since he knows who I am, that's weird. I follow up on my thought. "What are you doing here?"

"Brody recommended this place," AJ says casually.

Ah. Now this makes sense. I'll take his drink order, and he'll be off, headed back onto the streets of Georgetown with his coffee in hand.

AJ flashes me a grin and, oh damn, yes, that's just as sexy as I remember, even though my brain was in a complete post-fainting fog.

"It's kind of hard to forget someone fainting on you," AJ says, his eyes twinkling. "Or the conversation we had."

"I wish I could blame fainting for the babble that came out of my mouth, but I won't. That would be a lie."

"And future lawyers don't lie."

I furrow my brow. How does he know that? Brody must have told him.

"This future lawyer won't. Now, I'm going to tell you the truth. Because I think you can handle it, unlike what Jack Nicholson told Tom Cruise in one very famous legal movie."

This is a test. I'm eclectic. That's a nice way of saying I'm weird, but I am. And I embrace it. I love to refer to old movies for two reasons. One, I'm a movie junkie. I will watch anything to say I've seen it. I like to see if other people have seen what I have, especially if they are old movies. Two, I can see if people can handle the freak flag I'm waving. Thank you, Luke Wilson in *The Family Stone*, for that one.

"*A Few Good Men,* and go on. Like Frasier Crane, *I'm listening.*"

Whoa! AJ not only got the movie reference but now he's quoting TV shows?

I remind myself that is not a reason to elevate my crush on him.

The back door swings open, and Michael reappears before I can answer.

He stares at AJ and furrows his brow. Then his eyebrows shoot straight up as the light bulb goes off in his head.

"Wait, you're the dude from her phone!" he cries, his face lighting up in recognition.

I hate Michael.

"I'm on your phone?" AJ asks, raising an eyebrow at me.

Great. I was okay with flying my freak flag, but I'm not okay with looking like a stalker.

"The Soaring Eagles app is on my phone," I say, shooting Michael a "shut up" look.

Michael bursts out laughing. "She loves your *stats.* Katie has a particular interest in your personal ones."

Oh, dear God. Now it sounds like I'm obsessing over his height and weight rather than the distance of the home runs he crushes on a regular basis.

"Hmm. Any particular kind of stat?" AJ asks, flashing me a wicked grin.

He's so toying with me. I give up and react like I would to anyone else.

I give him an exaggerated eye roll. "Your game stats. Which were fantastic today. Congratulations."

He laughs. "Thank you."

"Did you get his drink order?" Michael asks, moving over to the espresso machine. "I'll get it started."

"Why can't Katie make it?" AJ asks.

Shit.

Since there is no other customer in the café, I tell the truth.

"I suck at making coffee," I say.

AJ appears confused. "Yet you work in a coffee house?"

"It's also a scone shop."

"So, you're good at making scones?" AJ asks.

"I'm extremely good at helping people pick the right scone to meet their scone personality," I counter.

"There's a scone personality test?" AJ asks.

My heart flutters. A man who can engage in rapid-fire conversation is freaking hot.

Like AJ needed to add to his already smokin' hotness ranking.

"Absolutely."

AJ wanders down the counter, to the part of the case that displays what is left of the scones.

"Now, you have to understand we are near closing," I explain. "So, our selection is down to two options today. Normally, I would have five in order to conduct this test."

"So, this isn't a valid sampling," AJ says.

So. Hot.

I clear my throat. "Exactly. My testing won't be quite accurate. Because I'm looking at two scones, the cherry almond and the maple bacon, there's only one obvious question for you today. Do you prefer a fruit-based scone or not?"

AJ laughs. "This is a horrible test tonight."

I laugh, too. "I agree."

"Which one do you prefer?" he asks.

"They are both very good," I say. "But I love the cherry almond one. Very delicate, with an almond extract glaze that I can eat by the bucket full."

"That's a lot of glaze."

"It's that good."

"That's enough of an endorsement for me. I'll take that one," AJ says, tapping the glass where the last cherry almond scone is.

Dammit. There go my scone dreams for tomorrow.

"And how about a maple bacon one, too."

"Absolutely," I say, retrieving a pastry box. "I can confirm that one has the perfect balance of sweet and salt."

"Is the maple glaze bucket-worthy, though?" AJ asks.

I chuckle. "Only because I prefer almond to maple, I'd have to say no. But that is a personal opinion, not a statement of fact."

Michael snorts, and we both glance at him, where he's watching us in obvious amusement.

I turn back to AJ and decide I will find a way to get even with him the next time we work together.

"I'll still say that's a fair endorsement," AJ says, scanning what's left in the case. "How about the cinnamon roll?"

Inside, I cry all the tears for my lost breakfast.

"Outstanding, if you love icing."

"Then I might as well clean out the case."

I retrieve the cinnamon roll and add it to his box.

"What coffee drink do you recommend?" AJ asks.

"Am I making it or is Michael making it?"

AJ smiles. "Let's say Michael is making it."

"Wise choice," Michael chimes in.

I ignore him. "I like an amaretto latte."

"And if you are making it?"

"Plain hot coffee with cream," I say, grinning at him. "It comes straight from the dispenser. Even I can make that."

"Then how about two large hot coffees with cream."

"Two?"

"Well, it's a nice night. You're about to close. Care to find a park bench and have a coffee with me?"

CHAPTER 3

I stare at him, wrinkling my brow.

What? Did AJ just ask me to have a coffee with him?

No, I must have misunderstood.

I'm the loon who fainted on him. There's *no way* AJ wants to hang out with me over cups of coffee.

Right?

"Is that a no?" AJ asks, interrupting my frazzled thoughts.

"Is this some kind of social curiosity thing?" I ask.

AJ appears confused.

"What?"

"Like you want to know more about me because I'm intriguingly odd. Is that why you want to get a coffee with me?"

Michael snorts as he takes it upon himself to get the coffee and cream AJ ordered. "You are being asked out, you dope."

I'm sure I look like a beet.

"Shut up," I snap at Michael.

"Well, you are," AJ confirms.

I shift my attention back to AJ. "I am?" I ask, shocked.

I give AJ my skeptical eye. The look I'm practicing for when I'm a lawyer in court someday.

"Yeah, you are," AJ says.

"And not because I'm weird?"

"Well, the fact that you're weird is a huge part of it," AJ confirms.

"So, you're looking at this from an entertainment prospective?" I inquire.

Before AJ can reply, Elise comes through the door, goes to the front, flips the "open" sign to "closed" on the door, and turns the lock.

"Katie, this young man shouldn't have to prepare a legal brief to make his case for a cup of coffee," Elise says. "If you say yes, you can leave now. I'll clock you out. We can handle cleanup without you tonight."

"Please say yes," Michael says as he slides the coffees over to us. "I'll gladly clean on your behalf so we don't have to keep listening to this."

"I'm sorry," I say, apologizing to AJ.

"I'm sorry as in no?" AJ asks, a disappointed expression filtering across his handsome face.

"I'm sorry I didn't say yes the first time you asked. Yes."

AJ flashes me a grin, and I find myself smiling back at him.

"I'll be right back," I say.

I scurry to the back room, take off my apron, and grab my nylon Kate Spade backpack. I shove my apron inside and pop into the employee restroom.

Crap.

My Mufasa hair is wild, the brown curls springing out of control. And as far as any future oil crisis, the nation needs to fear not. There is enough oil on my T-zone to fuel all the cars in the continental United States.

I fumble in my backpack for my makeup kit. *Come on, come on.* I shake my backpack sideways, balancing it against my knee, trying to find my oil blotting tissues. Lip gloss, no. Wallet, no. Ah-ha!

I pick it up and open it.

It's empty.

I internally do an *AAUGH* like a character on the *Peanuts* cartoon.

I exhale in defeat and chance another look in the mirror.

Crazy hair? Check

Makeup a grease pit? Check

Dressed in uniform of black T-shirt and jeans, with bonus of smelling like vanilla and dusted with flour? Check

AJ asking me for coffee after seeing this? A MYSTERY FOR THE AGES.

Screw it. He stood at the counter talking to me for five minutes. He knows what he's getting.

Me. In the rawest form.

I retrieve my Kate Spade black silk scarf with white polka dots and tie my out-of-control mane back with it. Hmm. I like the scarf in my hair, but it does draw attention to my round face and my oil slick. Which do I trade for?

I go with the hair under control look and head back into the café, where AJ is waiting.

I stop right in the doorway.

This is happening.

AJ is here. He asked me for a cup of coffee.

And now I'm leaving with him.

It's so surreal I don't have time to panic.

"Ready?" AJ asks, handing me a cup of coffee.

"Yeah," I say, smiling at him. "Thank you."

"Here, I'll let you out," Elise says, walking to the door and unlocking it. She pushes it open, and AJ escorts me out onto the streets of Georgetown. "Have a nice night!"

If she winks at me, I swear I'll quit.

Instead, she gives me a big, huge, toothy smile, which is nearly as obvious.

Insert mental *AAUGH* scream number two.

Finally, I'm standing on the sidewalk. With AJ.

"This is your neighborhood," AJ says, staring down at me. "Where's a good place for us to go?"

"Have you ever seen the C&O Canal behind M Street?" I ask.

"No," AJ says, shaking his head.

"Okay, this is a gem. Let's go there," I say. "We'll head over to M Street; it's right behind it."

I begin to walk down 34th Street, and AJ falls into step next to me as we move past row houses on the cobblestone streets.

"Do you realize I've never sweated out a girl saying yes to a cup of coffee before?" AJ asks as we pass a white brick home with beautiful bay windows.

I smile. "How many girls have you blindly asked out for coffee? Be honest."

"Blindly?"

"Yeah. Just show up and hope she says yes."

AJ pauses and takes a sip of his coffee. "One."

"So, I'm the second?"

"You're the first."

I stop walking.

"Okay, I have to ask. Why me? Why now? Why when I have Mufasa hair and a T-zone Sunoco could tap for oil?"

"Katie," AJ says, his eyes searching mine, "This is why."

I kind of can't speak after hearing how magical my name sounded coming from his lips.

"I wish I didn't have to say it's because you are different, because that's such a freaking cliché, but you are. You have this rapid-fire brain. After you fainted, you said the most interesting, off-the-wall things. You said what you thought. And I can't get that night out of my head."

I don't think I can breathe.

"You can't?" I repeat, stunned by his revelation.

AJ starts to walk again, and I move with him, my brain whirling from what he revealed.

"I like that you say what you think," AJ says as we go

down a small hill, passing under streetlamps and more illuminated windows in row houses. "You aren't thinking about what you say. You aren't curating."

He's smart, I think. Using a word like curating tells me all I need to know.

"I've dated a lot. I've been through painful conversations. I've been bored. I've had women say what they think I want to hear. I've talked to girls where after the initial introduction, we have nothing in common. So lately, it's been easier to hang out with the guys, you know?"

I nod. "I get that. My last date stood me up."

"No."

I laugh. "Oh, yes. It was my first and only attempt on an online dating app. A few weeks before Hayley met Brody. I met this guy. Pre-law, blah blah, and he suggested we meet at an Italian restaurant on the Capitol Riverfront. So, I get decked out—" I pause and flash him an apologetic smile. "Sorry, you didn't get that Katie tonight, but I flat-ironed my hair. Put on killer heels. I even wore a padded bra to make up for my lack of boobs for this guy, so I was going all out!"

AJ is laughing, so I keep going.

"I arrive there ten minutes early, and yes, Trace did make a reservation, so I'm seated. I ordered a wine, waited. Waited thirty minutes, th—"

"Whoa, you should have pulled that trigger at twenty unless he texted."

"I'll keep that in mind, Mr. Williamson," I say, flirting with him. "If you ever leave me waiting for twenty-one minutes, I'm out."

"I will never keep you waiting without a text," AJ says. "I will even text you if I'm going to be five minutes late. Now please tell me you left."

"No," I say, shaking my head. "The thing was, I was starving. And I could smell Italian food, which is one of the best smells in the entire world. So I thought, fine, dinner for one. So, I treated myself to dinner. And it was lovely."

"What did you have?"

"Well, it wasn't a pity meal, or that would have been a lot of lasagna. That's my comfort food. But I didn't feel like I was missing anything by being stood up by a law student named Trace, so I had wild mushroom rigatoni, a full-bodied red wine, and bread, and it was delicious. My brain is amazing company, since it never shuts off, so I was, if I do say so myself, a charming and witty date."

"Well played, Ms. McKenna," AJ says, grinning.

"I think so."

"What is this place?" AJ asks, pausing in front of a narrow, white-bricked row house. "Curry and Pie?"

I shoot him a mischievous grin. "It's not curry and dessert, if that's where your brain is going."

"I'm going to guess curry and pizza?"

"Ding! You win. It is a curry and pizza place, and it's delicious."

"What do you order here?"

"The saag paneer pizza," I say, taking another sip of my french roast. "Indian curry on a pizza. Italian and Indian fused together for an unexpected yet harmonious delight."

"Are you sure you don't want to be a food critic?" AJ asks. "Because you made that sound good, and I have no idea what paneer whatever-you-said is."

I smile. "Nah, I'll stick to law. Anyway, let's go down past M Street here," I say, and we begin to walk again.

Soon, we are at a street light where we will cross M Street, heading down past the Francis Scott Key Memorial Park. I sneak another look at him. I can't believe I'm standing here with AJ Williamson. AJ, whose career I have followed as he came up in the Soaring Eagles system. AJ, of whom I have a stash of pictures saved in my phone because he's so damn hot.

It's so absurd, I burst out laughing.

"What?" AJ asks, a bemused look on his face.

"You have to understand, this is totally weird. I'm a huge baseball fan. My parents have had season tickets since I was a kid. Fourth of July is coming up, and watching you play has been a part of that for me. Our family Fourth of July holidays revolve around the Soaring Eagles homestand that week, with watching the fireworks on the third and going to the early game on the Fourth. This is surreal, that I'm talking to you instead of watching you on the field."

AJ's expression changes, and I wonder what I've said wrong.

"AJ?" I ask as traffic whizzes by us.

"You've had the realization moment, haven't you?"

"I don't understand what you mean."

The light changes, and we walk on the crosswalk. As soon as we hit the other side of 34th Street, AJ exhales.

"You see me as the baseball star," AJ says, and I can't get over the sadness that is reflected in his eyes at this moment. "It's a completely normal reaction on your part. It comes with being famous. I get it."

"No, this is the funny thing, AJ," I say, shaking my head. "Yes, there is this very strange element of knowing I've seen you on TV and on the baseball field and that you are famous. That my neighbor, Dominik, and I have broken down your stats over babka and coffee. So yes, it is a little crazy that I'm walking with you tonight and if I reach out, I can touch your arm. But there's this bigger, more fascinating part."

AJ stops walking and gazes down at me.

"You're interesting," I continue. "I've only begun to scratch the surface here. So, if we throw the whole baseball player thing aside for now, I'd like to keep talking to you. AJ. Not about your batting average, but how on earth did you pull out a *Frasier* reference? How have you retained your Midwestern accent perfectly? If you like movies. Are you an adventurous eater? Do you wonder why Brody and Hayley eat so much cereal, like they would *die* if they somehow ran out?"

I see the sadness dissipate in his green eyes.

"That cereal thing they do is weird," AJ says, a smile tugging at the corner of his mouth.

"It is! Do you know they follow Instagrammers who talk about cereal so they know what new ones are coming out? I mean, who does that?"

"I think you tagged the wrong person as being weird," AJ says.

"You're right. I take it back," I joke. But then I grow serious. "We haven't even spent an hour together, and already a million questions for you are running through my mind. And none of them have to do with the game that made me aware of you. I know the man who wears a baseball uniform. I remember the guy in the white dress shirt who kept me from falling to the floor in a stadium. But it's this man standing in front of me in a gray T-shirt who has my attention at the moment. Now, do I have to file a deposition, or will you willingly continue this very odd yet engaging conversation?"

AJ cocks an eyebrow at me.

"You aren't an attorney yet. You can't make me sit for a deposition."

"That's a very minor detail."

"Oh, I'd say it's a major one."

"You are wasting valuable interview time on this."

"So now it's an interview?" AJ asks, and I think he's rather enjoying this.

"Well, it would be a mutual interview. Assuming you want to know more about me, too," I say. "And since you are the one who asked me for coffee, I am drawing the conclusion that this would be the case."

AJ stares down at me, as if he's processing everything I've just spit out at him.

Then I go serious again, as I need AJ to believe me. "AJ. I promise you, I'm not standing on this street corner right now wanting to know the Soaring Eagle I've watched run across the grass, throw his body against the wall, and take back what was sure to be a home run. I want to know this stranger standing in front of me, who now isn't sure if he's talking to a superfan or a girl from Scones and Such who can't make coffee."

His expression changes to one of surprise. I don't think he's ever had a girl talk to him with such raw honesty before.

"I won't lie, I am a fan," I say gently. "But I'm also a girl who is a mess, who is incredibly weird, who is intrigued by the guy standing before her. I want to know you. If you will let me. So we can head down this sidewalk, go over a bridge, and walk along the canal, or we can go back and forget this happened. It's up to you."

As I study his handsome face, I find myself holding my breath. Because every word I said was true. I do want to know AJ, and just AJ, tonight.

And it's up to him whether I get that chance—or not.

CHAPTER 4

Those emerald green eyes never waver. My heart begins to pound rapidly against my ribs.

I don't want him to say yes because he's a ballplayer. I'm not worried he can't live up to the image of him I've scripted in my head.

Because he already has, simply by being AJ Williamson, the man who showed up in Scones and Such tonight.

"Well, you've already been stood up once, so if I bailed now, I'd be an ass," he says, a smile once again tugging at the corner of his mouth.

"So?"

"So, I'm not going anywhere. I believe you, Katie," AJ says softly. "You're not a fan right now."

"No, I'm not," I reply, my heart hammering now. "I'm just a girl. One who wants to get to know you."

"Then let's do it. Starting with this canal," AJ says, gesturing for me to lead the way.

We walk down the sidewalk, passing the memorial park as we head toward the Towpath. I have such a feeling of excitement within me. I feel like I'm setting off on a fact-finding mission with this sexy, intriguing man.

"This canal," I say, "is called the Chesapeake & Ohio Canal. It runs along the Potomac River, 184.5 miles to be exact —all the way up to Cumberland, Maryland—and was used to move goods to communities along the river."

"Good thing I bought the pastries," AJ jokes. "Maryland will be a long walk."

I laugh and continue. "The Towpath is a great place to walk, and I use it all the time to avoid the sidewalk traffic on M Street. I pop down here, walk, and pop back up when I'm near my destination. Some parts of it are so beautiful, and I love walking past all these colonial houses. It always reminds me of how I'm a mere fragment in the history of Georgetown."

We reach the point where there is a pedestrian bridge that goes over the canal.

"Now, we can cross here, take a left, and go down the Towpath, past 33rd Street. There are some tables and chairs down there, where we can sit and talk. I'm sorry, I just realized I'm leading you on a very roundabout walk through Georgetown."

"I'm the one who suggested we take a walk, remember?"

"Oh, yeah. So, this is on you," I tease.

"Well, to be fair, I didn't tell you to take me on a roundabout tour of Georgetown," AJ says, shooting me a side eye that makes me snicker.

"Okay, so I'd make a terrible city tour guide. Which is sad because I've lived here my entire life."

"You've only lived in DC?"

"Think smaller. I was born and raised in Georgetown. Same house my whole life. I didn't even move out until I met Hayley and we got an apartment in Arlington."

"Seriously? The same house even?"

"Yes, same row house, East Village. Now even weirder: the original house was built in 1910, and it has been in my family that entire time."

"Wow. No shit?"

"I shit you not," I tease, taking a sip of my coffee.

"I can't even imagine. I've moved my entire life."

"How so?" I ask as we walk across the bridge.

"All over the Midwest. I went through one stretch where I went to three schools in four years."

I gasp. "AJ, that must have been awful. Starting over at a new school once is hard; I can't imagine doing it over and over like that. How did that make you feel?"

AJ continues to talk as we come down the other side. "Surprisingly, when you realize you are never going to stay someplace, it makes it easier. Whenever we moved, it was never home. Oh, my parents said it was home, this time we'd stay, blah, blah, but I knew better. Dad was a software engineer, and he's always got the opportunity for a better job. Combine that with his wanderlust? Well, if an interesting job came along, he took it. He just couldn't resist the opportunity for change. But his one thing was it had to be in the Midwest; that was the one place he truly liked to live. So, you name a state in that area, I've lived there."

"That's why your accent is so strong."

"What accent?" AJ asks as we continue our endless walk of Georgetown.

"You've got to be kidding! You have that total Midwest accent. Say this: I'm getting my bags."

"*What?*" AJ asks, laughing.

"Humor me. I'll prove my point."

"I'm getting my bags."

"Ah! You have such a strong one. Your bags sounds like *begs*."

"What? That is crazy. I said *bags*."

"Begs."

"Begs."

AJ stops next to a condominium building and gestures toward the stone wall next to it. "It's not a table and chairs, but could this work?"

I nod and take a seat on the ledge. AJ follows suit. He glances over at me as a warm summer wind blows across us, carrying the scent of his cologne toward me. Goosebumps prickle my skin. I remember it from when he held me after I fainted. Crisp and clean.

And absolutely divine.

"I can see why you would be a good lawyer," AJ says, interrupting my thoughts. "You like to argue, don't you?"

I laugh. "No, I really don't. Unless I feel someone is wrong. Or someone needs defending."

"What kind of law do you want to practice?"

"Employment law."

"Interesting. What made you pick that area as your focus?" AJ asks, taking a sip of his coffee.

I hesitate. This story is personal. Serious. And I don't want to mess up a fun evening by sharing this with AJ.

"You don't want to tell me, do you?" AJ asks.

I blink. "What?"

"Your expression changed when I asked you why."

"It's not that I don't want to tell you," I say slowly. "But it's serious, and I don't want to ruin our getting-to-know-you conversation with it."

"Katie, it's up to you whether you tell me or not, but please don't think you need to edit your story to keep things light. I didn't ask you to join me tonight with the intention that you would keep me entertained all evening. I asked you to have coffee with me because I find you intriguing. I find *depth* intriguing. I want to learn about *you*."

My breath catches in my throat. I'm moved by his words. And as I hear the water lap in the canal and see the lights from the building illuminate AJ's face in the darkness, I no longer see a baseball player I thought I knew.

I see the man who wants to know me.

"Very few people know this," I say softly, picking at the cardboard sleeve around my coffee cup. "But when I was a freshman at Georgetown, my initial interest was business. I wanted to work in sports management, and I had my whole path lined up. I was going to get my bachelor's, then get my MBA, and then I wanted to be a sports agent. I'm passionate about sports, and I like negotiating and reviewing documents. It seemed like a perfect fit."

I glance at AJ, who nods in understanding.

"I was so excited when I got an internship that spring semester at a sports and entertainment agency here in DC. This agency did everything, from preparing clients for draft day to working endorsement deals and developing community engagement plans. I was eager to do anything they asked, just to soak up the environment like a sponge. I even thought long-term. I wanted to do so well they would keep me on, maybe even offer me a job after I graduated and started working on my MBA at night."

I shift my gaze back to the canal, pausing for a moment, as this part of the story is hard for me to tell.

"I didn't know I was only one in a string of interns they hired for one quality only," I say softly. "I was hired because I was a young woman, and the agent I was assigned to help used these women for his sexual needs."

"Oh God," AJ gasps. "Katie."

I can't look at him. Humiliation burns in my face.

"I thought they wanted me because I was bright and ambitious. My boss made a comment the first week I was there. About how I should wear skirts more often, because that was feminine professional. And he bet my legs were amazing."

I turn to face AJ, whose is staring at me in shock.

"I honestly was so stunned I didn't say anything. Then, because time passed, I felt like I couldn't, because people would blame me for not filing a complaint immediately. It was my first internship. I didn't know what to do. I thought it would be best to ignore it, but then it escalated. He would drop things and ask me to pick them up, so he could check out my ass. Ask me to make copies, then come into the copy room and stand right behind me, so close I could feel his breath on the back of my neck. If I moved, he moved. I felt trapped. I made a plan that if he tried to touch me, I'd fight back. But he didn't. He loved knowing he was creeping me out, and he got off on that."

My voice grows wobbly, as this experience isn't easy for me to share. "Instead of this being an incredible career experience, it was an experience in sexual harassment. I was sick every day I went to work. I felt devalued. And powerless. Then I hated myself for not doing anything about it."

To my complete surprise, AJ reaches for the hand that I have resting on the stone wall between us. His skin is warm. Rough.

Comforting.

"You were a kid," AJ says, his eyes searching mine. "Don't be hard on that girl, Katie. You were harassed and preyed upon and you didn't know what to do. You had every right to expect you were entering a place where you would contribute and learn. And he took all of that away from you. This is all his fault, that sick bastard."

I wait for AJ to remove his hand after he speaks, but he doesn't.

And I don't want him to.

"So, what happened?" AJ asks, but this time, he picks up my hand and slowly threads his fingers through mine. He begins rubbing his thumb over the side of my hand.

I can't speak. All I'm aware of is how gentle his touch is, how AJ sensed my pain from talking about the past and instinctively wanted to comfort me. This is not the move of a guy who is bouncing from girl to girl, nor the guy looking for a hookup. When I see the concern in his emerald eyes, I know it's genuine.

And my heart tells me this is something different.

"I got sick of it," I say. "I gathered up all my courage and went to the internship coordinator. A woman." I laugh bitterly. "She told me that was just the way he was, the way men are, and it would be best for my career if I didn't take this to HR. That my life would become hell if that happened."

AJ stiffens beside me. His grip on my hand turns firmer, as if he's fighting back his own anger.

"That is disgusting, Katie," AJ says, his voice low. "They all knew, and they all hid it. And the woman who could have helped you buried you."

I bite my lip and nod.

"I'm so sorry. You never should have been put through that," AJ says, his voice taking on anger. "No person should."

I take a breath and continue.

"I quit the next day. I didn't tell anyone at first but Hayley, who wanted to get her Dad involved. He's a lawyer. She said I could file harassment charges and make sure this crap stopped, but I couldn't deal with that at that point. I just wanted to go to class and forget about it. But I couldn't. And then I got mad. Furious that some predator got away with treating me that way. With ruining what should have been an opportunity for me to learn. I thought, no, maybe this happened so I can stop it. I told my parents. I went to Hayley's dad, who got a friend of his who specializes in employment law onboard. We had a meeting with the owner of the agency and laid out what action we were willing to take if an investigation was not completed. Gemma Leary was the attorney. She's famous and a shark, and the owner of this firm wanted *nothing* to do with Gemma going to the press. Let's just say I was given a hefty payment, and after they completed their investigation, not only was that agent fired, but the internship coordinator as well."

AJ is silent for a moment as he takes in my story. "Holy shit, you took them down."

"I did."

"You have serious balls, Katie McKenna."

"I do," I say, smiling at him.

And from the smile he returns to me, I can tell AJ likes it.

"What happened next?"

"After what happened to me, and working with Gemma, I decided I was going to be a lawyer. I was going to help women who had been harassed. I was going to be that voice who helped. And now I can't imagine doing anything else. I've interned for Gemma every year since, but I took this summer off so I could decompress a bit before law school starts in the fall. All I'm doing is Scones and Such until August. Well, okay, that's a lie. I'm reading all kinds of books about preparing for law school and cases that interest me, filing notes on relevant articles on my laptop. And I have a law school prep course I'm doing online with webinars. I can't not read and study; it's a huge part of what makes me who I am."

"Katie, this is an amazing story," AJ says, shaking his head. "I'm so proud of you. Not just for fighting back, but for letting it define your future in a positive way."

He instinctively squeezes my hand in his after he speaks. I glance down at our entwined hands and back at AJ. He quickly removes his hand, and the second he does, I realize I want it back.

AJ clears his throat, but I decide to say what I'm feeling.

"I think I already miss your hand being where it was," I tell him over the pounding of my nervous heart.

I wonder if that was merely a comfort thing and that's why AJ removed his hand.

Slowly, AJ moves his hand toward mine. My heart is hammering against my ribs. I'm holding my breath. Will he take it again?

Then his huge hand, the one with the roughness that comes with playing baseball, reclaims mine in his.

Butterflies take off in force as AJ carefully laces his fingers with mine once again.

"Is that better?" he asks softly.

"Yes," I whisper.

AJ doesn't say anything, and neither do I.

"Good. Because I think so, too," he says quietly.

I can't breathe. My hand is entwined with his. Goosebumps prickle my skin.

As I stare at our hands again, I know the rest of the night is going to be amazing. I've shared something deeply personal with AJ, something that made me vulnerable, and AJ showed what kind of man he is in his response. He respects me. He's considerate.

He cares, I think as I lift my gaze to meet his. *AJ is genuine.*

And I know in my heart this night is going to change everything in my life. We've only started talking, but my gut is telling me this will be true. Everything will change from this moment on.

For the better.

CHAPTER 5

Best. Night. Ever.

I'm still sitting with AJ on the same wall, overlooking the canal as time stands still. We don't have phones out. AJ is wearing a watch, but he hasn't made a move to check it. All we want to do is talk and get to know each other, and with each question AJ answers, I find my crush on him taking a whole different direction.

Before tonight, AJ was my celebrity crush. The one I knew from Instagram and Soaring Eagles baseball broadcasts. I admired his jaw-dropping catches in the outfield. His powerful arm, one that can fire the ball to Brody on target to get a runner out at the plate. The way he can crush a ball and send it sailing 450 feet over the center field wall. One who was gorgeous and charming. A sports star who enjoyed the company of his best guy friends more than women.

That was AJ Williamson, the baseball player.

Tonight, however, I've met Andrew Joseph Williamson, or AJ ever since his younger sister, Lindsay, couldn't pronounce Andrew Joseph when she was a toddler.

AJ, the man, is becoming my new crush.

This man who loves big dogs and has rescued three Great

Danes that share his space in the Navy Yard area of DC. He's a mindless eater, and if you stick a bag of anything in front of him, he will eat his way through it. He likes fashion and enjoys breaking out a sharp suit. Because of the odd hours of baseball, he stays up at night and watches movies and TV, but not binge watching, because that ruins the experience of looking forward to the next episode for him.

"Your turn," AJ says, tearing off another piece of the cinnamon roll and popping it into his mouth.

I smile at him. AJ is sharing his haul from Scones and Such with me, as we both decided conversations are much better when there's food involved.

Now our conversation has evolved to a round of "this or that?"

"Amusement park or day at the beach?" I ask, arching an eyebrow at him.

"Pfft. Easy. Amusement park," AJ answers.

"May I ask a follow up?"

AJ gives me that easy smile of his, the one that makes my pulse flutter.

"Go ahead."

"Universal, Disneyland, or other?"

"Thrill Kingdom. I'd have a season pass if I didn't play baseball."

As soon he says it, I gasp.

"No. Way," I say the second he mentions the amusement park in Virginia.

"What?" AJ asks.

"I'm not kidding, that is my favorite, too! My family had season passes when I was growing up. I can't believe you love Thrill Kingdom as much as I do!"

"But do we love it for the same reason?" AJ asks. "You go first."

"All right. While I have to have a churro every time I go, it's not the food. It's the roller coasters. I'm an addict. I love that rush of getting to the top of the hill and careening toward the bottom. It's the best thing ever."

AJ's smile now reaches his eyes.

"Same."

"No way!"

"I'm a thrill seeker. The higher the roller coaster, the more inversions, backwards runs, all the better."

"Me, too."

"What's your favorite one at Thrill Kingdom?" he asks.

"The Fire-Breathing Dragon," I answer. "You?"

"The Escape Expedition. I love that two-hundred-and-twenty-foot drop."

"I like that one, too."

I snag another piece of cinnamon roll. "I can spend all day there. As a kid, it drove my parents nuts. They were ready to go by dinnertime, and I insisted it wasn't a full experience unless we stayed for the fireworks at the end."

"How often do you go?" AJ asks.

"This is a terribly sad stat to report, but I haven't been once this summer," I say. "I need to get it in because once I go to law school, my life will *be* law school."

"I can imagine," AJ says, gazing back out over the canal, across the street. "Georgetown is a prestigious school." Then he turns back toward me. "That's a pretty impressive achievement, to be admitted to Georgetown Law."

"Thank you. I worked very hard for it. I plan to work equally hard to excel there, too."

For a brief moment, I wonder what the hell I'm doing here, as I think of what my life will be at the end of summer. I will be a law student with ridiculous burdens put upon me. If anything happens with me and AJ—and I am crazy for even entertaining this thought—I will be in law school with no time for anything except school.

And where will AJ be? He will be a free agent after this season, and a highly sought-after one. He could be anywhere.

A twinge runs through me. One, for leaping this far ahead when we're simply talking and, two, at the idea of AJ taking a contract to go play somewhere else.

"I have no doubt you will be at the top of your class," AJ says, interrupting my thoughts.

Live in the moment, I will myself.

"Thank you," I say. I decide to redirect my brain to our conversation game at hand. "Your turn. This or that."

AJ rakes his hand through his hair. "Okay. When you sleep. Fan or no fan?"

"Oh, not only fan, but sounds."

"Sounds?"

"When Hayley and I were roommates at Georgetown, she talked in her sleep. Lots. I couldn't sleep, so I started playing sounds on my phone to block out the babbling. My current sound is rain. I love that sound. That and campfire."

"I've never had to sleep with sounds. Usually I fall asleep with the TV on."

"See, if I have the TV on, I'll start watching, and then the next thing I know, it's past two o'clock in the morning."

"That brings another this or that to mind. Morning or night?"

"Night. Definitely night."

"Baseball has made me into a night person. I don't leave the park until late, and then I'm wired. I have to unwind before going to bed."

"I do my best studying after ten in the evening. Then I'm crawling into bed around two. And ugh, it never failed, I had a morning class and I was so cranky because of it."

"So, don't speak to you before a cup of coffee?" AJ asks.

I snort. "Don't speak to me before I've had my eggs, toast, and two big cups of coffee, and skimmed my Instagram feed."

AJ laughs. "Well, at least you are detailed about it."

"I like details."

"I can see that."

AJ turns to me. "Got a question for me?"

Hundreds, I answer to myself. *I have hundreds.*

"Yes, but it's not this or that."

"I'm listening," he says.

I smile. He told me *Frasier* is comfort TV to him because he can always find it no matter where he is when traveling.

"Frasier," I say slowly, and he laughs. "Do you ever think about what your future will be like? The reason I ask: I'm always thinking a step ahead. Prepare for law school. Prepare for life once I pass the bar exam. I'm always looking at the next thing I want to accomplish. The next milestone. I'm never in the moment. Is that weird?"

I gaze up toward the sky, wondering why I'm like this. Why can't I just enjoy where I'm at? Why do I have to keep focusing on the next phase?

"For you, that makes complete sense," AJ says softly. I turn and see he's studying me. "It suits the future lawyer in you. Preparation is key in that field. I'd take that as a good sign."

He winks at me, and my heart melts.

"I'm different. I don't look that far ahead," AJ concedes. "I don't know where I'll be after this season. My agent is calling me wanting to talk about potential places where I can sign if I want a change, or if Washington doesn't want to come to terms on a new contract. But I don't want that distraction, so I told him we are not discussing it until the season is over. I live in this season. It will be July soon. I don't go past the Fourth in my mental calendar."

"I wonder what makes us like this," I say aloud. "I'm thinking five years ahead. You aren't thinking past five weeks. Yet for both of us, it makes sense."

I turn and study him in the darkness.

"I don't know why I'm telling you things I've never told

anyone else. Like what happened at the sports agency. Why I'm always trying to plan the next five years at a time."

"I don't know," AJ says, staring at me. "But I'm glad you are."

I feel my breath catch in my throat as his gaze locks on mine. He reaches for my hand again, and I get goosebumps the second his warm skin covers mine.

"I'm afraid to look at my watch," AJ says. "It has to be late, even for night owls like us."

I sigh. "I know, I'm sorry. I'm a talker, and if I'm talking to someone and the conversation is good, I can go on forever."

"If the conversation is good, I don't look at my watch or phone," AJ says. "If you've noticed, I haven't done either tonight. Until now."

He lifts my hand up with his, not letting it go, and I laugh softly in response. He glances down at his wrist and groans.

"One thirty."

"We've talked that long?" I cry. "I feel like we just got started!"

"I still have a million 'this or that' questions alone," AJ says, winking at me. "But I'll save them for another time."

AJ pops down off the ledge, and pulls me down, his hand remaining firmly locked around mine.

I glance down at our hands entwined, hardly believing this is happening. That I met this incredible man for real tonight, one I didn't know at all, but one I can tell is unique. Interesting. Fun. Sharp.

AJ is so much more than I ever envisioned him to be, I realize as we walk back through Georgetown. And to think earlier this evening, before he walked into my life, I thought meeting him would ruin things because he'd never live up to what I pictured in my head.

We continue to talk on our way back. AJ stops halfway up 33rd Street and looks at me.

"Where are you parked?" he asks. "I can walk you to your car."

Crap.

"What?" AJ asks, searching my face.

"I took the Metro, and the last train is gone," I say, smacking myself on the forehead.

"Who needs Metro? I can drive you back."

I exhale. "I owe you."

"You owe me nothing," AJ says. "It's my pleasure. Besides, selfishly, I get to spend more time with you, so I prefer it."

I could really like you, Andrew Joseph, I think as I stare up at him.

"Thank you," I say.

AJ leads me closer to Scones and Such and stops in front of a blue Audi R8. He opens the passenger door for me.

"Your ride for the night," AJ says, grinning at me.

"Nice car," I say, dropping down into the passenger seat.

"Thank you. I'm enjoying it this week."

As soon as I sink in, I get the scent of leather mingling with AJ's clean cologne.

Oh God, that scent is sexy as hell.

AJ slips in next to me and starts the sleek sports car.

"What do you mean, this week?" I ask, curious.

"I signed up for it for this week. Next week, I get something new," AJ explains. "Where do you live?"

"In Arlington. According to Hayley, only a few minutes away from Brody. And what do you mean, get something new? Are you in a car of the week club or something?" I tease.

AJ pulls up his GPS. "Easy enough. And yes, I belong to a driving club where you sign up for different cars for the length of time you want to drive them, and then turn them back in for something different. What's your address?"

I rattle off my address, and AJ eases the Audi onto the street.

"So, you don't own a car," I say.

"I have an old one for errands, but as far as what I drive every day? No. When I go on the road, I turn it in, and I don't get a new one until I return. I love it because I get to drive something new all the time. I'm never committed to one thing."

"I can't imagine," I say, thinking of how long I've had my own car.

"How come?" AJ asks. "Are you attached to your car?"

"I've had the same BMW since high school," I say. "My mom's old car. It's ancient. But I love it. Besides the fact that my life is in the backseat."

AJ doesn't need to know that my dad has termed my car "a trash can on four wheels" because of all the crap I manage to leave in it.

"Your life? Like what?"

Dammit.

"You know. My yoga mat. Library books. Dry cleaning."

I omit wadded up receipts, my water infuser bottle, three pairs of gym shoes, and way too many canvas shopping totes.

Among the things I can remember.

AJ heads back toward Arlington.

"You get library books?"

I shoot him a side eye. "Why is that weird?"

"I don't know, you seem like the type that would own a lot of books."

"I'm cheap. And I read a lot."

"I don't think I've been to a library since high school."

I gasp. "I can't imagine that."

"I can't even tell you where the library is."

"AJ! What kind of sorcery is this?"

"Sorcery," AJ repeats, that smile tugging sexily at the corner of his mouth again.

AJ is pulling up toward my building before I know it. He slides the car into a visitor parking spot, and nervousness fills me.

Will he kiss me?

No, I think, my heart hammering against my ribs.

Maybe?

Do you kiss after a cup of coffee, getting acquainted date?

I glance at him as he cuts the engine.

"I'll walk you in," AJ says softly.

No, he won't kiss me, I realize. He's doing everything right out of a gentleman's playbook. My heart tells me AJ isn't going to kiss until we've had a proper date, one that he asks me for in advance.

AJ takes my hand in his, and I lead him into my building. He stops me in the lobby and squeezes my hand, sending my stomach flipping upside down in excitement.

"Katie," he says slowly, "thank you for having a coffee with me tonight."

I can't breathe as I stare up into his green eyes.

"Thank you for asking me. And thank you for letting me get to know you, Andrew Joseph," I say softly.

AJ's expression changes when I say his given name.

"I hope you like him," AJ says.

"I do," I reply, speaking from my heart.

AJ is silent for a moment, and I can tell he's on the verge of asking me something.

At least I hope he is.

Because after tonight, all I want is more time with him.

"Katie," he says, squeezing my hand again, "what are you doing tomorrow? Are you off, by chance?"

Because I know the Soaring Eagles schedule by heart, I know AJ has a rare Monday off.

My heart leaps.

"I am," I say, smiling up at him.

A slow smile spreads across his face.

"I have a 'check yes or no' question for you," AJ says.

Ooh!

"Yes?"

"Katie, will you spend the day with me at Thrill Kingdom tomorrow? I'm up for it. But the question is, are you? Check yes or no."

It's all I can do not to squeal in excitement.

"I check yes," I say happily.

AJ's eyes sparkle at my reply.

"You probably like to get there when it opens, but since it's already two o'clock in the morning, will you settle for noon? Since we're not morning people?"

"I think you will be happier with noon Katie than eight a.m. Katie," I say.

AJ grins. "I'll pick you up tomorrow around ten."

He lets go of my hand, signaling our evening is over.

"Good night," he says.

"Good night," I reply, practically floating away from him on cloud nine as I walk across the deserted lobby to the elevators. I punch the button, and as the doors chime, I hear him call my name.

"Katie?"

I turn around and find AJ in the same spot he was standing a second ago.

"I think I could be equally happy with eight o'clock Katie and noon Katie."

Then he turns and heads out the door.

I stand still as the elevator doors close on me, in a state of euphoria and shock.

That just happened.

I had coffee with AJ, but it was so much more than coffee.

I met a man who is different, in the same ways I am. One who makes me laugh. Who is smart and quick. Who listens. For the first time in my life, I didn't want a date to end, and all we did was talk.

I punch the button again, and the elevator opens right back up for me. I step inside, lean against the back rail, and let out a huge, blissful sigh of happiness.

I have a date tomorrow.

With Andrew Joseph.

With that thought in my head, there's no way I'm sleeping tonight.

And I'm absolutely good with that, I think with a smile.

CHAPTER 6

Playlist Shuffle Song of the Day:
"Symphony" by Clean Bandit and Zara Larsson

"I am so excited!" I say as AJ and I go through the turnstile into Thrill Kingdom. "I'm at my favorite amusement park EVER!"

I look over my shoulder at AJ, that sexy smile tugging at the corner of his mouth as he enters through the gates behind me.

It's warm on this late June day, so I dressed accordingly in a light gray, Georgetown Law T-shirt, shorts, and my navy Converse kicks. With the summer humidity, there was no use fighting my Mufasa hair, so the curls are down and free, unlike last night.

I blush happily as I remember how AJ's eyes moved approvingly over my long legs when he picked me up and told me I looked gorgeous.

But AJ is the gorgeous one.

I drink him in—from the khaki shorts to the navy T-shirt that gives me a full view of his incredible arms, the gorgeous eyes hidden behind aviator sunglasses, and a backwards baseball hat covering his jet-black hair—as he follows me into the park.

I might be half dead due to about an hour of sleep, but I've never been more excited to do anything in my life. AJ and I talked non-stop during the drive, easily picking up where we left off yesterday. He arrived at my apartment right at ten on the dot, earning points for punctuality, and then earned more when I got to the car and discovered a Starbucks venti coffee with cream waiting for me in the cupholder, one on which he scribbled KATIE in Sharpie for me. Complete with a little stick girl with curly hair riding in a car on a little roller coaster.

As soon as I saw it, my heart melted right there in his Audi.

Andrew Joseph is charming and thoughtful and oh-so-sweet, and I might very well be half in love with him by the time we leave tonight.

"All right. The plan still in play? Hit every roller coaster once before we do anything else?" AJ asks.

"Yes, with the Fire-Breathing Dragon being the first," I say, referring to the roller coaster that goes upside down as we stroll into the medieval section of the park.

As we walk past a replica medieval inn, a blacksmith, a stable complete with horses, and a bakery, I sigh in utter happiness.

"I love being here. The second you walk through the entrance, it's like the real world goes away, and this world— of replica periods of time, rides, music, food—exists. I love this feeling. I love hearing the sound of the coasters running, the screams. The sweet scent in the ice cream shop that hits you the second you enter. I'm in this world for the next few hours, and it's the only place I want to be."

I look up at him, the handsome profile I now know by heart after studying him last night as we spoke for hours. AJ shifts his attention toward me.

It's just you and me in this world today, I think joyfully. *And I can't think of a better place to continue to get to know you.*

"All the things you described are what make amusement parks great. I like that I can escape. I go pretty much unrecognized, too. I've been to a lot of them, but this one is my all-time favorite. One of the reasons is because it has sick roller coasters."

"Yes, they are my favorites," I say as we work our way toward the huge castle at the end of this section of the park.

"Future counselor, you failed to follow up on the fact that I said 'one of the reasons' I like this place. I have another," AJ says.

"Oh, I'm sorry," I reply, smiling at him. "Please, AJ, elaborate on your second point."

"My second point," AJ says as we head toward the Fire-Breathing Dragon roller coaster. "This is my favorite park because this is my first amusement park date here. And I'm having it with you."

I stop walking. "I'm the first date you've brought here?"

Surprise fills me. AJ loves riding rides; this seems like a natural place for him to have taken previous dates.

AJ stops and gazes down at me. "This is one of my favorite places to be, for all the reasons you expressed. I can escape here. I can come back again and again, seeking the thrill, the rush of the coasters, with the familiarity of the park that is the closest feeling I've had to coming back home."

My heart aches as I grasp what he is saying. That AJ has never had the same home to come back to. Where the park might add enhancements and new rides, it's the closest thing he's ever had to the familiarity of a family home.

The kind of home his family never gave him due to constant moving. Not because they needed to, but because of the whims of his parents, not caring how it impacted their kids.

And now he's sharing this very personal thing with me, after one night of conversation.

I reach for his hand, linking my fingers through his and squeezing it.

"I'm glad you chose me," I say.

"I am, too," AJ says, squeezing my hand back.

Nothing more is said as park goers move around us. Then AJ clears his throat.

"Come on, let's do this," he says.

My heart is fluttering as he leads me to the bright red Fire-Breathing Dragon. I see the coaster going and hear the screams, and my excitement level shoots up.

"I can't wait!" I burst out. "We're here!"

AJ grins. "We are. Come on, let's go!"

We get in line and wait, but I'm enjoying it because we continue our flirtatious game. Light touching. Bantering. Getting to know each other as we wait to share this thrill ride together.

"I hope we get the front car," I say, showing AJ my crossed fingers.

AJ laughs. "Is this how we get the front car?" he asks, crossing his fingers like mine.

"I don't know, but if it works, we're doing it for every line we get in," I say. I slip my nylon drawstring bag off my back and drop my sunglasses inside.

"Want to put anything in here?" I ask, tilting the open bag toward AJ.

"Yeah, that would be great. I don't want to lose my hat or glasses," AJ says.

I'm pleased that he's taking his glasses off, because I really like gazing into those bright green eyes of his.

AJ takes off his aviators and drops them in my bag, followed by his baseball cap. He rakes his hand through his hair, and I find myself watching him. How his hair is longish, and he keeps it back with a bit of product. I love how it's black and thick, and I'm desperate to know what it would feel like if I touched it.

"Thanks for carrying my stuff," AJ says.

"No problem," I say, pulling the drawstring shut and slipping it over my back. We continue to wind through the line, and eventually, we move closer to the ride. Excitement builds in me, as it will be our turn soon.

Another coaster pulls up, and after it fills, we are able to get into the spot for the first coaster car.

I turn to AJ. "Crossing the fingers worked!"

He grins. "Are you going to implement this strategy going forward?"

I laugh. "Obviously."

Then I move my hand in front of me, where he can't see, and cross my fingers and hope AJ is having the same feelings develop for me as I am for him.

A coaster returns, and we slip in. My heart is thumping now in roller coaster excitement.

Or is that because AJ's leg is pressed up against mine, and I feel his skin lightly graze mine as we sit?

A shiver shoots down my spine as a result.

"I'm so ready to ride," AJ says, interrupting my thoughts.

"Me, too," I say, throwing my hands up. "You have to do it with arms up, like this."

"Duh, is there any other way to thrill seek?" AJ asks.

"I scream," I admit. "Loudly. You might regret sitting next to me."

AJ cocks an eyebrow at me. "So, I can blame you if I come off with ringing in my ears?"

I laugh. "Yes, I will take full responsibility."

We wait while everyone loads and safety checks are done. Then the coaster takes off for our thrill ride.

"Here we go," AJ says, a huge smile lighting up his gorgeous face.

My adrenaline is pounding as we head out into the

sunshine, the coaster track curving around the trees. We climb a hill, and my heart rate climbs with it, as I know we are building toward that first drop. The coaster is now high above the park, and I'm aware that we are towering over the trees.

"It's coming, AJ," I say happily.

We reach the top of the track, and I throw my arms up in delight as the coaster sails downward lightning fast, toward the water below us. My heart is slamming against my ribs, my hair is everywhere, and I'm screaming as the water comes closer and closer. It pulls back up in a flash, turning, twisting, and we're approaching the first loop.

"Here it comes!" AJ yells, his voice full of excitement.

The coaster flies up in a loop, and I'm shrieking as the water is now where the sky was, and the trees are growing upside down. The blood is rushing through me, an adrenaline rush taking over as the coaster completes the loop and surges ahead down the track. I begin laughing hysterically.

"Are you laughing?" AJ cries, laughing himself as he glances at me.

"Yes, because it's so fun!"

Now he's laughing because I'm laughing, and the coaster heads toward the dark tunnel.

"Into the darkness," AJ says as the coaster zooms closer.

We enter the tunnel, with more screaming behind us, but AJ and I both begin laughing again. We rush forward, popping back out into the summer day, and the coaster builds toward the second loop.

"I love the loops!" I cry in delight.

The coaster picks up speed. My heart is hammering again; I know I'm about to be turned upside down. The coaster goes down, then up, and I scream as the sky is at my feet and the water is above my head again.

The second I'm right side up I'm in a fit of giggles, which makes AJ crack up, and now I'm really laughing since AJ is losing it because I'm so weird.

And just like that, our ride on the Fire-Breathing Dragon is over.

"It goes so fast! Too fast!" I cry as the coaster slows before entering the starting point again. "AJ, we *have* to ride it again before we go."

"We will hit all the coasters twice before we leave. Hey, speaking of which, we should have a picture of us from our first coaster ride, shouldn't we?"

"Oh, you mean the ones the park takes?"

"No, I mean one that I take," AJ says.

Butterflies. Thousands of them take off when AJ says he wants a picture of us together.

"Let's get one with the Fire-Breathing Dragon sign in the background," AJ says as he retrieves his phone out of his pocket.

I follow him to the entrance of the ride. He pulls out his phone, and thanks to his height and reach, easily gets us with the sign in the background. But the second I see myself in his screen, I gasp.

"Oh, my God, I look like crap!" I blurt out.

The summer heat, along with being tossed around at high speed and upside down, has caused my curls to go insane. My hair is huge, and the infamous T-zone is once again ready for Sunoco to tap for oil.

"What are you talking about?" AJ asks.

"AJ! Look at me. My hair is *ridiculous*. And I'm shining! If there's a man on the moon, he can find Virginia thanks to my nose."

I'm about to take off my backpack so I can grab my oil blotting tissues and my Kate Spade scarf to tie back my hair, but AJ reaches for my wrist and holds it gently in his hand, his fingertips magically dancing across it while his thumb covers my pulse point.

"Katie," he says simply.

He releases my wrist, but then uses those same fingertips

and lightly brushes them across the top of my cheekbone. My heart explodes inside my chest the second I feel this rough skin touching my face.

"Your cheeks are flushed," he says, his brilliant green eyes searching mine as his fingertips explore my face. "You're glowing."

I can't breathe.

AJ's fingertips travel up toward my temple, to my eyebrow, and I shiver from the sensation of his gentle touch sweeping across my brow.

"Your eyes are sparkling," AJ continues softly. He slowly lifts his hand and gently pushes it through my hair, sending every nerve I have on fire. "Your curls are loose and free. I like that."

I can't think. I can't speak. I can't believe I'm having this moment with AJ.

AJ lowers his hand and, ever so lightly, brushes his index finger against my lips, sending shockwaves through me.

"When you smile, it's radiant. It's beautiful. You're beautiful, Katie."

I see myself through AJ's lens. I know why I'm glowing and radiant. It's not just from the euphoria of a roller coaster ride.

It's from being with this man.

I search his eyes. AJ thinks I'm beautiful, even when I'm a mess.

"Thank you," I say.

AJ moves next to me and, this time, slides one arm around my waist and draws me into his broad chest. I'm aware of the fresh cologne on his tanned skin and his muscular arm holding me, and I can't fight the rush I feel from being in his arms.

One greater than any coaster could ever give me.

"Picture," AJ says, holding his camera up with his other hand. "One, two, three."

AJ snaps it, and when he shows it to me, I know he's right. I'm radiant. My smile reaches up to my eyes.

All because of the wonderful man next to me.

"The Fire-Breathing Dragon is done. The Enigma next," AJ says, slipping his phone back in his pocket.

As his hand finds mine, we set off in the direction of The Enigma for our next thrill.

Although I know I will have no greater thrill than the one I have right now of being with AJ.

"Now this is the best dinner ever," I declare, dipping my spoon into a peanut butter sundae as The Enigma roars overhead. "Peanut butter counts as a protein, so I'll stand by it."

It's the perfect end to our day. We've ridden everything that has a rush to it, drenched ourselves on the water flume, had pretzels and craft beers for a snack, and then played games in the arcade, where AJ won me a ton of stuffed animals, which we happily gave away to the kids around us except for two that I kept, ones AJ got specifically with me in mind: a huge stuffed donut and a to-go coffee cup character toy.

Now we're sitting outside, tired and happy, and digging into sundaes before we head on out. We've already stayed an hour later than we planned, but we were having so much fun that we couldn't resist staying a bit longer.

"However," I say, pausing as I take another bite, "my dietitian mother would disapprove."

AJ gets that adorable crease in his nose. "Your mom is a *dietitian?*"

I can't help but laugh, as the disconnect in his mind is obvious.

"I know. The girl who loves food in a helmet and

oversized sundaes grew up with a dietician mom. She's the director of dietetics for a company that services hospitals."

AJ's eyebrows shoot up. "That's impressive. I see where the drive and the brains are in your genes."

"Dad is a cardiologist," I say, breaking off a piece of my waffle bowl. Then I raise an eyebrow him. "Don't worry, I don't eat only junk food. But I grew up in a house where a treat was a piece of fruit. When I started going to sleepovers as a tween, it was the first time I had ever had cereal that wasn't shredded wheat."

"Seriously?" AJ asks, taking a bite of his banana split.

"Yeah, it's weird, I know. And I have this high metabolism, so I was always given supplemental protein shakes to keep weight on, and I was like, 'why can't I just have some ice cream?' But now that I'm older, I get it. I needed healthy foods to help keep weight on, so I eat a lot of whole grain pasta, brown rice, proteins. I've had my thyroid checked, and that's not it—it's a genetic thing. And then you get people telling you you're so lucky to be so thin. Or I get accused of not eating enough. Worse, I've had people imply I must be bulimic."

I feel a heaviness coming on. I won't bore AJ with details of how in high school, girls started nasty, untrue rumors about me throwing up in the bathroom after lunch. Or doing drugs.

"Did that happen while you were in high school?" AJ asks, as if he has ESP.

"Yes," I admit, putting my spoon down. "I've never had an eating disorder. I love to eat! My parents made sure to raise me and Meghan with a positive body image of ourselves and what we can do to keep healthy with food. Yet, by making certain foods off limits, that sent a mixed message. I think it would have been better to teach us more about everything in moderation. I went crazy with crap my first year at Georgetown because I could, you know? That eventually got old, and one bad stomach ache cured that into moderation, but still."

"But that had to be hard at that age," AJ says, coming back around to his original thought. "Girls can be cruel to each other. My sister went through a lot with other girls saying things about her online."

I wince. "Yep, been there. With girls spreading rumors about bulimia and drug use, which is hilarious because I've never even smoked a single cigarette, let alone touched a drug. Guys went a different route. They loved telling me I had no boobs and a chest like a boy."

I freeze. What just came out of my mouth? I can't believe I told AJ that. Or any of this, for that matter. I haven't talked about this stuff in years. It's all memories of the past, ones I have left behind, but not ones I've ever talked about with anyone other than Meghan and Hayley.

"Teen boys are idiots," AJ says.

"AJ. Men like boobs, I know that," I say, digging in for some peanut butter cup goodness in my sundae.

"Katie. Men like other things. For some of us, the boobs aren't the end all."

"I can't believe we are talking about this."

"Oh, I want to talk about it. I'm not a boob guy."

Now I'm blushing.

"I made you blush."

"No," I lie, looking down into my sundae as if all the mysteries of the universe are tucked in there and keeping me riveted to it.

"I like eyes."

Now AJ has my full attention.

"A girl has to have beautiful eyes to get my attention," he continues.

Swoon.

"I remember when I had your head in my lap, and I was staring down at you. You had very long eyelashes, I remember that, but when they fluttered open, I was looking down into the most beautiful green eyes I had ever seen."

Electricity flows through me from his wonderful words.

"That's not all," AJ says, reaching over and brushing a lock of my curly hair between his fingers. "You had curls, all kinds of curls. I'd never even touched curly hair until that night. Then you informed me it was Mufasa hair, and you've had my attention ever since."

I can't breathe. His words are so heartfelt and wonderful, and I can't believe I'm sitting here with a man as beautiful as him, inside and out. One I never expected this baseball player to be.

I decide it's time for me to share more of myself with him, too.

"Before you came into Scones and Such yesterday, I didn't want to get to know you," I admit.

AJ continues to play with my hair, the crease reappearing across the bridge of his nose. "What? Why?"

"I was afraid you wouldn't live up to the picture of you I painted in my head. The one gleaned from your funny posts on Instagram or interviews you do on TV. The segments they've aired about you on *Soaring Eagles Live.* I already liked AJ Williamson, and I was afraid you'd ruin that picture. You couldn't live up to the person I envisioned."

AJ is quiet. "And now?"

"Andrew Joseph," I say, putting my hand over his, "has exceeded all my expectations so far. I like him. A lot."

That sexy smile tugs at the corner of his mouth. "So, so far, so good?"

"So far, so very, *very,* good," I say, smiling at him.

Now he flashes me that dazzling smile, the one that makes my breath catch in my throat. "Good. Because I feel the same way. You've exceeded my expectations, too."

Oh my, I don't think I can't wait until the end of the evening for him to kiss me.

We finish our sundaes, with AJ staring at me in disbelief as I polish off mine by myself, since it's big enough for two to share, and then we head toward the medieval section of the park on our way out. He's carrying my stuffed donut, I'm lugging the latte cup doll, and we're laughing about it as we move through the park. We head through Tudor England, on our way to the next section of the past.

We've barely crossed into Medieval Land when AJ stops.

"Come here. There's one thing left we have to do before we leave," he says.

AJ leads me over to the side of the bridge, one that is surrounded by loads of beautiful greenery.

He puts the donut down next to him and grabs his phone, unlocking it and then keying in something.

"What are you doing?" I ask, curious.

AJ finds what he is looking for and taps something.

"You love the fireworks show here, right?" AJ asks.

I nod. "Yes, but it's only on the weekends. Not on Mondays."

"I couldn't let you leave without seeing those fireworks," AJ says. "Come here."

Curious, I move around next to him, and he holds his phone up, like we're looking at the sky.

"These are Thrill Kingdom fireworks, compliments of YouTube," AJ says, tapping the button so they play for us.

I watch as the firework show plays out on his phone in front of my eyes.

"There you go, Katie," AJ says softly. "Your fireworks show."

I turn to him, studying his profile as he watches the fireworks on his iPhone.

AJ remembered what I said about the fireworks.

And he found a way to give them to me.

My heart is pounding. I'm not watching the fireworks, but

the profile of this amazing man that walked into my life only yesterday.

AJ must feel my gaze, because he turns and looks down at me. Our eyes immediately lock, and desire to kiss him bursts to the surface. I can't breathe. I'm searching his vibrant green eyes, wanting this moment now. To feel his lips against mine, to taste the sweetness of his kiss.

He lowers his phone, never breaking his gaze. My breathing picks up from the way he's staring at me.

I know he wants to kiss me, too.

AJ draws me into his arms. I drop my stuffed toy to the ground as his arms wrap around my waist.

The blood is rushing to my head. I'm dizzy with anticipation.

I allow myself to place my hands on his chest. The second I do, I feel his heart pounding through the fabric of his T-shirt, and the wall of hard muscle that makes up his athletic chest.

AJ slides one hand to the nape of my neck and begins caressing it with his fingertips. I tremble in response to his sensual touch.

"There's one more thing we need to do before we leave," AJ murmurs.

"What's that?" I manage to ask, although I already know what the answer is.

AJ's hand moves to my face, stroking it gently.

"This," AJ whispers, lowering his mouth to mine.

CHAPTER 7

I'm shaking as his mouth captures mine. I'm dizzy as I feel his lips—deliciously full, soft lips—sweetly press against mine in an innocent kiss.

AJ lifts his head and surprises me with a gentle kiss across the bridge of my nose. Then my forehead, sending the butterflies shifting in my stomach, all while cradling my face protectively in his hands.

He moves his hands and strokes them through my curls as he stares down at me.

His touch is like a drug, one that is exciting and thrilling and something I could easily become addicted to.

Because I will always want this man to touch me, I think. *I've had a taste of it now.*

And I already want more.

"Now we can go. I couldn't leave without kissing this beautiful mouth of yours to end our date here," AJ says, taking a moment to draw his thumb sensually across my lower lip before replacing it with another gentle kiss.

"I feel dizzy," I blurt out. "I—

"Are you okay? Do we need to sit down?" AJ quickly asks,

and I see he's having a flashback to that night at the ballpark when I fainted on him.

I put my fingertips over his lips to silence him. God, his lips are amazing. I can only dream of kissing them for hours on end.

"Bu—" AJ tries to protest, but I silence him with a kiss of my own.

I smile up at him. "AJ. Dizzy from your swoony kiss. Not pass-out dizzy."

"People say swoony?" AJ asks. "Is this a real-life thing or a Katie thing?"

"Um, I would say it's a Katie slash book thing."

"Tell me as we leave," AJ says, bending down, picking my stuffed donut, and handing it to me. "I'm listening."

"Okay, *Frasier*," I say, noticing how AJ is grinning as he retrieves the latte cup toy and tucks it under his arm.

As we head toward the exit, I resume speaking.

"Swoony is a word that I see in a lot of fiction I read. What can I say? I like romances to balance out my law reading."

"Well, one can't live by law books alone," AJ says, reaching for my hand again.

"Absolutely not," I say.

But come fall, I will, I think.

For a moment, law school enters my head. I know it's going to consume me. What if I'm still seeing AJ at that point? Will he understand I'm going to be buried in books for hours on end?

"Katie?"

I blink. I can't believe I went there. Hello, we're on our first official date. I have no business wondering how AJ will fit into my future. I don't know his annoying habits. I don't know how he argues. What he's like after a crappy game. Does he save money? That would drive me crazy if he didn't.

There are so many things I don't know.

One of them being if he will even return to DC with the Soaring Eagles after this season.

For once in your life, try not to think of the future, I tell myself.

"Where are you?" AJ asks as we walk out of the park.

"Thinking about books," I say, not elaborating on Crazy Katie who leapt ahead to visions of juggling AJ around classes.

"As in?"

I study his profile. AJ is more than perceptive, I realize. He follows with questions until he gets to the honest answer.

I've never been with a guy who has cared enough to do that.

"I doubt I'll be able to read for fun come fall," I say as we head toward the parking lot. "Which is hard for me, because reading is one of my greatest joys. The first year of law school is very intensive."

I watch as AJ's mouth frowns a bit as he takes in my words. My stomach tightens. Have I said too much? This is a first date. I shouldn't be giving him reasons to make this our first and last date.

But I'm being honest, I counter. *If we start dating, he should know this.*

AJ has the chance to opt out now before we get too involved.

So why do I feel nausea from that thought? Of AJ saying this was fun and wonderful but not practical, and we should quit while we're ahead?

Because I want to see him again, I think, swallowing hard. *And again. And again.*

AJ clears his throat. "I can't even pretend to know how demanding law school would be," he says slowly. "But I would imagine you'd have to give up some things in the short term to reach your long-term goal."

I swallow hard again. "I know you're right."

Would AJ be one of the things I'd have to give up? Not

because I wanted to, but because he wanted to leave DC after the season? Or he'd want a woman who could pick up and go where the wind takes them?

"But I also know you will figure it out. You'll find a way to carve out some time, however small it might be, for the things that matter, Katie. I believe you'd do that."

I shift my gaze to meet his. The knot in my stomach unravels when I see the sincere expression on his gorgeous face.

This is not the expression of a man who is scared off by either the conversation or where dating me could lead.

I squeeze his hand in mine. "Thank you. I needed to hear that. I've prepared for years for law school, but that doesn't mean I'm not worried."

Because I never prepared for law school with you in mind, I think. In my head, law school was going to be a solo journey for me. I was going to be in one relationship, and that was going to be with Georgetown Law.

And within the course of forty-eight hours, I find myself contemplating the journey with not only Georgetown Law, but with AJ Williamson, too.

AJ ESCORTS ME OFF THE ELEVATOR TO MY FLOOR IN THE apartment building. I'm exhausted. Happy. Wondering if he'll kiss me before we part for the evening.

Once again, we talked the whole drive back to DC. I'd never met anyone besides Hayley who likes to talk as much as I do, until I met AJ. He put me in charge of the music, and I made sure I didn't select any of the sappy, falling-in-love tunes on my playlist.

Because if he heard the words, they would seem like they were selected with him in mind.

The door to Barbara and Dominik's apartment opens as

we pass by, and Dominik steps out. I grin. Barbara and Dominik are my elderly neighbors, but they are more than that. They are my surrogate grandparents, and Hayley and I spend a lot of time with them.

Including going to Soaring Eagles games.

The second Dominik sees AJ, he stops dead in his tracks.

"Holy Moses, is that AJ Williamson? Do I need to change my prescription?" he says, squinting behind his thick glasses.

Oh, no. Dominik knows about my crush on AJ. In fact, he's been helpful in loaning me his binoculars to check out his baseball butt during games.

Crap.

"No, sir, your prescription is bang on," AJ says, smiling at him. "I'm AJ Williamson."

AJ steps toward him and offers his hand. Dominik stares at him in shock, then shakes his hand.

"First Brody, now AJ?" Dominik says, giving me the side eye.

I don't want to count how many times I've blushed today.

"AJ, this is Dominik, my next-door neighbor," I say, trying to steer the conversation away from any potential landmines. "Where are you going, Dominik?"

"Barbara has gas. I've got to go get some medicine. And air freshener, if you get my drift," Dominik says.

Oh, my God. We are not talking about gas. We are not.

I glance at AJ, who has an amused look on his face.

"Yes, I understand," AJ says with a straight face.

"Cabbage rolls. They're a killer. If you marry Katie, don't ever let her make those unless you are prepared for the consequences."

I want to disappear.

AJ looks like he wants to die laughing.

"Dominik!" Barbara calls out. "What are you talking about, Katie getting married?"

Suddenly, Barbara appears at the door in her fluffy pink bathrobe. The second she sees AJ, her mouth drops open.

"Oh, my God, you're AJ!" she says, moving toward us.

Say nothing about the crush. Nothing. Do not mention we check out his baseball butt daily during the season.

"And you must be Barbara," AJ says, extending his hand.

"Oh, it's a pleasure. All of us are big fans. Katie is your biggest, though. No doubt about that," Barbara says.

AJ glances at me and raises an eyebrow.

"My Katie knows who can rake," Dominik says proudly.

AJ grins. "I bet she does."

Barbara stares at the stuffed donut in my hand, a quizzical expression on her face.

"We went to Thrill Kingdom today," I explain. "AJ won both of these breaking plates."

"Oh, how fun," Barbara says, smiling.

"Do you want me to run and get your medicine?" I ask Barbara. "I'm going to be up for a while anyway. I'd be happy to save you the trip, Dominik."

"I don't mind taking you," AJ offers.

"Wait. What do you mean, *my* medicine?" Barbara asks. "He's not going out for me."

"I'm going, Barbara," Dominik says, adjusting his newsboy cap.

"You wait just a minute, husband," Barbara says. "You are the one with gas. Not me. Don't tell Katie that nonsense because you are embarrassed you're gassy." Then she turns to me. "I told him he either gets gas medicine and a new can of air freshener or he can sleep on the couch, that's what I told him."

I'm dying.

"Then quit making cabbage rolls; those always give me gas," Dominik says, shuffling toward the elevator.

"You not ask for cabbage rolls? Ha! We'll test that theory this week and see how far you get."

"Nice meeting you, AJ," Dominik calls out as he punches the elevator button.

"Likewise, sir," AJ says.

"I'd better get back inside. Coffee tomorrow, Katie? I made chocolate babka."

I see that gleam in her eyes. I know this invitation is not merely for breakfast, but to get all the details of what is going on with AJ.

"Can it be an afternoon coffee break? I have to work the early shift tomorrow."

"Of course. I'll see you then," Barbara says. "Nice meeting you, AJ."

"You, too."

Then she slips back inside her apartment and shuts the door.

I look at AJ. I really have no words to explain what he just took part in.

But AJ does, because he bursts out laughing.

"That was the greatest thing ever," AJ declares.

I begin to laugh, too. "Aren't they the cutest? They even make gas cute."

"Come on, gas is funny."

"You're a boy," I say as we head to my apartment. "You guys think all that stuff is funny."

I stop in front of my door, and AJ slides an arm around my waist. "Counselor, I saw that gleam in those pale green eyes. You thought it was just as funny as I did."

Electricity rushes through me.

"I'm not a counselor yet. And that's what a judge or another lawyer would call me, not you."

"I think you'd make an exception for me," AJ says sexily.

Why yes. Yes, I would.

He slides a hand up to my face, once again caressing it. The second he touches me, I grow hot.

"Katie," he murmurs, drawing his index finger across my

lower lip, "it's going to have to be a sweet good night kiss for now."

I nod, but as I stare at his sexy mouth, all I want to do is taste him.

"Before I do that, I have a question." He moves his hand back to my hair, looping his finger through my curls in a way that makes me melt.

"Proceed," I say.

He smiles. "Would you like to go to the baseball game tomorrow night?"

I bite back the squeal of joy that threatens to erupt from my throat.

"Yes," I say, nodding my head excitedly. "I would love that."

"I'll leave you a ticket and credential at will call," AJ says as he continues to play with my hair.

I swear, I can't concentrate as I think of going to his game tomorrow. Surreal.

"Okay."

"Maybe afterward, we can go out with Brody and Hayley," AJ suggests.

"That would be fun," I say, hoping he doesn't notice how my heart is beating against the cotton fabric of my T-shirt.

"Then it's settled. I'll see you tomorrow night. I'll text you tomorrow."

He moves to kiss me, but I put my fingertips over his mouth to stop him.

"Can you text me when you get home instead?" I ask.

He rewards me with a beautiful smile. "Okay."

Then he lowers his head and presses his lips against mine in another quick, sweet kiss. And another. And another.

"I don't want to stop kissing you," AJ murmurs against my mouth.

I'm burning up. "I don't want you to stop."

He brushes his warm lips against mine again.

I want to open for him, to explore his mouth with mine, but AJ pulls away.

"Tomorrow," AJ says, taking his fingertips and brushing them against my cheek. "I will kiss you the way I want to the second we're alone."

Oh, my.

"I'm holding you to that," I whisper.

"Don't worry, that's a promise," AJ says, handing me the stuffed latte cup toy. "Good night."

"Good night, AJ," I say, unlocking the door and stepping inside.

I close the door, lock it, and let out a huge, happy sigh.

That was, without a doubt, the best first date of my entire life.

AJ is proving himself to be so much more than I ever dreamed he could be. A gentleman. Thoughtful. Sexy. Fun. Charming. Genuine.

I like this man more than I should.

He just left me, and I'm already counting the seconds until I see him again.

And until we share our first real kiss.

CHAPTER 8

Playlist Shuffle Song of the Day:
"Connection" by One Republic

I step through these gates to Eagles Field, the ballpark of the Soaring Eagles, multiple times a year. I've had the thrill of getting off the Metro and walking toward the vintage-designed signs, knowing I would be going through that turnstile, getting my ticket scanned, and heading into my place of happiness. Where there's no clock managing how long each inning is. Where the grass is green, and I can hear the baseball hitting the wood of the bat. Where the blue sky is over head, and I can smell beer and hot dogs perfuming the air.

Baseball brings out a different side of me. It allows me to spend a few hours watching a game of strategy play out before my eyes. Wondering what pitch will be thrown. How the catcher will manage the game. I treat myself to my favorite foods, settle in, get out my scorecard, and allow myself to only be in this world for the time I'm here.

Tonight, however, is different. I draw an excited breath as

the Soaring Eagles park employee scans my ticket for entrance.

Because tonight I'm not entering as a season ticket holder with my dad. I'm not coming as a guest of Hayley's.

I'm coming because AJ Williamson wants me here.

That stupid, sappy, giddy, excited feeling sweeps over me at the thought of him. The same feeling that came over me when he texted me last night, and we ended up talking for another hour. The same feeling that came over me when I told Hayley about AJ this morning before dashing out the door to work. The same one that took root when I had coffee and babka with Barbara this afternoon and reappeared with the string of texts I've exchanged with AJ all day today.

AJ vibes are a legit emotion, I think with a grin.

"Miss, here you go," a man says, handing me a box. "For being one of the first fifteen thousand fans tonight."

I take the box and look down at it. Then I stop walking.

Oh my God.

It's a bobblehead.

Of AJ.

I stare down at it and burst out laughing. It's a hideous rendition of him. It doesn't even look like him. Why does he have a neck like a giraffe? And his teeth are half the face.

I can't decide what is stranger: that AJ's bobblehead looks nothing like him, or that I have a date after the game tonight with a man so famous they made a bobblehead for him.

Suddenly, I hear a snort laugh from behind, and I know without turning around that Hayley has received her bobblehead.

"Why is your boyfriend's neck so distorted?" Hayley asks, shooting me a devilish grin.

"Let's revisit that comment. Clarification for the record: He's not my boyfriend," I say, dropping Distorted AJ into my bag.

We begin to walk through the concourse, and I'm already leading Hayley to the vendor who has the food I'm craving tonight. Luckily, Hayley rolls along with me and puts up with my weird baseball food choices while sticking to her healthy eating plan.

"I think he wants to be," Hayley says. "AJ was the one who called Brody and asked if he could find out where you worked. Unlike me, it's not because he wanted a free day-old scone."

"This is crazy, Hayley. He used to be my phone screen saver. Computer wallpaper. I've looked at his butt a million times with Dominik's binoculars. I was a fan of AJ before, but now it's different."

"He's a person now," Hayley says, studying me. "Not a player."

"Yes," I say. "It's completely different now. That night we had coffee changed everything. I like the man I met that night."

"The player part is their job, but not who they are. That's what I loved about not knowing that Brody was an athlete. He's always been *Brody* to me. Now you see AJ that same way. I approve of the new screen saver and wallpaper. But don't give up checking out his butt. AJ won't know."

I laugh as we walk amongst the fans filling the concourse for tonight's game against Seattle. Before us is a sea of red, navy, and white, and I see multiple jerseys with WILLIAMSON 15 on the back.

Oh, crap. It hits me that *I* have one of those at home. I'll need to see if Barbara can hide that in their apartment for me, because that would freak him out. He knows I'm a fan, but he doesn't need to know I was the baseball fan who bought his jersey because he was my favorite player.

And my kinda sorta player crush.

Why am I lying in a conversation I'm having with myself?

Reset.

He was my huge player crush.

Was.

Until he became Andrew Joseph, the man who drank coffee with me along the canal in Georgetown. The man who rode every roller coaster with me twice and laughed because I laughed while riding them.

"So, what are you eating tonight that I'm going to be jealous of?" Hayley asks, interrupting my thoughts.

I blink, coming back to reality as my best friend waits for my answer.

"Totchos. In a helmet, of course."

"What?" Hayley asks, laughing. "What is that?"

"Tater tot nachos," I say, thinking I'll have to snap a pic to text to AJ. "What about you?"

"Curried chicken lettuce wrap," Hayley says, not sounding very enthused about it. "But I'll get something good when we go out afterward."

We get Hayley's wrap first, then my totchos, and head down the tunnel to our section. The second we reach the top, I stop and stare at the splendor of the field before me. I smile as I breathe in the air and gaze out over the immaculately kept grass. The white bases in place on the diamond. I hear vendors yelling out for people to buy peanuts and cold beers.

This never gets old, I think joyfully. I love every game I go to.

But tonight is even more special, knowing I'm here for AJ.

We head to our seats behind home plate. Hayley told me our seats are in the section where the other WAGS—wives and girlfriends—sit.

I follow Hayley down the row, with her greeting everyone by name, and we take our seats. I take a sip of my beer and dig into my totchos with abandon, scooping up crispy tater tots and cheese and beef.

"Are they as awesome as they smell?" Hayley asks.

"If you multiply it times a thousand, yes. So much awesome. And it's in a helmet, which makes all food taste so much better."

"Too bad they don't serve chicken curry wraps in a helmet. But I don't think that theory holds true for healthy wraps."

I reach for my phone and take a picture of my food so I can text it to AJ. I type in a caption to go with it:

Totchos. One of the world's greatest inventions, along with the helmet dish.

I hit send and then type a second message:

Can't wait to see you play tonight, but more than that, I can't wait to see you after the game.

I put my phone down on my lap and scoop up more totchos, this time making sure I have plenty of cheese and sour cream on this bite.

Just as I begin to eat, my phone vibrates on my leg. I glance down at it and nearly drop my totchos when I see it's a text from AJ:

Can't wait to see you either. I've missed you all day. I thought about stopping into Scones and Such on the pretense of needing to try a new scone, but you'd see right through that one.

I want to leap up and scream, "HE MISSED ME!" Better yet, he thought about stopping by Scones and Such simply to see me. I want to grab Hayley and show her the text. If we were in our apartment, both of us would be squealing and flailing around with Muppet arms in excitement.

Of course, if we did that here, that might be a little weird for everyone in our section, so I do that little dance inside my heart instead.

Before I can text him back, another message from AJ comes in:

BTW sending pictures of totchos is unfair when I had grilled chicken and fruit for a pre-game dinner.

AJ is typing…

Of course, according to someone I know, my food would taste infinitely better in a Soaring Eagles helmet dish.

Now I'm grinning like a loon. My hands are trembling in excitement as I text him back:

I missed you, too. BTW, don't you take to the field in less than a half hour?

AJ is typing…

I can see going out with a student of the game has a downside.

I smile, as I know he's kidding. I give him a witty reply:

I know from the Soaring Eagles Insider show that you should be dressed and stretching at this point as part of your pre-game routine.

AJ is typing…

To ease your mind that I'm somehow not ready

because I'm talking to you, I can assure you I'm not only wearing a uniform and stretched, but I'm listening to my pre-game playlist as I text. I'll be ready to face Castillo and his curveballs.

I nod as I read. I know Luis Castillo is the ace for the Seattle team and has a deep repertoire of pitches.

Don't let him get you with that wipeout splitter.

"Are you talking to AJ?" Hayley asks, raising her eyebrows.

Guilt sweeps over me. "I know, I shouldn't distract him from his game."

Hayley bursts out laughing. "Please. An hour ago, he was playing Fortnite with Brody. They have loads of time to kill, you know that."

"I know, but it's different thinking I'm going to mess up his game by distracting him."

Hayley takes a sip of her bottled water and shakes her head, sending her choppy blonde hair swishing from side to side. "You won't. When AJ steps on that field, he's all business. That's one of the things that bonded him and Brody together. They have the same passion for the game."

My phone vibrates in my hand, and I glance down and read AJ's message:

Showing off your baseball knowledge to impress me? It worked. I'm impressed. Unless you used Google, then I'm not.

I type rapid fire:

Those are fighting words, Andrew Joseph.

AJ is typing…

Fighting after one date would be bad. I'll trust what Dominik said. You are a girl who knows who can rake AND who can throw a good splitter.

I message back:

I'm a legit student of the game and have been long before you arrived in DC.

I pause. AJ doesn't have to know I followed him since he played Triple-A ball in Ocean City. Even if I'm a student of the game and follow the development of many players in the farm system, I would sound like a stalker to a guy like AJ, who is sensitive to fans liking him for the wrong reasons.

Ha! I sound like a contestant on *Is it Love?*, where the concern is if the contestants are there to find out if it is love or to build a career as a TV personality or professional influencer on Instagram.

Now that I've kissed Andrew Joseph, I'm one hundred percent here for the right reasons.

AJ replies:

I have no doubts you are legit, Katie. About many things.

Oh!

I try to think of how to reply, but it's hard when my heart is fluttering wildly inside my chest.

Another message from AJ drops in:

Gotta go. Have this game I need to play. Look for me on the field. I'm wearing 15. And I think I need to add a new pre-game ritual to the list.

I smile as I type back, as baseball players are notorious for their pre-game routines:

What is that? Fruit in a helmet?

AJ is typing…

No. I need to talk to you before every game. See you tonight.

Ahh!

The AJ vibes hit me with full force, like a wave of happiness washing over me and leaving me in a state of excitement and euphoria.

I put my phone down, almost too excited to eat my tater tots.

Then I grin. I don't care how much I'm crushing on AJ, I'm going to eat the totchos. I mean, come on. They are totchos!

I take a few more bites, and then the Soaring Eagles come out onto the field. I search the players until I find AJ, who trots out of the dugout in his pristine white uniform—one that looks stark against his tanned skin and dark hair—and begins running some sprints to warm up, as he always does.

I watch as he moves so effortlessly, his body in rhythmic motion as he runs.

"Do you wish we had Dominik's binoculars?" Hayley jokes.

"No," I lie.

"Ha! Liar. I know you want to see that baseball butt up close."

I sigh as my eyes shift down to his ass. Damn. Hayley is right. They should be celebrated, especially one as fantastic as AJ's.

Preferably in high definition optics.

The ceremonial first pitch is made, and we're inching closer to game time. When it's time for the anthem, the players line up and we all rise, and I watch as AJ removes his hat, holding it over his heart. The breeze ruffles his hair, and I find myself daydreaming about when I will be able to touch it as we kiss.

A tingle shoots down my spine as I drift back to Thrill Kingdom last night, how soft and gentle his lips felt against mine. What would it be like to kiss him in that first exploring kiss, the one that is full of wonderful discovery? I can't imagine anything better than being in his arms and kissing him for hours on end. Feeling his five o'clock shadow scratch against my skin. Inhaling the sexy scent of his clean cologne when I kiss his neck. Touching his hair, his face, his lips.

For the first time in my life, I keep my fingers crossed for a speedy game tonight.

I shift my attention to the field, where the players have gone back into the clubhouse. It seems like HOURS before they are ready to start the game, but soon players are coming out into the dugout and entering the field.

Excitement runs through me as I watch AJ jog out to his position in center field. Normally I'd have my scorecard out, studying our pitcher, Chase McLeary, but tonight I simply want to watch AJ from a new perspective.

The one of the woman who is going out with him at the end of the night.

I chat with Hayley as the first Seattle player, Chris Matthews, enters the box, and I focus on the batter instead of AJ. Though we can't see it from where we're seated behind him, I know Brody flashes the signal, and Chase blows a fastball right past the batter for strike one.

"Brody loves catching for Chase," Hayley says, shoving her empty wrap tray under her seat. "They have great chemistry together."

Chase shakes off one of Brody's signs, then nods, and delivers a perfect strike across the plate.

I glance back to the outfield, where AJ is standing, playing a shallow center field. Normally I cringe when I see players doing this, because while they can make the play on shorter batted balls, they are in danger of having one go sailing past them. But not with AJ. He has incredible speed and can make up ground to still get the long ball that others might not be able to reach.

I shift back to Chase, who shakes off Brody not once, but twice, before nodding.

Chase delivers the ball and whack! Chris sends the ball with a blast toward deep center field.

I wince as the crowd groans. AJ gets a jump on it, timing himself as he runs back to the 404 feet marker in center field, but the effort will be futile. This ball was jacked off the bat, and Seattle will take the lead with a home run.

This ball is gone.

AJ doesn't give up on the play, and I watch in disbelief as he leaps up on to the wall, half climbing up on it. AJ makes an unbelievable over the shoulder catch. He bounces off the green padding, landing on his back on the warning track, and the crowd leaps to their feet to see if he managed to hold on to it.

AJ raises his gloved hand in triumph, the ball still in his grip.

The crowd is roaring, and I high-five Hayley and the other WAGS around me in celebration. Chris Matthews is running past second when he stops, staring at AJ in disbelief.

My heart is racing in excitement as the entire stadium cheers in approval of the amazing catch. Ryder Asbury, the right fielder, runs over to check on AJ, who rises and turns to the crowd, grinning as he does.

He made an unbelievable catch, one that shows the outstanding defender he is.

Within two years of being in the majors, AJ's quickly rising to elite center fielder status.

I sink back down to my seat and smile as Chase gets ready to face the next Seattle batter. I have a good feeling about the game tonight.

And what will come after it.

CHAPTER 9

By the bottom of the seventh, the score is still tied at zero. The Soaring Eagles have two outs, and I'm keeping my fingers crossed that we get on base, so AJ can bat again.

Not only did he have that highlight catch in center in the first inning, but a good night at the plate, too. AJ has gotten on base twice and moved runners into scoring position each time, but no Soaring Eagle has managed to cross home plate.

Ugh. I really don't want to go to extra innings tonight.

Not when I have a date with AJ when this game is over.

"Your boyfriend is up next if we can get on; let's hope he gets things moving," Hayley says.

"Not my boyfriend."

"He's your boyfriend."

"Stop."

"Did you stop when I started dating Brody?"

Dammit.

I groan.

Hayley laughs. "Maybe we should get out our bobbleheads and wave them for good luck. I mean, doesn't he have to score? It's his bobblehead night."

I give her the side eye. "Is it? That bobblehead doesn't even look like him!"

Hayley snorts. "I think it's the worst one they've done yet."

I groan. "Poor AJ. Forever cast with a giraffe neck and teeth half the size of his face."

"Yet people will bid on the horrible bobblehead on eBay."

This thought gives me pause. Yes. People will be bidding on bobbleheads of a man I've kissed.

Two days ago, my life was Scones and Such, hanging out with Hayley, watching baseball games, and thinking about my plans for law school in the fall.

Now I've met a man who is changing the game on me.

I watch AJ in the on-deck circle, and he moves in sync with David DeLeon, the batter in the box, almost as if he's taking the pitch himself, getting the tempo before it is his turn at the plate.

The Seattle ace is still in the game, still throwing strikes like crazy. Ugh. His pitching is on point, and I'm beginning to think the Soaring Eagles' bats won't break through this evening.

David takes the first pitch, and it's a ball. The crowd cheers in response.

The pitcher delivers again, and it's ball two.

"Oh, maybe he's starting to lose it," I say hopefully as the Seattle catcher goes out to the mound to talk to the pitcher.

They chat for a moment, covering their mouths with their gloves, then the catcher trots back to the plate and resumes his position. David steps back into the box.

Ball three.

Now the crowd is getting excited. If David gets on base, we get to the heart of the order, starting with AJ. The players who are known for driving in runs.

Strike.

"Ugh," I say, screwing up my nose. "If only we could get David on."

"I know," Hayley says.

We both wait for the next pitch. AJ is still in the on-deck circle.

Strike two.

"Oy," Hayley groans.

"Come on, David," his girlfriend sitting behind us yells. "You've got this!"

We all start cheering for David along with the rest of the Soaring Eagles fans.

Ball four!

We erupt into cheers as David tosses his bat aside and heads toward first base.

"Center fielder, number fifteen, AJ WILLIAMSON!" the PA announcer roars.

One Republic's "Make a Connection" is blaring from the speakers, and I love the choice for him. For AJ, it's making a connection between the bat and the ball.

But this song could be ours, too.

Our connection is about two people who seemed so unlikely to meet, let alone make a connection, but that's exactly what happened from the moment we met. One we built upon when AJ sought me out at Scones and Such and with the best first date ever, riding roller coasters and sharing fireworks and sweet kisses.

Now I'm here, cheering him on as he walks up to the plate. My emotions are a mix of excitement and anxiousness.

AJ gets into position on the right-hand side. I find myself mindlessly tapping my feet on the concrete as I wait for the pitch to be thrown.

The pitcher fires a fastball that comes in high and inside, and I gasp as AJ jumps back to avoid being hit in the face.

"Oh!" I exclaim, anxiety overtaking excitement for a moment.

The crowd boos as the manager for Seattle comes out of the dugout, making a slow trek to the mound. A reliever has been called in to get AJ out.

I continue to tap my feet until Hayley places her hand on my thigh. "This is why you are so thin," Hayley teases. "You never stop moving when you are wound up."

I smile sheepishly. "It's still genetics, but my restless energy doesn't help, I'm sure."

"Do you know what you need?" Hayley asks, a wicked gleam coming into her eyes.

"I'm afraid to ask," I say as the Seattle reliever trots toward the mound.

"Brody and I found this amazing brunch place that has Fruity Pebbles french toast. It is the greatest invention ever."

I shoot her a quizzical look. "I thought that award went to your brand-new cantaloupe skin peeler."

I don't even repress my smirk. Hayley is obsessed with random gadgets, and whenever one is delivered to our apartment, she declares it's either life-changing or the greatest thing ever, or in the case of the magical cantaloupe peeler, both.

"I have categories for the greatest things ever. And the greatest *french toast* ever is one covered in Fruity Pebbles," Hayley declares.

"I see."

"Anyway, that's not the point. You need this in your life."

"As my best friend, I'll trust you on that," I say as the Seattle reliever, Jay Thompson, begins throwing a few warmup pitches.

AJ is standing off to the side, his white uniform now caked with dirt. Hmm. There's something sexy about him being all sweaty and dirty and being put in a critical position to break this tie and get some runs on the board.

After a few more pitches, we're ready to go again.

AJ steps back into the box. I hold my breath.

Thompson throws a ball that AJ takes a swing at but fouls off.

Ugh, the count is now one ball, one strike.

AJ steps out of the batter's box, adjusting his feel of the bat, and steps back in.

I'm not a nail chewer, but I'm fighting the urge to start.

The reliever nods after receiving the signal from the catcher.

He throws a fastball right down the middle for strike two.

Hayley and I both groan in unison with the rest of the crowd.

Come on, AJ, I will him. *You know what Thompson is going to serve up to you. You can beat him.*

Thompson goes to deliver, and another fastball heads AJ's way, but again, he fouls it off.

My fingernails make a connection with my teeth.

The reliever shakes off the first few signals from his catcher. Then he nods, and I bite down on my thumbnail as he delivers the ball.

It's right down the middle again, and AJ takes a huge swing. Whack! AJ's bat splits in half the second it makes contact with the ball. He's holding the end of it in his hands as the rest of the bat flies into the screen behind him.

But somehow the ball is crushed toward right center. How is this ball traveling like that after a broken bat?

Thanks to the power AJ has in his swing, that's why.

Everyone rises to see the ball soar toward the right field seats, where the Seattle outfielder stands still as it goes over his head.

I gasp as I realize what AJ has done.

AJ has hit a broken bat home run.

"AJ!" I cry excitedly.

The crowd goes wild in approval, as this is a rare feat, and I have butterflies as I watch AJ rounding the bases, following

David, who has already crossed home plate. I'm exchanging high-fives and cheering wildly for AJ.

The Soaring Eagles are up by two runs.

All thanks to a powerful blast from AJ.

I watch as AJ crosses the plate, high-fiving David, who is waiting for him. He takes off his helmet, and his jet-black hair is all over the place. His expression is serious, and damn, AJ is freaking hot as he rakes a hand through his hair, pushing his longer locks off his face. And knowing he had enough power to hit a home run off a *broken bat?*

Incredibly sexy.

And I might just have to tell him that this evening, I think with a grin.

I LOOK AT MY PHONE AGAIN. EXACTLY FOUR MINUTES HAVE GONE by since I last checked it.

I've always been patient, but now I'm not.

Not when I'm waiting to see AJ and celebrate a Soaring Eagles win tonight.

It turned out David's run was all they needed to beat Seattle, winning two to zero. Hayley told me they'd be out sometime after eleven. I know AJ will have to talk to the media, get treatments, and normally, eat a post-game meal. However, he and Brody are skipping it tonight so they can eat with us instead.

The AJ vibes are so strong that I don't think I can eat. Which is crazy because I can always eat.

But right now, as I kill time with Hayley in the WAGS lounge, I'm eager to see him. I want to congratulate him on his performance tonight. I want to talk about that busted bat home run. I want to sit next to him at a restaurant and pore over a menu with him and discuss what sounds good. I want to sip a cold beer and laugh as he and Brody tell some stupid joke. I want to feel his rough, masculine hand on my bare thigh. I want him to steal a look at me, one that I will catch, with his emerald eyes shining brilliantly with affection.

With a whoosh, all my romantic desires that I had given up on last year, all my hopes that some man could exist like this outside of my Kindle, thoughts I was content to shelve until I was done with law school, have come back to life with AJ.

"Brody says they are on their way out," Hayley says, typing on her phone. "We'll meet them outside the clubhouse doors."

Electricity zips through me. My heartbeat picks up as I follow Hayley out into the corridor, taking the short walk between the clubhouse and the WAGS lounge.

I see the doors open, and some of the Soaring Eagles players step out—players whose stats I know backwards and forwards. I remember the last time I was here, with Hayley, how I couldn't believe I was going to be introduced to some of these players. How I knew I would internally fangirl the second I saw AJ.

While the excitement is still the same, the sentiment is completely different now.

I'm not here to fangirl over AJ.

I'm here to have dinner with the man who kissed me last night outside my door.

We stop in the hallway outside the clubhouse, and more players come out.

But not the right players.

Chase McLeary exits next. I can't get over how much brighter his hair looks in person. He's got flame-red curls, ones I usually only see peeking out from his baseball cap. But in street clothes, with no cap, his ginger hair is head-turning.

"Hey, Hayley," he says brightly as he heads out.

"Nice game tonight, Chase," Hayley says.

"Your man called it brilliantly," Chase replies, giving all the credit to Brody as he stops in front of us. "Have I told you how glad I am we stole him from Miami?"

"I might be biased, but I'm glad you all stole him, too," Hayley says. "Chase, this is my friend, Katie McKenna."

Chase extends his hand. "Hi, Katie, nice to meet you."

I shake his hand. "Nice to meet you, too, Chase."

"How's Hannah?" Hayley asks. "I haven't seen her this week."

Chase's light-brown eyes flicker for a moment.

"She's been crazy busy with work," Chase says. "After the Fourth of July, things should calm down for her."

Chase turns to me. "My girlfriend covers events for *DC Scene* magazine's Instagram account. Summer is insane for both of us, but this June she's had a lot more assignments than usual. I joke that I hope to see her by September."

I notice he smiles, but it doesn't reach his eyes.

"Tell her I said hello," Hayley says. "Maybe when it slows down for her, we can do brunch or something."

"She'd love that. I'll let her know," Chase says. He smiles that half-smile again. "I've got to run. See you, Hayley. And nice meeting you, Katie."

Then he heads off down the concourse.

"He's such a sweetheart," Hayley says. "I'm glad he and Brody have become close."

"What's Hannah like?" I ask, thinking of how Chase wasn't truly happy when he spoke of her.

"A mystery."

"A mystery?"

"Let me start off by saying she's been nothing but pleasant to me."

Ah. The set up for Hayley's "but" comment.

"But," Hayley says, right on cue, "she's not engaged when

87

she's here. Not with the WAGS. Not with the game. She'll smile and chat if you talk to her first, but she doesn't follow up with any question about you, you know what I mean? At first, I thought maybe she was just shy or socially awkward. But then I found out she covers the social scene for that digital magazine, and it didn't make sense. I'll show you her Instagram later. She's all over it, having fun at every cool opening in DC. But when she's here, in Chase's world, she's disengaged. That's the best way I can describe it."

I consider this information. "Do you think maybe that's why Chase likes her? Because she's not a fan?"

As I say the sentence aloud, I wonder if AJ will ever have doubts about me because I was a fan first. It's already been an issue with him. Brody likes the fact that Hayley doesn't know anything about baseball. Maybe Chase is the same.

Hmm. I don't like where my logical brain is going with this train of thought, so I abruptly make a mental U-turn and go back to thinking about Hannah.

"I don't know. But Chase is so friendly and talkative with anyone he meets, it's weird for him to be with a girl who doesn't interact with any of his teammates' wives or girlfriends," Hayley says.

I make an assessment. I can't help it. I love taking in information and building arguments for something or against it, laying out the facts as I know them.

My gut tells me in this case opposites won't attract for the long-haul.

And Chase's smile, and the expression in his eyes, are my key pieces of evidence.

I hear the clubhouse door click again. I hold my breath, hoping this time it will be AJ.

David DeLeon steps out first, followed by Brody.

And then AJ.

Every crazy feeling I have for the man goes into overdrive

the second I lay eyes on him. AJ's dressed up, with a fine green tattersall shirt, jeans, and tobacco-colored leather blucher shoes.

His eyes meet mine. My pulse leaps. My stomach goes upside down, the same feeling I get when I go down that first hill on a roller coaster. I'm beginning my own thrill ride, the one of spending the rest of the night with AJ.

A smile lights up his face when our eyes connect, and that dimple pops out in his cheek.

Hashtag romance novel moment.

Because I'm melting from the way he's staring at me.

"Katie," AJ says, stopping in front of me.

"Hi," I say, ecstatic to be with him again.

Before I can even wonder how he will greet me in front of our friends, AJ draws me into his solid chest for a hug.

I relish every single sensation of the moment. How the fabric of his shirt is soft against my cheek. How his large hand seems to span the small of my back. How tall he is, how hard his chest feels against my body. I close my eyes and breathe him in, the scent of freshly showered skin with his clean cologne lingering on top, and one word comes to my mind.

Bliss.

AJ releases me and takes my hands in his, stepping back so he can get a view of what I'm wearing. His deep green eyes flicker over me, taking in the navy-and-white striped T-shirt dress I'm wearing, with a denim shirt tied around my waist in case I get cold while we are at a bar or restaurant later. I'm always cold.

However, I'm anything but cold now as AJ's eyes flash sexily while he moves down my legs and back up to my eyes.

"I like the dress," he says, drawing me in closer. "Very nice."

"Who cares about my dress?" I say, laughing. "You were on fire tonight! You were incredible, AJ."

The smile tugs at the corner of AJ's mouth, causing my heart rate to fluctuate.

Into the high, dangerous zone.

"Well, thank you, but I do have to counter your point. I care about the dress. And the woman who is wearing it."

Feels. Swoon. Butterflies. You name it, I am afflicted with it in this moment.

I keep the romance vibes to myself and smile up at him. "Thank you. But I didn't get the opportunity to do a wardrobe change like you did."

And when we are not standing next to Hayley and Brody, I'll tell him how he is super sexy in both a dirty baseball uniform and a tattersall shirt and jeans.

"You don't need to. I love it."

I'm running out of words to describe my emotions. I obviously need to binge read some new books. Or go back and re-read Holly Martin's books. She always knows how to capture the feels.

"Katie, good to see you," Brody says, interrupting my thoughts.

"Hey Brody, you called a masterpiece tonight," I say.

"I wouldn't call it a masterpiece. McLeary had everything clicking on the mound."

"The whole team did," Hayley says, squeezing Brody's hand in hers.

"It was a good game," he replies, grinning. "Now, though, we need to get down to what really matters. What do you feel like eating? We both skipped the postgame spread in the clubhouse so we can eat with you two."

Hayley affectionately runs her hand through Brody's golden locks. "Which means we need to eat now, right?"

"Yes."

I'm beginning to think of a place when AJ lets go of one of my hands and brushes a curl back that has gone awry.

"While you are thinking, remember, it has to be a place that's open after eleven o'clock," AJ adds.

Oh, right. I can see this will be the interesting part about going out with a professional baseball player. The hours are … different.

"What about that empanada place?" Hayley asks. "They're open late."

Brody's eyes light up. "Oh, great call, Cherry Blossom. I love those jamaican ones."

I smile. Cherry Blossom is Brody's nickname for Hayley.

She turns her attention to me and AJ. "The restaurant has a bar that faces the street and opens up, with tables and chairs on the sidewalk. They serve until like two or three."

"Works for me. How about you, Katie?" AJ asks.

"I love empanadas," I say.

"Then we have to do it," AJ says.

He holds my hand as he leads me to the player parking lot, with Brody and Hayley walking alongside us. As soon as we reach it, Haley and Brody get in his old Jeep while AJ leads me to his Audi, as we agreed to meet at the restaurant so we can leave separately.

"New car next week," AJ says as he opens the door for me.

I slip inside. "What are you getting?"

AJ shuts my door and walks around to the driver's side of the car to get in. "A Tesla. I can't wait to see how that drives."

As AJ fastens his seatbelt, I wonder if the need to swap out cars is somehow linked to his childhood. He trades in cars every road trip, never keeping one as his.

I find it hard to breathe as the rational, lay-out-the-facts-and-study-them side of my brain begins to go into analysis mode.

I begin putting together all the pieces that I've learned about him so far. His Instagram pictures pass through my head like evidence exhibits. He travels with his crew of guy friends during the off-season. It seems like he was gone more than he was ever home, and I never found a post on his account that showed his house, now that I think about it. If he *was* home, he showed pictures of his dogs, but always in a park or somewhere outside, and never tagged with the word home, or even a location. As if he couldn't bring himself to identify a place as his home.

The cars follow this same pattern. He doesn't want to own one, which I get, and he can't go longer than a few weeks with the *same* one. Even for the short term, AJ doesn't want to commit to a car.

Heaviness sinks into my heart.

Will I follow this pattern, too?

Whoa. I didn't go there.

I did NOT.

Why am I even thinking about this?

We've had one date.

One amazing, wonderful, perfect date.

I need to take this for what it is.

And be realistic.

I'm going to law school in a few months.

AJ might be going to another team.

Everything says I should live in the now and have fun. Something my brain is not good at.

And apparently my heart isn't either.

Not with this man.

I mentally put the evidence away. I can only hope that if my feelings are right, and if AJ's are headed the same way, all the images we take together will give me a different picture than the one my brain is guiding me to.

My heart lifts as he drives out of the lot, entwining his hand with mine and resting it on my thigh.

This is what I need to focus on. The man who is taking me to dinner, the man who is holding my hand, who is taking steps with me into something we don't know.

But something I know will change my life all the same.

I smile as he squeezes my hand.

There's one part to the future I will allow myself to look forward to, however.

And that is sharing our first real kiss at the end of the night.

CHAPTER 10

My stomach twists as AJ drives us from Dupont Circle back to his place in the Navy Yard neighborhood in the wee hours of the morning.

My stomach *could* be knotting up from the obscene number of empanadas and glass of beer I piled in on top of the totchos and a hot pretzel shaped like a big E that I plowed through earlier at the ballpark.

I know the real reason, though.

My bottomless pit slash cast-iron stomach is not having food issues.

My stomach is excited—and anxious—to share that first big romantic kiss with AJ.

The evening has been fantastic so far. As I've been up since five, you think I would have fallen asleep face down in my empanada platter, but I'm anything but tired in AJ's presence.

I'm *alive.*

I study his profile as he drives. We grabbed a table at the back of the restaurant, hoping to have a little privacy away from the eyes of baseball fans who might recognize Brody and AJ. We lucked out, with it being so late on a Tuesday night, and they were only approached by a handful of fans during our meal.

Which left us to a fun evening talking and laughing over combo platters and a pitcher of beer.

AJ kept in constant touch with me, putting his hand on my leg as we sat side-by-side in the booth or casually draping his arm across the back of it, both of which sent a thrill through me each time they happened.

He's into me.

I'm into him.

We've had another great date.

So why does the idea of making out with him suddenly make me so nervous? We shared sweet kisses last night. All day long I thought about kissing him, and now that the moment is here, I find anxiety swirling in the pit of my stomach.

I think of past dates, of how we would have great evenings and then we'd get to this part and the BIG KISS was a big fat disappointment. I remember making out with one guy in his dorm room, and it was so boring that I ended up watching TV over his shoulder while we kissed.

Gregory. That was his name.

Really nice guy.

Incredibly boring kisser.

On the other hand, I did find that kissing chemistry with two guys during my university years. Ones I allowed myself to fall for. They both crushed my heart, leaving my romantic dreams in a pile of disappointed ruins.

In those cases—Brent and Matthew—the chemistry burned bright.

And for them, burned out.

I don't want that to happen again. I want the chemistry. The friendship. The romance. My heart is telling me AJ could be these things, if the kiss is right.

And if it is, I don't want that chemistry to burn out.

Not with AJ.

I shift my gaze straight ahead to the Capitol Building—the glorious white dome overlooking the city in the inky black night—and try to distract myself from my thoughts by talking to AJ.

"I love how the Capitol always glows bright in the darkness," I say as I gaze upon it. "It's so beautiful. It's tradition in my family to go every year and take our picture on the steps for the annual Christmas card. Dad said he wanted us to remember the importance of democracy, because that is a tremendous gift we received being Americans, and even more so, being lucky enough to grow up in the midst of the history of it here in DC. We still do it, although Meghan and I have refused to wear matching outfits since we went to college. As Meghan says, we needed to celebrate the freedom of fashion."

"I like that you still do it," he says. "Even though you and Meghan are on your own, you still take the annual picture."

"Oh, I can't imagine not doing it," I say. "Those traditions mean so much to my heart. My parents were good at finding those things to create shared experiences. That was one of them. So is staying in on New Year's Eve. We always have a spread of food and play board games. Family, friends, neighbors—the house is full, and it's always a blast. It's potluck, so everyone brings a dish and there's tons to eat. Oh, and it's a requirement that I make my baked cheese and ham mini sandwiches, and Mom pretends not to notice I'm eating stuff she thinks I shouldn't. It's not a party without those. And no, they are not served in a helmet because they are so fabulous they don't need a helmet. It's all about my super-secret sauce."

I glance at AJ in the darkness, and his face is lit up with a smile.

"You have your own secret sauce?" he asks, playing along with my crazy, nervous, rambling conversation.

"Well, it's not a secret because I found it in a vintage cookbook, but nobody can figure it out because I'm the only one who likes to go to old bookstores and flea markets and rummage through nineteen seventies cookbooks. Oh! Have you ever seen those crazy recipe cards from that time? I have a collection of them. You have to see them, AJ. Like those crazy molded foods. They molded everything, isn't that insane? I even have one card that has a mold made out of those canned spaghetti rings. You have to see that one to believe it."

AJ is silent for a moment. He's listening to me, I can tell, but his expression has changed to serious.

"Did I go a bridge too far with molds?" I joke.

"Yes, but not in the way you think," AJ says.

I don't understand what he means. I'm about to ask when he makes a detour onto Pennsylvania Avenue, headed toward the Capitol.

"Where are we going?" I ask, confused by this sudden change of direction.

"There's something I need to do," AJ says.

The area in front of the Capitol is practically deserted at this time of the morning, and AJ swings into a parking spot next to the reflecting pool in front of the building.

"Come on," he says.

Curious, I get out of the car and shut the door. AJ comes around and takes my hand in his.

"AJ, what are we doing?" I ask.

AJ doesn't say anything. He leads me up toward the edge of the reflecting pool, so we're facing the Capitol. The reflection of the building shimmers in the water, creating a breathtaking sight.

"You're right," AJ says softly. "It is beautiful here."

My heart begins to hammer inside my chest. I hear the water rippling in the pool and crickets chirping on this warm summer night as the Capitol glimmers in nightlights in front of us.

"You're beautiful, Katie."

I turn to find he's already staring at me.

He takes my hand, the one he's holding, and draws me into his strong body. AJ gently places my hand over his chest, holding it still against the soft fabric of his shirt, while his other hand glides down to my waist, right at my hip.

His body radiates heat that I can feel through his shirt, along with that hard, muscular chest my palm is flattened against.

I can't breathe as his emerald green eyes gaze down at me.

"You're all I've thought about all night. How fearless you are with food, telling the waitress to surprise you with a combo of her favorite empanadas. How your legs look amazing in this dress. That you say what you think. How you laugh with delight on a roller coaster, then scream your head off in terror the next minute. Down to weird recipes for molded foods that you find fascinating."

I smile at that, and so does AJ.

"You get me," I say.

"I do," AJ says, removing his hand from mine and bringing it to my face. I flicker with heat the second I feel his warm, rough skin caressing my cheek. "I like who you are, Katie. I like you a lot."

I swallow hard. "I like you, too."

AJ stares down at me. My heart is still slamming against my ribs in excitement.

"When you stare at me with those light green eyes of yours, I know you see Andrew Joseph, not AJ."

"It's true," I whisper back. "You're only AJ when you are on that field, but even tonight, when I watched you, you're Andrew Joseph now."

My Andrew Joseph.

"I know," AJ says, his fingertips trailing along my jaw.

Neither of us speak for a moment.

"I couldn't wait to get home to kiss you," he says, breaking the silence. "When you were talking about how much the Capitol means to you, how many memories you have here, I had my answer. I want to give you a new memory here. Let me kiss you, Katie."

I tremble in response to his request. Anticipation burns through me.

Just like that, my fears about kissing him evaporate into the DC night.

Because I know I am meant to kiss this man.

"Please kiss me, Andrew Joseph," I whisper back.

AJ slides his hand up underneath my hair, stroking his fingertips across the nape of my neck.

He lowers his head toward mine. I close my eyes, and his lips softly, gently graze against mine with a whisper-light touch.

I stifle the groan of need that threatens to erupt in my throat as AJ eases my mouth open with his tongue, parting my lips, slipping it inside as his hand moves down to my back. I'm pressed up against his hard body. We entangle as his mouth begins to discover mine for the first time.

It's electric. Thrilling. Sensual.

Everything I've ever dreamed of a romantic kiss being.

AJ takes from me, exploring me with abandon. I taste him, the beer that is lingering on his tongue, and all I want to do is consume more. I kiss him back, matching him kiss for kiss. Our tongues tangling is a beautiful, sensual harmony as his powerful arms hold me tightly to his athletic body. I feel his heart pounding against my palm, and I know I'm creating that same feeling in him that he is creating in me.

I find his face, feeling the five o'clock shadow, allowing my fingertips to graze across the rough stubble that is there— the same stubble that is prickling sexily against my skin—and he continues to kiss me more deeply. I inhale his clean scent, the one that reminds me of a fresh shower, and find myself wanting to taste his neck, but I can't tear myself away from his mouth, not yet.

My head is spinning as he is moving his hands everywhere, from my hair to my back to my hips, and I feel waves of pleasure rippling up through me. I need his touch. I need his taste, I need his scent.

I kiss him harder, more passionately, wanting to consume him. A groan escapes AJ's throat. He plunges his tongue deeper into my mouth, his hand gripping my hip and making me choke back a cry of pleasure simply from his kiss. I push my fingers into his long, dark locks, and AJ shivers against me as I do.

"Katie," AJ murmurs against my mouth. "Katie."

Then he opens the seam of my lips with his tongue again, quickly plunging inside with urgency.

My heart rate is frantic. My pulse is burning. My blood is pounding in my ears. I'm dizzy.

All because of this kiss.

We tangle again, giving and taking, our hands caressing each other while the water in the reflecting pool laps gently next to us. AJ breaks the kiss, and I gaze up at him in wonderment.

Whoa.

That was the most incredible kiss I've ever experienced.

AJ brushes his lips against mine, slowly and sweetly this time, in a caressing kiss that has me melting in his arms.

He breaks the kiss and gazes down at me. "I could kiss you like this all night."

"Then we should get comfortable," I tease.

AJ grins and takes my hand in his. He walks a few steps to the edge of the reflecting pool and sits down, then carefully pulls me down so I'm sitting across his lap.

"Comfortable?" AJ asks, his eyes shining mischievously at me.

All the feels.

AJ cradles me protectively to him. A giddy, warm feeling takes over as I run my hand over the powerful forearm wrapped around me.

"It's after two in the morning. Don't you have a game tomorrow?' I ask, resting my head against his chest. I close my eyes and inhale his cologne, loving that I'll be able to smell it on my dress later when I'm alone.

"I'll sleep at four."

"Four?" I ask, lifting my head to look at him.

AJ gently moves his hand through my hair, and his finger catches on a tangle of curls.

"Ouch," I say, laughing.

A flustered look sweeps over his handsome face. "I'm sorry. My finger is stuck in there."

"Mufasa hair for the win," I say, reaching up and untangling my curls from his finger. "Now why are you sleeping at four?"

"That gives me six hours. More than enough. Because I have more important things to do with my time tonight than sleep."

I smile at him. "Anything in mind?"

"Yeah," AJ says, nuzzling his nose to mine. "Making more memories."

He kisses me again, slowly and sweetly in the shadows of the nation's Capitol. I can't think of anything I want more than this.

And without a doubt, kissing AJ at the steps of the reflecting pool will be my favorite memory here of all.

CHAPTER 11

Playlist Shuffle Song of the Day:
"On My Mind" by Ellie Goulding

I flick through racks of perfectly preppy sundresses in a boutique in Georgetown. Not my style, but this store is one of the holy grails of shopping for my sister Meghan. Since I'm not working at Scones and Such until this evening, I was able to meet Meghan for lunch and shopping as we had planned last week.

Of course, I didn't get much sleep, because after making out with AJ for an hour, and then him having to drive me home instead of seeing his apartment because we couldn't stop kissing each other, it was well past four in the morning by the time I tumbled into bed.

The idea of sleeping was ridiculous, however, because all I wanted to do was replay the evening in my mind like that favorite movie you always have to stop and watch when flipping channels. I happily relived every kiss, remembering his mouth claiming mine over and over and over in front of the Capitol.

I glance down at my phone. It's five minutes past ten now,

and AJ should be up within the next hour. I've already sent him a little good morning text to greet him when he wakes up, and I'm eager for him to reply to it. While I can't go to his game tonight due to work, we decided that he would meet me back at my place, so we can hang out together this evening before the team flies out tomorrow after a day game for a Midwest road trip.

I remember Hayley saying in the beginning that it's hard dating a baseball player because the hours are so screwy. Luckily, I'm a night owl, so it hasn't been hard on me yet.

Of course, I'm not going to law school now, either.

I flick through a bunch of navy-and-white striped shirts, and for once in my life, I'm annoyed at myself for thinking ahead. Why can't I just live in the moment like normal people?

But right now, I want to run right into something with AJ, thinking of a future, the consequences of the situation come fall be damned.

I go through all the clothing while Meghan tries on the first of twenty-some-odd items she has in the dressing room, looking for the perfect preppy outfit for a boat party she's going to in Annapolis on Saturday night.

I move to the next bay, filled with more chambray. More white. More eyelet.

I can't help but smile. Meghan and I couldn't be more different. I love T-shirt dresses. Stripes. Cute jeans and flowy tops and sundresses in vibrant colors.

Whereas Meghan is all about perfect prep. She likes chambray. Gingham. Navy. Cords and cable knits in the autumn. Her hair is glossy and straight, her nails always in a delicate nude-pink, a smile always present on her face.

Whereas I like to participate in a good debate and love spending days sifting through junk at a flea market and happily digging into messy food with abandon, Meghan prefers writing poetry. Working on her bullet journal.

Blogging about her life at American University, where she is a senior studying literature. Meghan dreams of a life on the bay, in Annapolis, where she can write and live in a rambling old house that she will lovingly make the perfect home for her and Whitaker and their perfectly preppy children, with names like Crew and Brownyn, and a golden Labrador named George.

Those are the names. Meghan has already told me that. Along with the fact that I will be the godmother to both of them.

Ha-ha. It must be in our genetic makeup, seeing as how Meghan has her *Town and Country* magazine future already laid out just as I have my law career mapped out.

But Meghan is planning this future based entirely on Whitaker, without any promises of this future, let alone a ring on her finger.

Once, I asked if Whitaker had mentioned this rambling house in Annapolis with hollyhocks growing outside and if he had talked about when they would get engaged, and my always happy sister, the one with sunshine in her eyes, grew cloudy for a brief moment before saying she knew it would happen, that Whitaker often talked about how when *h*e got married he'd have a house in Annapolis, save to buy a boat, join a certain country club where he could enjoy golf and his wife could play tennis, and she knew he meant *her.*

I cringe when I recall that conversation, as I don't think Meghan is planning a future outside of Whitaker. She doesn't talk of finding a job after college, but apartment hunting in Annapolis, Whitaker's hometown.

If I'm going off my romance novel education, the foreshadowing is looming large here, like a big, black thunderstorm that is rolling ahead in the distance but very visible.

My pre-law brain, laying out evidence, agrees.

"What do you think, Katie Bug?"

I turn and see Meghan twirling around me, in a beautiful white eyelet dress. Her long, shiny, chestnut-colored hair streams around her as she moves.

"You look beautiful," I say, and my voice grows thick when I think of the storm that is most likely headed her way.

"Katie?" Meghan asks, stopping in place. "What's wrong?'

I force a smile on my face. "I love you, Meg. I hope Whitaker knows how lucky he is to have such an intelligent, sweet, beautiful soul like you."

I think of all the times I've met Whitaker. I've always found him lacking personality, like Meg ordered him out of a high-end preppy clothing catalog—he looks great in pictures and polo shirts and doesn't have much else. He's blond and handsome in that preppy way, but when I talk to him, I'm bored to tears. Whitaker will speak if you speak to him first, answer your question, and then fall silent, as if he's done his bit to speak a few pleasantries to you. To get him talking more than a few sentences, I'll bring up boating, which is one of his things. Along with financial investments.

Man. He is a catalog cutout. You could show him on the deck of a boat in sailing gear, then headed to the office in traditional suit and tie.

Which would be great if he had a personality and showed interest in the people around him, but he doesn't. After three years, I honestly don't know if he knows much about my family other than the fact that we are the people Meghan is attached to.

More to the point, I don't think he cares.

And what do I know about him? He likes talking about Annapolis. Boats. Investments.

Himself. That is his favorite topic, hands down.

Ugh.

He's boring. Self-absorbed.

But I could survive all of that if he honestly showed love and respect to Meg.

Which he doesn't.

When I raised my concerns to Meghan, it led to the biggest fight of our lives. I told Meg that he didn't seem to appreciate her. That he liked for her to jump when he commanded. That I didn't see the respect coming from him that she deserved. Well, that conversation didn't go over well, and Meg didn't speak to me for a week, which was the worst week of my life.

For reasons unknown to me, Meg is determined that Whitaker is the one.

But it's a future that I don't think will ever happen.

For all the times my dad asked Whitaker about what he wants for the future, the talk was always about himself. Never what he hoped for Meghan, or even referring to the future as a "we."

After four years, I've never heard Whitaker talk of the future like that.

Now a huge sense of foreboding surges through me. They are about to enter their senior year of college. Will Whitaker freak out and break up with Meghan? I can't tell you how many times I saw that this past year, the "we're too young to get so serious" breakup speech, with people Hayley and I knew.

"Hey, you look like you're going to cry," Meghan says, coming over to me and putting her hands on my shoulders. "Are you okay?"

I sniffle. "I'm feeling protective of my little sister."

"I'm only a year and a half younger than you."

"I know, but I'm still older. And all I want is for Whitaker to give you all the happiness you deserve."

"Why are you talking like this?" Meghan says. Her light green eyes, identical to mine, show confusion in them. "Of course Whit makes me happy. I'm the lucky one, I promise you that. He's amazing and smart, and he's got his future lined up for us. We're going to be so happy. Disgustingly so, I promise."

Ugh, if I were flipping the page in my book, I'd know the breakup was coming the next chapter.

"You know, if you could change your schedule at Scones and Such, you could come with us to Annapolis this weekend," Meghan suggests, a wicked smile playing at the corners of her mouth. "There are going to be loads of single, successful men there. You always say no when I ask you to join us, but Katie, it's been forever since you've gone out with a guy. Come on, there are some delicious ones you can make out with at a minimum!"

I grin and move over to a display of wicker purses, absently trailing my fingers over one. I was going to save the AJ conversation for lunch and give Meghan the details over salad and iced teas, but I decide now is the time to share my news.

"I made out with a guy last night, thank you very much," I say casually, as if I do this all the time.

Meghan is silent.

I think I've rendered her mute.

"What?" she finally gasps. "With whom? Why didn't I know about this?"

"I wanted to tell you in person. But I've met somebody. And he's amazing. He's sweet and funny and sexy, and I'm so smitten with him that you're the one who is going to be sick."

Meghan is standing next to me, her mouth wide open.

"Forget this dress. We're going to lunch right now so I can hear everything!"

I smile. This is what I love about Meghan. When it comes to people she loves, she's all in with needing to hear details and asking questions and sharing in your joys, your successes, your pain—all with unwavering love.

"No, get your dress and bag and whatever *Town and*

Country says you need to wear for yachting," I tease. "This will keep until the bread is placed on the table."

"Oh, no. I'm buying this dress, so you can expand all you want right now. Who is it?"

"You know him."

I nearly burst out laughing at the look on Meghan's face. We don't run in the same social circles, so I can see she is racking her brain for someone we'd both know who isn't a cousin or neighbor.

"You don't know him," I say. "But you know who he is. He's famous."

"*What?*"

"I know. As improbable as it sounds, I've had a couple of dates with a celebrity."

"A *couple?* And you didn't tell me?"

I wince when I see the hurt look on Meghan's face.

"I know, but I wanted to make sure he was real. And he is, Meg. He's wonderfully, perfectly real, and I really like him. More than I've ever liked anybody."

"Is he a politician?"

I snicker at the most normal assumption when someone is dating a celebrity in DC. "Noooooooooooo."

Meghan stamps her Tory Burch-clad foot impatiently onto the hardwood floor.

"Tell me right now, or I'll never forgive you for keeping him a secret!"

I lean in closer to her, so only she can hear me, even though the shop only has a few customers and sales people in it.

"AJ Williamson," I whisper in her ear.

I step back and see her brain clicking into place.

"The baseball player you have on your *phone?*" Meghan asks, her eyes wide.

I nod. "Yes. Him."

"No. No way."

"It's true."

"The one you fainted on?"

My face grows warm. "Apparently, I intrigued him."

"Shit. I need a chardonnay at lunch to take all this in!"

"Good thing you turned twenty-one last month, then," I say with a smile.

"And he's smart and kind?" Meghan asks, circling right back to AJ.

"Both. In abundance," I say. And as I think of AJ, warmth spreads through every inch of me.

"You're glowing!" Meghan cries.

"We've only spent three days together, but I have this feeling about him, Meg. I really do."

She squeals. We've both inherited the romance sucker gene.

"Okay, I'm getting changed. And then you are telling me everything over lunch and a glass of wine."

I watch as she sails back toward the dressing room, practically running across the floor as she does.

As she closes the door behind her, my phone buzzes in my hand. I tap it open, and excitement shoots through me when I see I have a text from AJ:

I love waking up to a text message from you.

I'm tingling all over as I message him back:

Good morning. I hope you got enough sleep.

AJ is typing…

I eventually crashed. Had to get up and walk the dogs but then fell right back asleep. Now I'm going to get some breakfast. Wish you could join me.

Ahh!

I type back:

**Are you sure about that? I'm NOT a morning
person.**

Then I hit send.
AJ is typing…

**I'm more than sure. I don't have to talk to you. I just
want to be with you. Even if you're cranky.**

My heart leaps as I read his words. I already know what
sappy words I'm going to say to him before I even type:

**I want to be with you, too. I might even talk to you
before eggs. Which means I like you a lot, Andrew
Joseph.**

Then I hit send.

As Meghan returns from the dressing room, I know how
much I do like AJ.

Best of all, I'm pretty sure he likes me just about as
much, too.

"This is so romantic," Meghan says. "You fainted in his
arms, and he fell in love with you, and he's been your secret
crush for years."

"Who are you, Holly Martin?" I tease. We trade her books
back and forth between us.

"No, but I know a romance plot when I see one."

"It's not like that," I protest. We're seated on the patio at
our favorite bistro in Georgetown, sipping chardonnay in

celebration of my dates with AJ and the prospect of maybe, just maybe, finding the love that I have been waiting for.

I reach for a piece of hot sourdough bread from the basket the server has just placed on the table, and I can feel Meghan watch me as I put my bread on my plate.

"How is it not like that? Oh, side note: I want that bread so badly I'm almost willing to eat it."

I stare at her. "Then why not eat it? You're not gluten intolerant," I say, reaching for the butter and my knife.

"Whitaker and I are both low carb. It makes me so stabby sometimes," she says, wrinkling her nose.

"Better you than me. Give up bread? So much NO."

"Back to AJ," Meghan says, pausing to take a sip of her wine. "Do you see this going somewhere?"

"I do for the summer," I say cautiously. I set the butter knife on the side of my plate and put the slice of bread down next to it. "I'm trying not to think about what will happen when fall rolls around. His contract is up. AJ has wanderlust. He loves going from place to place, and that's not a life I can live, not while in law school."

"You can't really do it once you are in a firm, either," Meghan points out. "Beside that fact, you aren't a wanderlust type of person. You like routine and roots. Always with the five-year plan in front of you. You always have."

I think on Meghan's words. She's right. I can't imagine living out of a suitcase for months on end. Not only because of the profession I want to pursue, but because I would hate that. That's not me. I love having a place to come home to, the same place, with my things that make me happy and comfortable.

"Hey," Meghan says, reaching for my hand across the table, "don't second guess everything so much. Let your heart fall and feel wonderful."

"Oh, it has," I say. "I can't stop thinking about him. Which makes me worry about what might happen in the future."

Meghan appears thoughtful for a moment.

"I believe," she says, squeezing my hand to comfort me, "that love finds a way to work things out."

"But there's no flexibility on my end, and that's not fair to AJ. I won't have a lot of time for him, and he'd have to stay here. What if he resented me for it?"

"What if he didn't?"

I blink. "I just told you he doesn't have roots. How could he not hate being stuck here and then getting minimal time with me for it?"

"Because maybe he'll want roots with you," Meghan says simply.

I release her hand. "I shouldn't think that far ahead."

"Katie, it's me. I know you. And I know you already have."

Ugh. She's right.

"Don't worry. It can work. It won't be easy, but love never is. Except for me and Whitaker. Everything fell into place for us so easily."

Despite the sunny skies overhead, I feel an imaginary storm cloud moving toward me with her words.

"Okay, enough of this," I say, picking up my glass of wine. "Cheers to us. For being not only sisters, but friends. And to our happiness."

"Cheers to that," Meghan says, smiling brightly as she clinks her glass against mine.

As I take a sip of the chilled wine, I decide to put all thoughts of the fall aside.

I'm going to live in the now.

Which means seeing AJ later tonight, I think with a smile.

CHAPTER 12

I finish running my flat iron over my hair and study the image in the mirror. Seeing Meghan today made me want to straighten my hair for a change.

And it's something I can surprise AJ with, too.

"You look so different with your hair straight," Hayley says, dipping her brush into her glimmery, champagne-colored eye shadow and tapping the excess off.

I glance in the mirror, watching her as she applies it to her lids.

A smile lights up my face. It's like we're right back at Georgetown, with a playlist cranked up as we spend our time being all girlie, getting ready for the evening. I had to work, and Hayley had a sponsor dinner for the non-profit she works for, so neither one of us was able to go to the game tonight.

"I love doing this," I say, turning off my iron and unplugging it. "There's something exciting about getting ready for a date."

"It reminds me of school," Hayley says, her eyes meeting mine in the mirror. "But this time, we're not getting ready for boys. We've got *men*."

I once again get a flashback to AJ kissing me.

Oh, yes, there's no doubt about that, I think.

"Men who won tonight," I add as I reach for my new lipstick.

The Soaring Eagles won the second game of the series against Seattle, with AJ hitting a sacrifice fly to put the first run on the board for his team. They ended up winning three to two.

Obviously, making out with me until three in the morning didn't impact his game, I think with a grin as I take the cap off my lipstick. I begin to apply it, and I notice Hayley is watching me.

"Ooh, what is that? It's so pretty on you," she says.

"It just came today. It's Morphe liquid lipstick in Spotlight," I say. "Isn't it gorgeous?"

"It is. Too bad it won't stay on long tonight."

I shoot her a look, and she gives me a mischievous grin.

"Are you implying I intend to make out with AJ for hours tonight? If so, then you are correct."

We both laugh.

"Promise me when we are getting ready for bingo at the retirement village, we'll still put on our lipstick together, Katie."

I smile back at Hayley. She has been my best friend since we met, and I know she will always be my closest friend. We have even promised each other we'll live in the same retirement community as we grow old.

Hayley is my other sister, and she always will be.

"We'll not only put on our lipstick together, but I'll be honest and tell you when it's feathering into your wrinkles," I tease.

Hayley grins. "I'll tell you when it's on your dentures."

"Deal."

I put my lipstick down and take a moment to press my lips together to evenly distribute the color. I peer at my outfit and take a moment to adjust the neckline of my off-the-shoulder black blouse, tugging it back down into place.

"You look very sexy in that top and jeans. AJ is going to die when he sees you," Hayley says.

I grow warm from the thought.

"I have never been this excited to see anybody," I admit, watching as Hayley picks up her signature Jo Malone perfume and sprays it on her wrists. "I couldn't stop thinking about him all day."

"It's a wonderful feeling, isn't it?" Hayley says, smiling warmly at me. "Even when that super excited feeling eventually fades, it's replaced by the happiness of knowing you're going to be with him. I'm always happy knowing I'm going to see Brody. And I always miss him when he goes on the road."

I nod. The Soaring Eagles are leaving for Chicago tomorrow after a day game. They'll play a three-game series there, and then another series against St. Louis before coming home next Friday.

AJ is going to be gone for a week.

I frown as I pick up one of my silver, honeycomb drop earrings off my porcelain jewelry tray and put it in my ear.

"I hate that I'm just getting to know him, and he's going away so soon," I admit.

"That's the hard part," Hayley says. "But that's not going to change how AJ feels about you. If anything, it will make him more excited to come back to you and pick up where you left off. Technology will be your Cupid. Texting and FaceTime will help."

I slip in my other earring. I hope she's right. That we can continue where we are and pick up where we left off when he returns.

"I'm right," Hayley says, expertly reading my mind. "AJ will miss you and come back dying to see you."

"I should pick up extra shifts next week," I think aloud.

"To keep me distracted. I can't believe I'm saying this, but I know I'm going to miss him."

"Of course you'll miss him. You *like* him," Hayley replies. "You glow when you talk about him, and it's not just your bronze, summer-kissed makeup."

"I know I've told you this before, but it has nothing to do with him being a baseball player," I say. "I like the guy I know outside of the uniform."

"Katie, you thought AJ was hot before, and that's not a crime," Hayley says. "We all create judgments based on first impressions, and that's all you knew about him. But now you are falling for the man he is, and that's what matters. You don't have to convince me or AJ that your feelings are genuine. You are a genuine person, Katie. Everyone who knows you knows that."

"You know what? You're right," I agree. "I don't need to justify it. AJ knows who I am."

And that my budding feelings for him have nothing to do with what he does for a living.

"Back to needing distractions," Hayley says. "You already have one on your schedule. Remember, we are going out Friday night with Addison."

I nod. Addison works with Hayley at Expanded World to the Shelf, a non-profit organization to support research and provide tools to help people with dyslexia. I met her at a big gala a few weeks ago, and she is a super sweet girl.

"I can't wait. Are we going to try that new rosé garden?" I ask. "You know I've been dying to go."

"I think we must do that," Hayley says, her eyes shining brightly at me.

Hayley's phone buzzes on the counter.

"I bet it's the boys," she says, picking it up. She taps her phone and reads. "Yep, they are leaving the ballpark now. Brody says he's going to drop AJ here and take me back to his place."

"Okay, so I can take AJ back to his place later," I say.

I exit the bathroom, and Hayley follows behind me, flipping off the light as she leaves.

"You could let him sleep over if you want. I'm staying at Brody's, so you have the place to yourselves."

"Is it weird to say that I want to wait a little bit longer before having sex with him? I'm enjoying dating him. Making out with him. It's romantic to me. Not that I don't want to have sex with him."

"No, of course not," Hayley says, sinking down on the sofa next to her gray ball of fluff called Pissy. The most appropriate name for the world's crankiest kitten.

"And I totally reserve the right to change my mind."

"Absolutely."

"I mean, if his shirt were to come off and things took a turn, I might be thinking of things other than romance," I say, sinking down on the other side of Pissy.

She hisses in disapproval.

"Pissy thinks romance first," Hayley teases.

I snort. "Pissy wishes I'd evacuate her space. I cramp her style."

"Why are you so rude?" Hayley says, stroking her tiny head. "Katie is sweet, you little dork."

Purring immediately ensues.

"I'll take her with me, too," Hayley says. "She's used to riding in the car, and Brody likes having her around."

"Brody is weird," I tease.

"Ha-ha. She loves Brody, just like her mama does."

"Hopefully AJ's dogs will like me, unlike tough stuff here," I say.

Hayley and I talk while we wait, but the whole time I have to resist the urge to get up and walk around, fiddle with my bracelet, tap my foot—anything to work through this anticipation building up within me. How can I be so excited to see someone I just saw last night?

My phone beeps.

I quickly swipe it off the coffee table and unlock my screen, which now has a picture of me and Meghan as the new wallpaper, and see I have a text from AJ:

On our way up. Waiting on an elevator. It needs to hurry up. I can't wait to see you.

Ooh!

I text him back:

I can't wait to see you, too. That elevator better be hitting the lobby floor any second now.

"Was it AJ?" Hayley asks.

"Yeah," I say happily. "They are waiting on an elevator. AJ says he can't wait to see me."

All the vibes kick in as I read his text again.

AJ is as anxious to see me again as I am him.

"Who knew under that dude's dude exterior was a romantic who needed the right girl to set him free?" Hayley asks.

I wonder if that's true. If I'm the girl who is different. If things go well, maybe I could be the one worth staying put and putting up with law school for.

"Ugh, I hate my brain," I say, putting my phone back on the table.

"What do you mean?"

"I've been out with him three times, if we include when we got coffee. Three. And I'm already wondering where this can go. I need to live in the moment. The future is so complicated."

"Everyone's future is complicated, Katie. But lots of people fall in love and date and stay together. If it were impossible, nobody would do it."

I grow quiet. In my head, I argue her points one by one. *Yes, but those people aren't dating a professional baseball player and going to law school. They aren't dating a man who hates being grounded and in one place. They aren't going to be first year law school students struggling to keep grades up and praying their partner doesn't resent them for not having time to do all the things they did before school started. Who doesn't resent them for making them stay in one place for years, if not forever, if they told the truth.*

There's a knock at the door. Pissy hisses, and I put my arguments away. As if I had written them all in a notebook, I slam it shut and shove it under the bed, so I don't have to think on it.

Living in the now is happening.

And that includes a night in with AJ.

With that thought replacing my worries, I leap off the couch.

Hayley laughs. "No need to run. I won't race you to it."

"Shh!" I say, putting my finger over my lips. "I don't want them to hear us."

"Are you going to count to ten before answering?"

I mouth "shut up" to her as I go to the door.

And Hayley starts laughing as I stand there and mentally count to ten in my head.

Now that I waited enough so it doesn't seem like I was either standing next to the door, waiting for AJ, or running to the door to open it the second he rang the bell, I unlock it and pull it open.

My eyes widen. I know Brody is next to him, but I can't see him.

Because my eyes are only for AJ in this moment.

He's standing before me in a summery linen button-down shirt, one that is a pale blue-green and shows off his dark, tanned skin and deep green eyes. He has on khaki shorts, and my eyes skim once again over his powerful legs, and then back up to his face. AJ is freshly shaven, and all I want to do is bury my face in his neck and inhale the scent of soap and cologne that is now lingering on his skin.

As my eyes meet his, I realize his expression is one of shock.

"Katie," AJ says slowly, "your hair. It's straight. The curls are completely gone."

"I flat-ironed it," I say, smiling at him. "Come on in."

"It's like a different Katie," he says, his eyes still taking me in. "I can't get over it."

Brody steps past AJ, as he's still staring at me.

"Hi, Katie," Brody says, moving inside.

"Hi, Brody," I say, although my eyes never leave AJ's.

"Do you like it?" I ask, wondering what he truly thinks of my hair change.

AJ takes strands of my hair between his thumb and his index finger, slowly sliding them down the length of my long locks before gently tucking them behind my ear. Goosebumps prickle my skin as a result.

"I do," AJ says. "But I like Curly Katie just as much as Straight-Haired Katie. I don't care how you wear your hair. Either way, you're beautiful to me."

If I were to use an emoji to describe my feelings, I'd have hearts shooting out of my eyes.

"You look incredible tonight," he says.

"Thank you," I say. "Come on in."

AJ steps past me. As soon as I shut the door, he draws me into his arms for a hug.

I slide easily into his body, his arm looping around me as I press my cheek into his chest, inhaling his clean scent and closing my eyes as he holds me to him.

Absolute bliss.

The moment is over far too quickly as AJ releases me. I only hope I'm cradled right back against him as soon as Brody and Hayley leave for the night.

"Hey, AJ," Hayley says, smiling at him. "Nice game."

Right! Game!

"Oh, yes, I kept up with it at work the best I could," I say.

"Hey. You don't have to follow every game. You don't expect me to follow you around Scones and Such and take notes of every order you take, do you?"

I grin. "Well, when you put it that, way, no."

"Brody, I'm going to bring Pissy with me tonight so she's not a pain in the ass to Katie and AJ," Hayley says. "If you'll take her, I'll get her carrier."

"You know my place is her place. Come here, my girl," Brody says, taking Pissy and holding her to his chest. "How are you?"

I know AJ is an animal lover, and his eyes light up when he spots Pissy. "What a cute kitten," AJ says, moving toward Brody. "She's so tiny!"

"She's evil," I warn. "There's a reason why she's named Pissy. For pissed off. She will hiss at you."

Brody laughs good naturedly. "She's selective about who she likes, that's all."

"And she likes you?" AJ jokes, looking at Brody. "She's so cute."

He goes to pet her, and Pissy lets out a sharp hiss that has AJ jerking his hand back at record speed.

"Shit!" AJ gasps.

Brody and I both begin laughing.

"I warned you," I say.

Brody puts her up around his right shoulder. Pissy simply hangs out up there, curving around his neck, surveying us from her perch with her watchful eyes.

"She won't bite you. But she doesn't want you near her, either."

"Pissy is all hiss, no bite," I say. "She's hated me since the day Hayley brought her home."

"But she let me pick her up the first time I was over here," Brody counters.

Pissy's motor kicks in as Brody scratches her head over his shoulder, and the sound of her purrs fill the air.

"How can anyone hate Katie?" AJ asks.

"Right?" I say. "I love animals!"

Hayley returns with her soft-sided carrier and her bag and sets them on the sofa.

"Okay, let me take her," she says, retrieving Pissy off Brody's shoulder and putting her inside the carrier.

Brody moves around Hayley and picks up her bag.

"There we go," Hayley says, zipping it up.

"She doesn't fight you on that?" AJ asks in surprise.

"Nope. She knows she's going to Brody's. Someday, we'll surprise her with a trip to the vet, and then she'll never trust me when I put her in it. But she'll forgive Brody if he does it. He's her person."

"I hear I'm yours, too," Brody says affectionately, his blue eyes gazing at Hayley with adoration. "Are you ready to go?"

"Yep," Hayley says. "Good night, guys. I'll see you tomorrow, Katie. What shift are you working?"

"Evening. If they have the Earl Grey scones, I'll save you one," I say, knowing those are her favorites.

"I was hoping you would say that," Hayley replies, flashing me a grateful smile. "AJ, I'll see you when you're back from St. Louis. Have a good trip."

"See you, Hayley," AJ says.

As soon as they leave, I move over to the door and lock it. I turn around to face AJ. My stomach flips upside down in excitement, as we are alone now.

"Hi," I say, walking toward him.

AJ slides his arms around my waist. Anticipation shoots through as he holds me close.

"Hi," he murmurs, lowering his mouth to mine.

He slowly eases my mouth open with a kiss. AJ is kissing me gently, deliberately, taking his time, as if he's savoring the taste of me. I melt into him, my heart dancing from this wonderful feeling.

He slides his hand up underneath my hair and laughs against my lips, breaking the kiss.

"I'm sorry," he says, gazing down at me. "I'm used to your curls. It was weird to feel straight hair."

I smile up at him. "I'm glad you like them."

"I like the girl they belong to," AJ says. "So, you just want to hang out tonight?"

I nod. "If that's good with you. I thought we could watch TV or something."

Like kiss you for hours. That would be a lovely something.

"Whatever you want to do I'm good with."

"Do you want anything to drink?" I ask. "My options are limited, however. Water, iced tea, orange juice, or rosé."

AJ flashes me a smile, and that dimple pops out in his cheek. "I'll take a water."

I smile and go into the kitchen, retrieve two bottles of water from the refrigerator, and come back into the living room. I hand him one and pick up the remote from the coffee table before I sink down on the sofa. AJ sits down right next to me.

He put his arm across the back of the sofa, oh-so-lightly grazing my back and sending a rush through me as he does.

"What are you in the mood to watch?" I ask.

"What's your routine? What do you watch when you get off work?"

"Legal dramas," I say seriously. Then I flash him a smile. "Kidding."

AJ grins. "I would have bit on that."

"I know, that's why I said it."

"Touché. So, in all seriousness, what do you watch?"

I wince. "I'm embarrassed to tell you."

"Why? Is it sappy chick stuff?"

If only.

"Not that I don't enjoy good 'sappy chick stuff' as you say, but there's always one thing I watch nightly."

"You're making this very dramatic. You're going to be great in court one day, Counselor."

I exhale. "I watch the *Soaring Eagles Postgame Show*."

AJ studies me after my confession. He knows I'm a big fan, but anyone who watches every postgame show is a serious one.

He's quiet for a moment, as if he's pulling together his thoughts before speaking.

"Katie," AJ says, "my first impression of you was that you were a big fan. When I went to see you at Scones and Such, I wasn't sure what I was getting into. Would you be able to see past the uniform? Would you act like you liked me simply because you wanted to be with AJ, the baseball player? Or could you see me apart from baseball? From the person you saw on TV and read about? I honestly didn't know if you could."

"What made you take that chance?" I ask, curious. "It would have been easier to start with a girl you walked up to in a bar. You'd know from the way she looked at you if she knew who you were or not."

AJ reaches for my hand, lacing his fingers through mine. "I didn't want a girl at a bar. I didn't want a setup. The second you started talking, I had to know you. I knew I was taking a risk, that you might not be honest with me, or you might talk yourself into believing you like me because you wanted to like me. But I believe you. I know you like me as me, and that has nothing to do with you being a fan. I see you as Katie. Katie who likes roller coasters and wants to help other women and protect their rights in the workplace. One who says the funniest things and is the most unique girl I've ever met. Not Katie the baseball fan. That's a part of you. But it's not all of you. No different than me being a center fielder isn't all of me."

As the depth of his words reach my heart, I know how different this conversation is. AJ is not like any man I've ever gone out with.

I could fall for you, I think as I stare into his brilliant green eyes.

"I'm glad you believe me," I say.

"I do," AJ says.

He releases my hand and exhales. "I can't say what is going to happen between us. I've never seriously dated anyone. Have I gone out with women? Yes. But I never let anything go beyond the casual stage. I didn't want that responsibility. I didn't want to have to answer to anyone. But here I am with you."

He raises his hand to my hair, stroking it and sending shivers down my spine.

"When I'm not with you, I'm thinking about you. Thinking about when I'm going to see you next. I've never had this feeling in my life. I can't get enough of you. Talking to you. Touching your soft skin," AJ says, trailing his fingertips down the side of my neck. "Knowing that if I were to bury my face right here," he continues, his voice dipping low as his fingers dance at the spot above my collarbone and at the side of my neck, "I'd inhale the sweetest scent of vanilla perfume."

My heart goes haywire. I swallow as my throat goes dry.

"I want more of this, Katie. I want to keep seeing you. I want these nights. I want to keep discovering you. And I want to take my time doing it. I don't want to rush into the physical, and I can't believe I'm saying that, because trust me, I want that, but I want this first."

Elation swirls in me.

We're on the same page.

With everything.

"I want the same things," I say softly. "I want to date you. I want to talk to you when you're on the road. I want to see what this could be between us. And I want us to take our time, too."

AJ slides his arm around me and lays me back on the sofa. I drop the remote as his mouth finds mine, and we both chuckle.

"TV is overrated," I murmur as I slide my hands up his arms, feeling his powerful muscles beneath my fingertips.

AJ chuckles softly, and I feel his breath on my cheek as he lowers his lips to that very spot he described a second ago.

"Very overrated," he murmurs, pressing his lips against the side of my neck.

I close my eyes and shiver in response to this sexy kiss, and a gasp escapes my lips as I feel his tongue flicker across my skin. I run my hands up to his neck, to the back of his head, and caress his hair with my hand as he kisses my neck.

Slowly, oh so slowly, his mouth travels up my neck, to my jaw, and finally his lips meet mine. Pure heat fills me as his tongue parts the seam of my lips, opening me, his mouth caressing mine as he tastes me gently. Deliberately.

Sensually.

It's the kind of kiss that can go on for hours.

Which is exactly how long I plan to kiss AJ tonight, I think with happiness.

CHAPTER 13

Playlist Shuffle Song of the Day:
"Nervous" by Shawn Mendes

"Cheers, ladies," Hayley says, lifting her glass of rosé. "To the beginning of girls' night out!"

I raise my glass of rosé and tap it against Hayley's and Addison's glasses. It's six o'clock, and we are sitting in Whaley's Rosé Garden in the Navy Yard. We couldn't have picked a better spot on this June evening. We're outside, with a view of the Potomac River, seated at a white metal table under a completely girlie pink-and-white striped umbrella, surrounded by potted plants and sipping chilled fruity wine.

Bliss.

I take a sip of my wine, the one the menu described as having hints of grapefruit, and savor it. Mmm. Delicious.

"I needed this after this afternoon," Addison says, setting her glass down and tracing her finger up and down the stem of the glass. "I found out I didn't get the job with the animal rights group."

"Oh, Addison, I'm so sorry," Hayley says, reaching out and touching her hand. "I know how badly you wanted that."

I do, too. Addison was down to the final round when we talked that night at the gala, and she was trying hard not to be too optimistic about her chances of landing that social media coordinator position with them.

But I could tell when she spoke about the job that she was so excited about the opportunity, about the chance to work with a group that held a place in her animal-loving heart.

"I was one of two," Addison says, frowning. "They told me it was incredibly close, a hard decision, blah blah blah. It's kind of like being dumped. It's not you, it's me, we feel it's better to go in the opposite direction of the one where you are standing."

A memory clicks into place for me. I remember Hayley telling me Addison followed her boyfriend to the University of Virginia, only to be dumped a few weeks later.

"I could tell you that you were one of two out of all the people that applied," Hayley says, pausing to take a sip of her wine.

"Technically, you did just tell her," I say, smiling.

"Shut up," Hayley says.

"I know you're right," Addison says. "I need to pick myself up and apply for the next one that comes along."

"Allow yourself to wallow in rosé first," I suggest.

"I think that sounds like the perfect antidote," Addison concurs. "I'll wallow about that, and my lack of meeting any men I'd like to date here, and tomorrow, I'll wake up with a wine-induced headache and a new attitude on the job. On men? I'm not so sure."

"How have you tried to date?" I ask, curious about this. "I gave up on dating after I met a guy online and he stood me up in a restaurant. A few months later, I met AJ, and believe me, after fainting on him and babbling like a fool, he was the last guy I ever thought I'd be dating."

Addison groans. "I'm afraid to try online dating. If it's anything like the weird friend requests and messages I've gotten from guys sliding into my social media inbox, no thanks. You should see some of the pictures these guys sent. I won't go into detail, but you can guess what body part made an appearance. Gross."

"Thank you for sparing us," I joke.

"Trust me, I'm doing you both a tremendous favor," Addison says.

"Back to finding a guy," Hayley says. "Sometimes it happens when you least expect it. When I accidentally threw that coffee on Brody, I NEVER thought I'd date him."

Addison grins. "Okay, so I either need to faint on a guy or throw coffee on his crotch to get a date."

"Obviously," I tease.

Addison laughs. "I think I'm going to be single for a long time. Just me and Willy," she says, referring to her pet ferret. "I'm going to focus on getting a job working with an animal organization and hope the right animal-loving man will fall into my life when I least expect it."

"It's so weird how it can just happen," Hayley says. "Even when common sense says it's all wrong. Brody and I are completely different people on a lot of levels, and we make it work."

I gather up my courage to ask Hayley a question.

"The thing I worry about with AJ is how this will work if we keep dating," I say, admitting my fear aloud. "Right now, I can see so much potential between us. But everything will change in the fall when I start law school. I know what I'm getting into. I'm going to be in a relationship with law school. My life will consist of reading and studying and, other than eating and maybe squeezing in some sleep, not much else. AJ, on the other hand, will be in his off-season. Is that how he's going to want to spend it? Watching me study? Watching me cry when I'm exhausted from lack of sleep? That's what he will get if he remains in DC when the season is over. And for someone who is used to traveling and never staying in the same spot, I don't see how this will work."

I stop talking. I said everything out loud that has been looming in the back of my mind. Hayley and Addison are staring at me, not saying anything. I reach for my wine and take a big sip, trying to wash away that last sentence I spoke.

I don't see how this can work.

"Katie," Hayley says gently.

I put my hand up to stop her. "I'm so sorry, that is crazy babble. I've only been on a few dates. Who knows where we are going to be months from now. I'm not talking like a rational woman, but a pre-teen with a crush. Forget I said that. Please, forget I said that."

"I'm not going to forget it," Hayley says firmly, shaking her head. "You feel something for AJ. Of course, you can't help but think ahead, and because you know what is going to happen, you have every right to be concerned. A few weeks ago, you were only going to be in a lopsided affair with law books and study groups. Now you're trying to figure out how AJ can fit into a very demanding life."

I wrinkle my nose. "How can I ask him to put up with that? With me ignoring him because I have to read? The fact that I can't just spend all my free time with him like I am now?"

"He'll put up with it if he wants to be with you," Hayley says simply.

I take another sip of my wine. If only it were that simple. She has no idea about AJ's life, how he's never claimed a home, how he's never committed to any serious relationship, how he has a permanent case of wanderlust.

Shit. If this is the case, I should stop seeing him now before my heart gets any more invested.

"Your heart is already in, so forget running from AJ."

I blink. Hayley is staring at me, reading my thoughts with a scary kind of ESP ability.

"It might save me a lot of heartache," I admit.

And as soon as I say it, my chest draws tight.

"Losing him altogether might be worse," she counters.

"I know I don't know you as well as Hayley does," Addison says quietly, "but if I had a man who made me feel all the things, I'd put up with any schedule to have him. How do you know AJ doesn't feel that way about you? Shouldn't this be his decision if it gets to that point?"

"You've only heard the horror stories from year one," Hayley chimes in. "You need to talk to people with good experiences. Like my dad. He and Mom were together while he was in law school and look at them now. Married for twenty-eight years!"

I glance between my two friends. One old, one new. One in a relationship, one not.

But both thinking the same thing regarding me and AJ.

"You know what? This is a stupid waste of our night," I declare. "This is not 'worry about a future that might not even happen' night. This is girls' night out. I want to drink. I want to laugh. I want to go home and devour a pizza with more wine after we are done with our happy hour."

"We're still going to talk about AJ," Hayley says. "Like how good of a kisser he is."

I think my cheeks are the same color as the wine in my glass.

"Sexy," I say, grinning wickedly at her. "His lips are full. Soft. And he knows exactly what to do with them. In short, he's a delicious kisser."

Hayley laughs, and Addison lets out a heavy sigh.

"I want to date a sexy kisser like that. Hell, I just want to kiss somebody. It's been too long."

"How long?" Hayley asks.

Now I think Addison has beaten me and is the color of a nice cab.

"No."

"No what?" I ask.

"It's too embarrassing," Addison says.

"How long?" Hayley demands.

Addison reaches for the bottle of rosé out of the bucket and pours more in all our glasses.

"This requires more drinking," she declares. "But it's been four years."

Whoa.

Even in my crappy dating period, I didn't go a year between kisses.

"Maybe tonight we need to find some cute guy for you to go make out with for a while," Hayley suggests.

"No, no, no. I don't want to kiss a stranger. I want that electric, butterfly-filled, oh-my-God I can't wait for this guy to kiss me feeling. You only get that when you like somebody."

"I know you said you are afraid of online dating, but would you entertain the idea?" I ask. "I mean, I didn't get good results, but that doesn't mean you wouldn't."

Addison picks up a strand of her copper-red hair and twirls it around her finger. "No. I keep thinking he'll magically cross my path someday, but maybe I'm going about this all wrong."

"When you are ready to date, you'll put out the right vibe," Hayley says. "But you'll have to put yourself out there in the position to meet somebody, too."

"I don't even know how I'd do it. Or how to do an online dating site intro. I hate listening to myself speak, let alone shooting a video of myself and basically saying, 'I'm a dork, I don't know what I'm doing, but I'm fun-sized and love ferrets?' Who would date me? WHO?"

I'm dying laughing. "Did you call yourself 'fun-sized?'" I ask.

Addison giggles. "I'm short. I know I'm like the fun-sized candy."

Now I'm really laughing. "You have to say that in your video."

"I'm not doing an online dating video!"

"Would you stop? You aren't conducting surgery," Hayley says.

"No, only potentially mining for a future husband. No big deal if I look like a weirdo and attract back what I put out!"

"I agree with Hayley. You are overthinking this," I say, taking another sip.

Mmm. My head is starting to feel lighter already.

"We'll prove it," Hayley says, picking up her phone. "I'll shoot a mock one for you right now."

"I'm not doing it," Addison cries, shaking her head in horror.

"Here." I pick up my phone. "I can do one for myself in like five seconds. I'm going to show you how easy this is."

I swipe a few things and turn the video app on, holding the phone up to my face.

"Hi. I'm Katie McKenna. I'm looking for a not-so-ordinary man to spend quality time with. Must love animals. Stadium food. Roller coasters. You have to be able to laugh with me at my goofiness, as well as yours. You will like going out to a fusion restaurant but like being at home, too. You have to put up with my Mufasa hair and getting your fingers stuck in the snarls, because hello! Curly hair? It snarls. I snore. I'm notorious for spilling things on my shirt."

"Wait, you would not say that!" Addison protests.

"Oh, she would," Hayley says.

"I'm taping, shut up," I tease. I clear my throat and continue. "Odds are very good by the end of the night there might be food crumbs wedged in my bra. If it's something tasty, I might even eat it."

Now Hayley bursts out laughing.

"Like if it's a potato chip crumb. Or a cereal marshmallow. I'd totally eat that out of my bra."

"You would?" Addison says. "Ew!"

"Why ew? It's like it's been in a little holder. I wouldn't eat it off the ground!"

I clear my throat again, as my demo is still going, and they both go silent.

"I'm not glamorous. But one thing I can assure you is that you are getting the real me. As far as the real you, serious bonus if you have a bobblehead made in your image."

Hayley snort laughs. "Does he get extra points if the bobblehead is all teeth and has a giraffe neck?"

I grin and continue, as now I'm going to go on about AJ. Why? Because we're joking around. Or because I'm drinking wine too fast, and I kind of feel like being mushy about him at the moment.

"Additional bonuses: having a glorious ass in baseball pants, delicious lips, and a smile that makes my heart flutter. You give me fireworks. You're romantic and swoony, and I have all the feels. By the way, I'm Katie McKenna, and my heart belongs to Andrew Joseph."

I tap on the stop button and glance up.

"I really like him," I say, my emotions going into AJ overload.

"I can tell," Addison says.

"She does. You might have a law mind, but you totally have a made-for-TV romance movie heart," Hayley says.

"I do," I agree, sipping more wine.

"So let's do this," Hayley says. "We'll finish this bottle, Uber home, and stuff ourselves with pizza and more wine. You can stay over, Addison. It will be a like a big sleepover."

Addison frowns. "I can't, I have to go home to Willy."

I burst out laughing. "If only you could go home to a different kind of willy tonight!"

Addison begins to laugh, and so does Hayley, and we all lose it at the table.

I smile at my friends. I can already tell tonight is going to be a good night.

≈

I'M SO BUZZED.

I'm sitting on the sofa with Hayley in our living room. We've eaten a ton of pizza. Drank red wine. On top of rosé wine. My head is floating. Everything is funny. Well, it's not funny that the Soaring Eagles lost the first game of the series with Chicago, but everything else is hysterical.

Hayley reaches for the bottle and pours what is remaining in my glass.

"Only because I love you," she says. "Otherwise, I'd drink it."

"Should we open another bottle? I mean, Addison drank out of this before she left, so we really have not drank two whole bottles between the two of us. If you did maths, it's not a bottle per person, so we're not runks. Drunks," I correct, as the words trip over my tongue.

Shit. I'm not buzzed.

I *am* drunk.

"I feel sleepy," Hayley says. "I'm going to bed."

I remember this from college. On the rare occasions we did get our drink on, Hayley always went to bed.

"Night, Hayley. I love you. You're my best friend," I say, feeling sentimental.

Hmm. Now everything is sappy instead of funny.

I miss AJ now. I want to be all lovey and sappy on him.

"You're mine, and I love you more," Hayley says, interrupting my thoughts as she pushes herself up to standing. "Night, Katie Bug."

"Night," I say, watching her head off down the hall, with Pissy following behind her.

I reach for my phone and check it. Hmm. AJ hasn't texted me from Chicago, but maybe he's in a bad mood after a loss.

Maybe he doesn't miss me like I miss him.

I so miss him.

He has to miss me.

It would suck if I missed him and he didn't miss me.

I think I'll text him.

I begin to type:

Ajjjjjjj I now u lost but I miss y9ur fce

Shit. Typing is hard when you're buzzed.

I try to back up but accidentally send it.

Gah! Dammit! Why isn't there a recall button like with email?

I quickly try to type another message to explain:

Sry I had wine and can't tp. Tye. Tpye. Dammit.

Okay this isn't going very well. Should I call him? Oh, God no. I'd probably tell him I love him.

Which wouldn't be awful because I'm kind of there, but I shouldn't tell him that because I feel sappy due to wine.

And I should KNOW I love him rather than be kind of there.

Okay no.

I decide to text a final message:

AJ. I miz yor. Yu. U.

I pause. I need an emoji. I scroll through my favorite ones and add some and then hit send.

I reach for the glass of wine Hayley gave me. She really is

my best friend. And now I owe her forever because she introduced me to AJ.

I'll miss her when I start law school.

Oh, I'll miss AJ so much.

Now I'm sad. I reach for my phone and type AJ another message. I sniffle and text him a few more things, then I lay down on the sofa. Wait. I forgot something. I need to tell him something important. I type another message, trying to concentrate. Okay. It has typos. So what. I put my phone down, my brain sorting through all kinds of thoughts whirling through it.

Which is a challenge when you are tipsy. I'll pick one.

Why does law school have to suck your soul dry?

I stare up at the ceiling. I don't want to lose my friends because I can't see them.

What if Hayley and Addison forget me?

Meghan will hate that I won't have time to go shopping and sip wine.

Ugh. Wine sounds awful now. Need to tell Meghan too much chardonnay is bad.

Wait. I drank red wine tonight.

Isn't rosé more white than red?

I don't want to lose AJ.

But I'm NOT giving up law school. I was born to be a lawyer.

A really badass one who sticks up for women who need it.

I can't wait to cross-examine someone.

That will be freaking fantastic.

I love that AJ is a good man.

Why is being an adult so hard?

I wish I would have met AJ last year.

That would be easier. We'd already be in love, and he'd put up with me because he loved me.

My eyes grow heavy.

Did I text him something about my hair?

So tired.

I think I'll just rest my eyes while I wait for him to text me back.

≈

Playlist Shuffle Song of the Day:
"U Got the Look" by Prince

UGH. I FEEL LIKE CRAP.

I open my eyes. I'm on the sofa. I'm twisted like a pretzel to sleep on my side and fit on the couch, and the whole left half of my body is achy. My throat is dry. My head hurts. I lift my hand to it, and my bracelets clank as I move my arm, making me wince. Wait. I passed out in my clothes?

Geez. This is worse than college. One, because I'm supposed to be more mature now, and two, when Hayley and I got drunk together, it was girls' night in and we were smart enough to put pajamas on first.

I need water. Then coffee. And a shower.

Ew. I didn't even brush my teeth. Gross.

I feel disgusting.

Of course, one might feel like crap after polishing off two bottles of wine with friends.

Wait. Did Hayley and I open a third bottle when we got back?

I glance over on the coffee table.

I wince. Yep. Two bottles.

And a bottle of wine at the bar.

Ugh.

I wonder what time it is. I don't hear Hayley, so she must still be asleep in her room. I stretch my arm across the table, as I can't face sitting up yet, and get my fingertips on my phone, dragging it closer so I can retrieve it.

I unlock it. It's nine thirty in the morning. Luckily, I'm not working today.

I shift onto my back and see I have messages from AJ.

Did I text him last night?

Oh, no. I did.

I drunk texted him.

I wince. Do I even want to see what I said?

It's not a good sign if I can't remember.

Oy. That's a bad sign.

I bite my lip. I probably said a bunch of nonsense. AJ knows I don't go out and get drunk on any kind of any regular basis, so he probably thought they were funny.

I man up and swipe open his message:

I see you have become Smashed Katie tonight.
Luckily I can crack the Katie code so I was able to
decipher your texts. You're cute when you're drunk.
But I think you're cute regardless.

I don't even have to scroll up to see what I said. It's all good if he thinks it's cute.

I get to one more message from him:

I do have to ask though: Do you only eat cereal
marshmallows out of your bra? I would think those
would get sticky. The cereal probably holds up better
for consumption upon discovery.

Wait. Wait.

I bolt upright on the sofa. Did I text him about the video I made as an example for Addison?

DAMMIT.

I fumble through my phone, my hands shaking. I scroll up, and with horror, I see I've not just texted AJ.

I sent him a video.

The goofy intro video I made as a joke for Addison.

Where I talked about eating food out of my bra.

Oh no. No no no no.

But there it is, my video in all its glory, where I talk about eating out of my bra and how smitten I am with AJ.

"Shit!" I yell, hurling my phone toward the end of the sofa. "Shit shit shit!"

I TOLD HIM I EAT CRUMBS OUT OF MY BRA. HOW UNSEXY IS THAT?

I exhale and retrieve my phone. I replay the video, and it's so much worse than food in the bra. I told him I loved his butt and his lips were delicious and my heart belonged to him.

GAH nooooo!

No man wants to hear that after a few dates! He'll run. AJ will block me from his phone and social media, provide my picture to Soaring Eagles security to keep me out of the ballpark, and label me this obsessed girl he had a few dates with, and she said it was love.

And it's not love.

Not yet.

Now it might never be if I freaked him out.

Which is favorable, between using my bra as a food holder and declaring AJ has my heart.

If he wants to go out with me after that fact, it will be a miracle.

Or he's my person.

And I guess I will find out as soon as I talk to him.

CHAPTER 14

I turn the phone face down, because if I don't see AJ's text there, it doesn't exist.

If the string of messages doesn't exist, he doesn't think I'm a step away from picking out china patterns at Bloomingdale's and randomly dropping my ring size in casual conversation.

I'm going to turn on selective memory for the time being.

Nope. I never sent him a video where I claim he gives me all the feels and has my heart after a whopping handful of dates.

And I absolutely did not tell him I eat food out of my bra.

Oyyyyy.

I stand up. I head down the hall, and since Hayley's door is open, I peek my head in. I see Hayley is curled up in her bed, with Pissy sleeping on the pillow next to her. The kitten lifts her head and shoots me the stink eye. Then Pissy adds a hiss for good measure, just to remind me that she loathes my presence.

I roll my eyes. Drama cat.

I step across the hall to my room, going past the bed and

entering my bathroom. I flick on the light and glance into the mirror.

As soon as I see my reflection, I gasp in horror.

Holy hell.

My mascara is all over my face, like someone punched me in both eyes. My makeup is caked around my nose. The Mufasa hair is huge and snarled. My eyes are rimmed with red, and my blouse is rumpled and has a red sauce stain on it.

I vaguely remember dropping pizza on it.

I wonder if I have crust in my bra.

Okay, that's not food I want to retrieve.

In fact, I'm certain I will never eat out of my bra again.

I turn on the water and reach for a washcloth from the basket. If there was a video of me now, my looks could be compared to Madeline Khan in the old *Young Frankenstein* movie.

Oh. That might be a fun one to watch with AJ.

If he hasn't run screaming by then.

I wash my face, getting the grime of last night off. I then brush my teeth for a long time and, convinced I look somewhat better, move over to my closet. I have everything meticulously organized thanks to Meghan, who lives to do things like re-arrange closets, paperwork, and pantries. In fact, I think she'd be an awesome professional organizer.

But Meghan has her eye on writing about her glorious old home with hollyhocks growing along the side and looking beautiful in a chambray dress while she picks out fruit at the market, so I guess going through someone's old T-shirts and telling them, "No, this goes in the throw away pile, it's yellow and has fifteen holes," isn't as appealing.

Although she organizes for me with glee.

Which I'm grateful for this morning, since my head is pounding, and I don't want to think about where my favorite shirt is.

I retrieve from the built-in shelf a pair of shorts and my

Vineyard Vines blue-and-white striped nautical T-shirt. I change into those and put my feet into my flip-flops. Ah. That's a start.

I don't feel like fighting with my hair, so I leave the Mufasa wildness alone. I go back down the hall and into the kitchen.

Coffee. Next priority.

The biggest one at the moment.

I head to the machine and open the drawer for the coffee K-Cups. Wait. What the hell? Why is there no coffee?

I jerk it all the way open, hoping a K-Cup will roll forward.

Noooooooooooooooo.

In all my AJ love, I forgot to put this on my shopping list.

I close the door. I can't handle going to Scones and Such right now. Or even the closest café.

Suddenly, a solution appears in my head.

Barbara.

Yes, Barbara! She and Dominik go out for breakfast but always have sweet breads and a pot of coffee on for the entire day.

I need her coffee. Her pastries. Maybe she might have some sage advice about dealing with embarrassing moments. She can guide me on how to handle this.

I leave my phone on the couch, as I still don't want to see if AJ has woken up and texted me about any more of my embarrassing video moments, and pick up my purse. Then I head down the hall and knock on the door to their apartment.

A few moments later, Dominik opens the door.

"Katie, coming over to break down the Eagles' loss last night?" he says.

I smile. I can't count the number of times Dominik and I have broken down the game from the night before at his kitchen table.

"I know you'll be shocked, but I haven't seen the game

yet," I say, stepping inside the tidy apartment. "I went out with the girls last night and, um, enjoyed some wine. Maybe a bit too much."

Dominik grins as he shuts the door behind me. "Tied one on, didn't you?"

I wince. "Yes. And we're out of coffee and I—"

"Say no more," Barbara says, coming out of the kitchen and wiping her hands on a dishtowel. "Do you need some aspirin, too?"

She's an angel.

I nod. "And any kind of bread you might have?" I say, heading into the nook and taking a seat at their old wooden table.

"Oh, you're in luck there," Dominik says, shuffling over to his recliner chair and picking up his copy of the *Washington Post*. "She made cake during the game last night."

Cake *and* coffee for breakfast?

Yes.

"Sour cherry," Barbara says. "I saw cherries at the farmers' market that were calling my name."

"Please," I say, nodding.

Barbara brings me a ceramic mug filled to the brim with fresh coffee and some cream, just the way she knows I take it. The mug is covered with cartoon-looking owls and makes me smile.

"Now let me get you some aspirin," she says, patting my shoulder.

"Not that baby stuff you take for your heart," Dominik chimes in.

"Dominik. Does she look like a child or an elderly person who has been directed to take baby aspirin for heart health? No. I know what aspirin to give her."

"Just making sure, wife. Sometimes you get excited when the girls visit. You'll get your gossip on soon enough, so keep your focus."

Despite my headache, it's all I can do not to burst out laughing.

"Get your gossip on?" I ask, wondering where Dominik— all news-channel and baseball-watching Dominik—heard that phrase.

"I know what's up," he says, flicking a page in his paper.

I begin to laugh. Which makes my head hurt.

"He reads my gossip magazines when I'm not around," Barbara declares, placing a bottle of aspirin and glass of water in front of me.

"I do not," he protests.

"You do so. Would you like more coffee?" Barbara asks.

"Yes, please," Dominik says.

Barbara takes the coffee pot and pours him a cup of coffee. After she is finished, she leans down and places a loving kiss on his bald head.

I watch the moment of tenderness between them, and I know that's what I want. Someone who will bring me a cup of coffee and drop a kiss on my head, even after forty years of being together.

"Thank you, wife," Dominik says.

Barbara comes back into the kitchen and picks up a cake plate holding a beautiful golden cake studded with cherries that are bursting through the sides in glorious baked goodness.

She places the plate in the center of the table, and I swear, it's all I can do not to tear a chunk off with my hands and shove it into my mouth.

That would totally fit with my true self.

But instead, I take the aspirin and find my courage for what I need to talk about.

I pop the tablets and take a sip of water. "So, I made a complete fool of myself with AJ last night."

"Pfft," Barbara says, setting down a dessert plate and fork

in front of me. "I doubt it. But that doesn't mean you don't have to tell me everything."

I sigh as she takes a knife, cuts off a huge wedge of the cake, and gently lowers it to my plate.

I pick up my fork. "I drunk texted him."

"So?" Dominik asks. "Who hasn't done that?"

"Says the man who only uses his phone to call his grandkids," Barbara says, sinking down into the chair across from me.

"I think a phone is for calling people. All that other stuff is ruining society, but with that said, I'm sure everyone your age has done it."

I resist the urge to point out he's always asking me to show him stuff from the Soaring Eagles app and take a bite of cake instead.

"What did you say?" Barbara asks.

I can't speak for a moment as I indulge in buttery, sugary, cherry goodness.

"Oh, my God," I mumble with my mouth full. "So good."

Barbara simply looks at me.

I can tell she doesn't want cake compliments now.

I swallow my bite. "I went out with Hayley and another friend last night. We were having fun—girls' night out, you know. Nothing crazy. Drinks at a patio bar. Anyway, we were trying to talk our friend into online dating, and I demoed how to make an introduction video."

"Here's where it's going to go sideways," Dominik says.

"You're practically *Sherlock*," Barbara says dryly. She shifts her attention back to me. "Let me guess, your demo wasn't straightforward."

I wince. "No. I had to be funny, for some reason, and I said all kinds of stupid crap. Embarrassing self-truths that AJ didn't need to know."

"Like?" Barbara prods, leaning over her coffee and awaiting my answer.

Ugh.

"Um, that if a crumb fell down my bra, I would eat it."

Barbara furrows her brow. "You do that?"

"AJ will say you're a keeper for that," Dominik chimes in. "That's practical *and* frugal."

Ughhhhhhhhhhhhh.

"Why would you eat a crumb out of your bra?" Barbara asks, clearly mystified by this.

Now I'm thoroughly embarrassed.

"I don't know, because it's there?" I answer lamely. "Anyway, that's not the worst of it. That's embarrassing. But the rest of it might be too much for AJ to handle."

"Do you eat food off the floor?" Dominik asks. "Five second rule?"

"No," I say, turning around and shaking my head.

"I do. Of course, by the time I bend down and pick it up, it's more the thirty-second rule, but people are too obsessed with germs these days."

"Ignore him," Barbara says. "What did you say?"

I shove a big piece of cake in my mouth to delay answering for a moment. But as soon as I swallow, I confess. "I was totally mushy. I said I had feelings. That my heart belonged to him. Things you do not say after having a few dates, Barbara."

"Who says?"

I stare back at her. "Common sense?"

"That is nothing."

"Barbara," I say, reaching for my coffee, "AJ has never been in a relationship. He's avoided them. What if spouting off about how much I like him within days scares him off? What if he thinks those feelings are rushed because I'm a fan?"

I take a sip of coffee, and Barbara stares at me in a contemplative way.

"Are they?" she asks simply. "Are you caught up in the fact that your celebrity crush is interested in you?"

"No," I say, shaking my head firmly. "The first time we hung out, we got coffee in Georgetown and sat along the canal. We talked for hours, and the more he revealed about himself, the parts that had nothing to do with baseball, the more real feelings popped up. Not for AJ the ballplayer."

"Then you're fine," Barbara says simply.

"But how can AJ be sure of that?" I ask.

"Because it's the truth. The truth always reveals itself."

"What if it's too much, too soon, and it freaks him out?"

"Then he's not the man for you," Dominik says simply.

"Did you ask him to marry you? Say you wanted to move in with him in a few days?" Barbara asks. "Say you loved him?"

"No."

"Then all you admitted to is liking him. A man who likes you would like hearing that. Strokes the ego."

"He'll be more fascinated with the food in the bra," Dominik adds.

"Husband, read your paper," Barbara says. "Is this embarrassing? Of course. But you have always been straightforward, Katie. I don't think it will shock AJ at all that you put your feelings out there."

"But what if it does?"

"Dominik answered that. If it does, he's not the man for you. You aren't going to be the coy, play-hard-to-get woman. You will say how you feel. You said your heart belonged to him. You two are only dating each other; this shouldn't scare him."

"Ugh," I say, eating another bite of cake, "the *my heart belongs to him* is kind of bad."

"Unless he likes it," Barbara says. "You won't know until you talk to him."

"He texted you last night about the video?" Dominik asks.

"Yes."

"I'm no Georgetown Law student, but wouldn't that be evidence of the fact that he wasn't bothered? That he initiated communication after watching it?"

Clarity breaks through my hungover brain. I was so wrapped up in being embarrassed that I overlooked that rather obvious fact.

"Dominik?" I ask.

"Yes?"

"I love you," I declare.

He smiles. "See that, Barbara? I do know what's up."

She snorts, and I see Dominik smiling.

"Would you like to take that coffee and cake back to your place?" Barbara suggests. "You might have a call to make."

"She'll FaceTime or text," Dominik, who indeed knows what is up, says sagely.

I rise from my chair. "I will take these to go," I say, picking up my mug and plate. "Thank you for feeding me and clearing my head. I'll return these later this morning."

"Send Hayley back with them," Barbara says, her eyes twinkling at me. "I need to have my one-on-one with her next."

I smile. "I shall."

I head back to the apartment and carefully juggle the cake in the crook of my arm while retrieving the key from the pocket of my shorts. I unlock the door and am greeted by Pissy, who is glaring at me from her spot in the hallway.

"Your mommy hasn't fed you, has she?" I ask her.

She growls and turns around, heading back to Hayley's room.

I roll my eyes. That cat has issues.

But apparently I do as well, as I flipped out over the texts without thinking about how AJ had, you know, texted me back.

I glance at the clock on my phone. AJ is most likely up by

149

now, unless he went out with Brody in Chicago. If not, I can get him later. I park the mug and cake on the coffee table and sink down on the sofa.

Okay. This will be embarrassing, but only for a moment or two. Then it should all be good with AJ, and he can tease me about this for eternity.

I text him first, deciding to make fun of myself and own my stupidity:

> **Good morning. You'll be happy to know I'm sober now. And eating a delicious cherry cake baked by neighbor Barbara. So good that if a crumb did fall into my bra, it's totally worth eating. By the way, you're probably right about the marshmallows. Unless you grab it the second it drops, you know.**

I hit send and have another sip of coffee. Damn, what is it about Barbara's coffee that is so good? I can detect a mixture of spices brewed into it, and it's so tasty.

It's warm. Comforting.

Much like Barbara herself.

AJ is typing …

> **I'm going to video call you. Hold on.**

I set the coffee mug back down and wait for his call to come through. When I see it, I tap on it, and AJ's handsome face fills my phone screen.

"How are you feeling?" AJ asks, grinning at me.

Heat burns my cheeks. "Physically? Hungover. Emotionally? Embarrassed I sent you that video."

"That," AJ says, a gleam coming into his deep green eyes, "was hilarious."

"I can't even blame being drunk, because I wasn't at that point. Everything I said was true. I was trying to be funny at first and loosen Addison up about doing a video for online dating. Then I got all mushy about you."

AJ's expression softens. "That was my favorite part about the video."

My heart holds still. "Yeah?"

"It's nice that you missed me," he says. "I've never had that before."

Now my heart is fluttering.

AJ is silent for a moment, simply staring at the screen, and I wish I knew what he was thinking.

"I miss you, Katie," he says softly. "I'm used to being on my own. I'm used to hanging with the guys, going place to place, and I've always been good with that, but I found myself missing you last night."

I smile. "You know I miss you."

He grins. "And it wasn't all wine-induced?"

"Nope," I say.

"How hungover are you?" AJ asks, a smile tugging at the corner of his mouth.

Swoon.

"Very. But I have coffee and cake thanks to Barbara; I'm coming to life. How are you this morning?"

"Good. Waiting on room service. Then I'm going to take a walk around Michigan Avenue. It's always weird to be here. This is one of the cities that was part of my growing up tour. Spent eight months here. I was a freshman in high school, and we lived in the north suburbs. This was the one place I begged my parents to stay. I loved it here. I was on a good team, I was just starting high school. We left in April. That's when I vowed not to get attached to any—"

A knock on the door interrupts AJ.

"Room service," a female voice calls out.

"Coming," AJ replies. "I've got to eat. I'll call back, okay?"

I nod. "I'll be here eating cake."

AJ flashes me a wicked grin. "Watch those crumbs. But I know your bra has your back on that one."

I blush furiously, and he laughs as he disconnects.

As soon as he's gone, my mind goes back to what he was saying before the room service person knocked on the door. How he vowed to never get attached. He didn't finish his sentence, but it doesn't matter if it was anyone or anything. Whatever he got attached to it, it was taken away from him.

I know missing me is a huge thing for him to feel, and my heart is elated by that fact. But I'm also scared. I must be enough for him to want to be attached. Come fall, can I offer him enough when I'm immersed in school?

My elated feeling crashes out with my next thought.

Can I give him what he deserves, after all these years of avoiding attachments to places and people?

I reach for my coffee, needing to feel that comfort that Barbara's whimsical mug and spice-infused blend can give me. AJ deserves the world. He deserves to be happy. To feel like he can have a home, and a woman who can give him everything instead of scraps of time squeezed in-between papers and books.

My phone beeps. I glance down and see it's AJ:

What is it about you that makes me miss your beautiful face already?

I stare down at his words. Before I can answer, another text comes in.

I know that answer, though. It's because it's YOU.

I read his words over and over. I'm the factor that's different.

Just as he is for me.

I decide I can't obsess about the future. I want to fall for

AJ. I want to experience all these new and wonderful feelings and live in this moment. My brain is leaping ahead of my heart in this case. I have to trust my heart will lead me to the right place. To trust AJ.

I take a sip of coffee, comfort seeping through me. Both from the homey brew and AJ's delicious words.

We can do this, AJ, I think with determination. *If we fall in love and are meant to be, we can handle anything.*

I put the future away with that thought and focus on the now, except for one date next week.

And circled in my head is the day AJ returns home.

CHAPTER 15

Playlist Shuffle Song of the Day:
"One More Cup of Coffee" by The White Stripes

"I would like something off the secret menu," the twenty-something girl says, looping her finger around a lock of her glossy brown hair and smiling at me in a conspiratorial way.

I panic. It's a half-hour until we close. I'm going to AJ's as soon as I'm done here, as he has finally come back from his road trip. This is so not how I want to end my evening at Scones and Such.

Michael called in sick. Conveniently, a day after he returned from a gaming convention in Austin. So, I've had to work solo with Sharon, our assistant manager. Who just went to the back to work on the books and left me alone because things were "quiet" and surely, I could handle a few coffee orders out here if any happened to come in.

So far, I've only had to pour iced coffee and iced tea and one drip brew, so it's been bueno.

Until Ms. Secret Menu walked in.

And those two words—secret menu—bring one thought to my mind.

WHAT SECRET MENU?

We aren't Starbucks. We don't have a secret menu. I have no idea what this girl is talking about.

"Secret menu?" I ask, wrinkling my brow. "We don't have a secret menu here at Scones and Such."

The girl leans forward, as if she's about to fill me in on some great mystery.

"I know you have to act like you don't know. But I would like," she says, pausing for dramatic effect, "one extra-large Unicorn Sparkle."

What?

"I'm so sorry, but we don't have a drink called the Unicorn Sparkle," I say, praying she would just like a simple iced tea instead.

She stares blankly at me.

"Is this part of the secret menu hype?" she asks.

"No," I say, shaking my head. "We really don't have one. The drinks we have are all on the board."

The girl begins drumming her manicured nails—I do have to give her credit, she has a fabulous pale pink polish on her expertly shaped nails—and she seems very put out that I don't know what a Unicorn Sparkle is.

She snorts. "Online, it said you sometimes have to guide an inept barista through it."

It's all I can do not to snort laugh. If she only knew she hit the complete jackpot on getting an inept barista.

The girl drops her mammoth Elizabeth and James tote on the counter and lets out a loud, heavy sigh as she rifles through her bag. I hear keys and coins, and while I thought Hayley's bag was always a mess, Ms. Secret Menu might have her beat.

"Where is my stupid phone," she mutters to herself as she

continues to dig. Then she triumphantly finds it. "I'll tell you how to make it."

Oh, no. I feel sweat prickle the back of my neck. I would rather do mock trial than do this. Wait, I love mock trial. I'd rather take one of my law school exams than make this drink.

My brain sifts through the evidence. Unicorn Sparkle doesn't sound like anything that would have coffee, so that's a big advantage. Coffee is where I usually mess up.

She taps her phone and lets out another heavy sigh, as if my not knowing what a Unicorn Sparkle is has ruined her evening.

"Now where was that drink," she says, scrolling through her phone.

I would like to helpfully reply, "at another coffee house," but keep my lips zipped.

"Ah! I found it," she says triumphantly. "See?"

She turns the phone toward me, and sure enough, the Unicorn Sparkle is indeed on the secret menu.

Of a coffee house two blocks over from here.

"That's the secret menu for French Press," I say.

"So?"

"This is Scones and Such."

She stares at me. "So?"

I furrow my brow. "That's why I don't know how to make it."

"Which is why I'm telling you how!" she snaps, annoyed.

I suddenly regret my decision not to spend my summer working at the law firm, thinking I needed one last relaxing summer hurrah before school.

Because this is not my idea of relaxing.

"Okay," I say, forcing a smile on my face. "Please tell me what I need to do."

As I finish speaking, the door bells clang and, oh crap, a group of five teenagers walks in, all on their phones and laughing and chatting.

How is it I can totally go head to head in a debate competition and not be bothered at all, but the mere idea of whipping up six assorted beverages sends me into panic?

Katie. Grip. Now.

"One portion simple syrup," Ms. Secret Menu begins to rattle off.

"Ooh, I want a salted caramel mocha latte," one teen girl says. "What are you going to get, Emberly?"

"Oh, I totally want a french press coffee," she says.

French press?

I think I'm going to have a stroke.

"One pump raspberry syrup," Ms. Secret Menu continues.

I frantically begin typing the directions into the cash register, so it prints on the label.

"Hi, welcome to Scones and Such. I'll be with you in a moment," I say to the teens, who are now moving their way down the pastry case and deciding what they want.

"Are you listening?" Ms. Secret Menu snaps.

"Yes, I am," I say. "One half-pump strawberry syrup."

"One pump toffee syrup," she continues.

How many ingredients does it take to make a freaking Unicorn Sparkle?

"Half a packet of sugar in the raw," she says.

Half?

"Then one half Splenda …"

She is totally making this part up.

"I'm so starving, I can't wait to get a cinnamon roll," another teen says. "And a cappuccino to dunk it in."

Oh, my God. I'm up to three specialty coffees after making this stupid unicorn drink.

I hit my headset to call for backup.

"Sharon?" I say.

She picks up. "I can't right now!" she yells into my ear. Then she bursts into tears. "I just had a fight with Philip. It's over this time, for g-g-good!"

Then she hangs up.

I decide I hate three things right now:

Secret menus.

Michael for pretending to be sick.

Philip for his on-and-off-again crap with Sharon, which always sends her straight into the emotional dumpster.

"Coconut milk," Ms. Secret Menu goes on. "Oh, and let's go back and make that a full pump of strawberry syrup, not a half."

One of the teens rolls her eyes.

I'm feeling that right there with you, girlfriend.

"Light ice. There," she says firmly. "Now you should be able to make it."

"Of course," I say. I get her name for the order and ring her up first, and then take the orders for the teens, so they can be seated while I work.

I regret it, though, as they rattle off complicated coffee drinks. Including one for a bone-dry cappuccino, which means no milk. Yes. A cappuccino with no milk, but she wants the bubbles.

Send. Help.

I ring them up, process all their debit cards, and then hurry back to get the Unicorn Sparkle drink started.

Now my shirt is sticking to me, as I have six orders in all to complete. When I make coffee, I usually get a few "remakes" requested because I'm so fantastically awful at it.

Oy.

I measure the syrups, the coconut milk, rip open the packets of Splenda and raw sugar, hit blend. Then I hurry back to the espresso machine to get the coffee started for the latte and the stupid cappuccino that is NOT a cappuccino.

French press. Shit. I've got to do that.

"Is my drink almost ready?" Ms. Secret Menu calls out over the music.

The White Stripes are singing "One More Cup of Coffee," and I tamp down the urge to shut the music off, because the last thing I want anyone to do is ask me for another cup of coffee.

The blender stops running, so I hustle back to that. French press coffee. Must start that next. Don't forget.

Is it hot in here?

I think I feel my curls exploding in the humidity and, ick, is that sweat on my upper lip?

I pour the Unicorn Sparkle into a plastic cup, pop a paper straw into it, and call out the order.

"One Unicorn Sparkle for Shauna," I call out.

If she demands I remake it, I swear I will lose my mind.

She saunters back up to the counter, swoops the drink up in one swift move, and strolls out the door without so much as a thank you or goodbye.

Okay. Done. I move back to the espresso machine and, oh crap. The girls ordered pastries. I shift to the case and begin putting cookies and scones and cinnamon rolls onto plates and setting them on a tray. Then I carry them over to the girls and serve them.

"Oh, would it be much trouble to change my order?" french press girl asks.

Only if you say it's for a drip cup of coffee, I will her.

"Of course," I say with forced cheerfulness, "what can I get you?"

"A flat white french press coffee," she says.

The world is completely against me.

"Sure thing," I say with the faked confidence of a kick-ass barista.

Now I have to pray I put the right amount of spice in the cup and that I alternate the hot milk with the french press coffee to get the perfect drink.

I repeat: Send. Help.

I'm beginning to make the salted caramel latte when the

door bells ring again. Oy, more customers. I think I'm going to cry.

I turn around to do my spiel of "Welcome to Scones and Such," but I freeze on the spot.

It's another customer all right.

AJ.

My mouth falls open in shock. I was supposed to go over to his place as soon as I was done here. He casually strolls toward the counter, and my heart races with each step closer he takes toward me.

Once he's at the cash register, AJ flashes me that sexy smile of his.

"So, are you are my barista tonight?" he asks.

"What are you doing here?" I exclaim, delighted that he surprised me.

"I could say I came for coffee, but I'm more interested in the girl who is making it," AJ says.

Lightness fills my panicked barista soul from his sweet words. I turn back to the coffee machine just in time so he can't see the goofy smile that I know is spreading across my face.

"Oh?" I say, pouring the steamed milk into the latte and then making a caramel drizzle across the top. Except I squeeze too hard, and the drizzle becomes a quarter-sized blob in the middle of the cup.

Dammit, this looks like crap.

I bite my lip. I don't want to remake it. Maybe I'll sell it as extra caramel bonus.

I put that cup aside and begin whipping up bubbles in the stupid bone-dry cappuccino.

"What's on the top of that one?" AJ asks.

I turn around, and because AJ is so tall, he can see over my shoulder. And he's staring straight at the ugly blob in the middle of the salted caramel latte.

"Extra caramel," I say, picking up the drinks and heading over to where the teen squad is sitting.

I move across the café to the table they have commandeered for their time here.

"One salted caramel latte," I say, placing it in front of a girl who is busy typing away on her phone. "I hope you don't mind, but I love extra caramel on mine, so I gave you some extra, too."

She glances up at the blob in her cup.

I bite my lip, praying she doesn't ask me to remake it.

"Score," she says, picking up her spoon and scooping the blob out before popping it into her mouth.

I feel like I've just cleared one coffee-making hurdle.

"Bone-dry cappuccino," I say, placing the cup in front of her friend.

"Thank you," she replies.

"I'll be back with the flat white and two frozen mocha coffees, okay?" I say cheerfully.

I hustle back toward the counter, and AJ is leaning over the glass, studying what remains of our cookie collection for the day.

"I have three more orders to make," I say, pouring more milk into a pitcher so I can steam it. "And I have to say, turning around and seeing you at the door is the best surprise tonight."

"So, you're the barista on duty?" AJ asks, his green eyes shining in amusement.

"Indeed," I say, heating the milk. "Michael is hung over from his gaming convention. Oh, I mean *sick*."

I get the milk to the right temperature. I draw a breath, tell myself one-fourth of a teaspoon of secret spice blend is the right amount, and dump it into the ceramic mug. Then I begin the process of alternating milk and coffee and layering and hoping to the heavens above this will be a decent drink.

As soon as it's done, I walk it over to the table and place it in front of the girl who ordered it. "I'll be right back with the frozen drinks," I say.

So far, the other two teens are drinking their coffees and laughing so ah-ha! Cue the sound of trumpets, because I made coffee they don't hate.

Now I'm left with the easy stuff. Throw chilled coffee into the blender with some chocolate syrup and ice and a splash of cream and hit blend.

AJ is watching me come back from the table, and his eyes haven't left me the whole time I walk across the café and slip back behind the counter.

"Two more drinks to go," I say, opening the refrigerator and pulling out some iced coffee and cream. I begin to fill a blender with ice. "We close in half an hour. But then there's cleanup and stuff, which takes about an hour and a half. I'm sorry, you'll be sitting here a while."

"I'm capable of entertaining myself," AJ says.

I hit the blender and let it create frozen coffee magic. As it's whirling, I see the girl with the french press flat white approaching the counter with the cup in her hand.

Shit.

I stop the blender and wipe my hands on my towel. She gets in line behind AJ.

"Oh, I'm not in line," AJ says, sliding over. "Please, go right ahead."

She stares at him, her lips parting as she does. I repress a smile. This can be for one of two reasons. She recognizes him from some recess of her brain or because he's hot.

Maybe both.

The girl blinks. She moves past him and slides her cup across the counter.

"This tastes burnt," she says, wrinkling her nose.

Inside, I die. I hate that I'm a crap barista.

"I'm so sorry," I say, immediately removing the cup. "Would you like another one? Or something else to drink?"

"No, I think I just want a refund. That was really bad."

A smile plays at the corner of AJ's sexy mouth, and I can tell he's amused by the fact that I'm such a fail at coffee.

"Absolutely," I say swiftly, moving to the cash register.

Because in my limited capacity as emergency barista, the one thing I've become excellent at is issuing refunds for my shitty cups of coffee.

After I give her a refund and gift her a bottle of water on the house, I notice it's moving ever so much closer to closing. Thank God.

"You weren't kidding about the bad barista part," AJ says, dropping his voice.

I feel my face burn red. Even my scalp feels hot.

"I hate not being able to master things," I confide.

"You're not used to struggling, are you?" AJ asks.

"I've always been a quick study," I say, turning and pouring the coffee drinks into two glasses. "Studying for school comes easily to me. I grasp difficult concepts quickly. Yet as hard as I try, I'm terrible with coffee. I've studied it. Watched YouTube videos on it. Had Elise, the owner, coach me. So why can't I get this?"

I retrieve two more paper straws and put them in the drinks, and I hate the fact that I can hear frustration in my voice. Now that's an attractive quality for AJ to see. Me whining about how coffee is hard.

Wow. Between drunk texting, telling him I eat food out of my bra, and complaining about how coffee is hard for me to grasp, AJ must be falling in love with me at a rapid rate this week.

Oy.

"I'll be right back," I say, and vow to redirect the conversation as soon as I return.

I approach the table and make a quick assessment of the evidence sitting there. Salted caramel girl and bone-dry girl are still drinking their coffees. I must have mastered those.

Or they can't tell a crap coffee from a good one, I muse.

I serve the frozen mochas and head back to the counter, deciding to do one thing I'm very good at with AJ.

Make fun of myself.

I slide back behind it and face AJ, flashing him a wicked smile.

"I don't suppose you want me to make you a coffee drink, do you?" I say. "Michael isn't here to save you."

"I didn't come for coffee tonight," AJ says. "I came because I couldn't wait to see you."

I realize he has given me my first romantic movie-type moment. He missed me so much he came to the coffee shop because it meant gaining extra time with me.

I want to do that happy dance that the one character in *Love Actually* does.

"I'm glad you did, AJ." I lower my voice so only he can hear me. "I missed you."

"I'm glad I got to see you in action," he says as I begin to wash out the blender pitcher.

I snort. "Right."

"No. It's good to see you struggle at something," AJ insists. "Otherwise, you're pretty much perfect. That's intimidating."

I stop my scrubbing. "What? I'm not perfect."

"Katie, you're insanely smart," AJ says. "You're going to a top law school. You have this desire to make things better for other women and a whole plan laid out as to how you will accomplish your goals. Hell, you're immersing yourself in law school reading when you are not even in law school yet."

"That makes me *driven*, not perfect," I say, not wanting AJ to visualize me as something I'm not.

"I don't know. Beautiful. Intelligent. Hilarious. Fun. If I hadn't seen the burnt-coffee complaint first-hand, I'd think you were."

I laugh. "I'm so not. So, so far from it. I don't think a

perfect girl would send you her mock online dating bio and confess to certain tricks with food."

"No, that's perfection right there," AJ says, flashing me that sexy grin of his.

The back door swings open. Sharon's eyes are swollen and red. She looks awful.

"I need to scrub," she says, taking the milk pitcher and beginning to clean.

"I can sweep," I tell her, as I mopped earlier in the evening when it was slow.

See, that's the thing about working in a coffee house. You clean on a scheduled basis, and we do a lot of it in times when we expect slow traffic. So usually between five and six, I can get a lot done. But it still takes an hour to close. Probably longer tonight, thanks to stupid Michael.

At least when Sharon is upset, she loves to clean because she can take out her misery with a scrub brush and soap.

Seeing how vigorously she is scrubbing that pitcher, we might be out faster than I thought.

I turn back to AJ. "As much as I love that you're here, I don't expect you to wait an hour for me to finish. Are you sure you don't want to go home? Play with your dogs?"

AJ smiles. "I picked up the crew first thing this morning. Went to the dog park. Chilled at home. They're good."

Confusion hits me as I think about AJ taking his three big dogs out. "Wait. You are always trading in sports cars. How do you drive your dogs around?"

"That's a valid question. I'll answer it when we get back to my place."

I laugh. "Your transportation has to remain a mystery?"

"Yes," AJ says. "But I think you are brave enough to handle it, so I'll share it with you. In due time."

"You are making this rather dramatic," I say dryly. "Because if you're renting another car for them, like a luxury

SUV, I won't be surprised. Your Insta is full of your dogs. I bet they only have the very best transportation."

"Maybe I have my own imperfection to share with you," AJ says mysteriously. "Now if you don't mind, may I please have a coffee with a lot of cream? I'll read my book on my Kindle app while I wait for you."

He reads. This is a new discovery for me.

"What are you reading?"

His eyes hold steady on mine for a moment, and my breath catches when I see the shift in intensity in them.

"It's a new one; I just got it last week," AJ says slowly, his eyes never leaving my face. "It's called *How to be the Man She Deserves.*"

Then he turns and heads across the café, dropping down at a small table for two and swiping open his phone.

I stare at him in shock.

I can't breathe.

Because the book he's reading, the one he's recently picked up, tells me everything.

AJ wants to be the man for me.

CHAPTER 16

By ten, Scones and Such is spotless, and I'm free to leave. With AJ, who sat there the entire time reading on his phone while I cleaned. Every now and then, I'd feel his eyes on me as I worked, and when I glanced over at him, he'd smile at me.

My heart is being won over by this man.

This man who wants to be the man for me.

I still can't believe what he's reading. And that he *told* me what the book was.

I glance at him as he drives his ride for the next week, a Tesla, through DC.

AJ put a card down on the table for me to read tonight.

And I don't have to be a tarot card reader to know he wants to be a part of my future.

But I don't understand why he's reading the book in the first place. Doesn't he know he's incredible the way he is?

"What are you thinking?" AJ asks.

I'm not ready to put my card out on the table just yet, so I come up with something else.

"That I smell like coffee beans and baked sweets and

instead of bringing a change of clothes for tonight, I should go home and take a shower and start over."

I instantly smack myself inside. Wow. AJ will be pulling that card back in five, four, three, two—

"You don't need a shower," AJ says, putting his hand on my knee and giving it a squeeze. "Your sexy skin smelling like coffee and frosting? I might not be able to keep my mouth off you."

Hello!

I grow hot from the thought of AJ's tongue dancing across my neck. Down my collarbone. Toward my bra an—

I clear my throat before I allow that intimate thought to go any further.

Besides, I did eat a chocolate chip cookie on my break, and I'd die if he found a crumb down there.

"So, you plan on kissing me tonight, Andrew Joseph?" I ask coyly.

AJ grins. "The only question is, for how long? Do you work the morning shift tomorrow?"

Now I'm the one grinning. "Nope. In fact, I'm off."

"I could kiss you until it's very late. Might be too late for you to go home."

I pause. Is he implying I should spend the night?

"You might want to sleep over," AJ says as he drives. "Then we could get up and take the dogs to the dog park, get some breakfast. You can come to the game, too, even though it looks like it might be a rainout."

While I love the sound of all of this, I need to clarify one very important fact.

"Define sleep," I say, wanting to make sure I understand the situation.

Not that I don't want to have sex with AJ. Of course I do. But I don't want to rush it. I know this is contrary to my "living in the now" mantra I'm trying to do, but I can't lie to myself.

I don't want AJ to be the now.

I want him always.

And I want us to be different. I want us to wait. I want it to be right.

I want to give him my heart and body at the same time.

I smile. Author Holly Martin would be proud of me.

"Katie," AJ says slowly, "I hope you don't take this the wrong way, but I want you to let me speak and explain what I mean without questions. Counsel can cross-examine after I finish."

I furrow my brow. His tone is serious.

"Okay," I say softly, curious as to this shift in his demeanor.

"No woman has made me want the things I want with you," he says quietly.

My heart thunders in my chest as DC rolls past the car windows. I'm oblivious to everything except the words coming from AJ's lips.

"I've never worried about screwing things up with a woman because I never allowed things to go anywhere. I never wanted that. I was young. I wanted things to be fun. I made it clear we were casual upfront. That if we had sex it wasn't going to lead to a relationship, let alone love," AJ flinches at the last sentence. "Romantic, right?"

"You were being honest," I say. "Women would rather hear that than a bunch of lies and then wonder why you didn't call ever again."

"I was even upfront about that. If I felt things were cooling off, I told them why I wasn't going to ask them out anymore. All women deserve to be respected. If some guy strung my sister along with false promises, I'd want to punch him in the face. While I wasn't going to be serious, I wasn't going to be an asshole, either."

AJ pulls up to a red light, and now he shifts his gaze toward me.

"I don't want to mess this up," he says, his emerald eyes reflecting nothing but concern for me. "I don't want this to be just about sex, although I think about having sex with you all the damn time. I want this to be more. I know relationships are work. I know I have a weird schedule with baseball. I know you are going to law school. Yet not for one freaking moment do I question that I want this. I want to set us up right. I want us to succeed. And I know waiting for a while before having sex might sound weird, especially when it's something I want so badly. I know this isn't what you expected to hear. I know for a guy my age, this is freaking strange. But you already know I'm not like other guys. And while I want to make love to you more than I've ever wanted to with any woman, I want us more. I want to see if there can be an us, Katie."

A huge lump swells in my throat. I can't speak. AJ has spoken everything that is in his heart, and he wants the same thing that I do. He knows it's not going to be easy, but he doesn't care. He wants to be my man, and he's hell-bent on doing it right. While we have only gone out a handful of times, AJ sees the future in us.

A future he wants.

The blood rushes to my head. I feel faint. Dizzy. Unable to breathe.

My heart is responding to his words, from this man who wants to build something with me, who has laid his heart right out for me at this stoplight. One who has only known me a short time, but his heart is already speaking to him in a way that makes him determined to build the bonds of friendship and partnership first before adding the intimate layer.

Because with us, we both know it won't be just sex. It won't be casual.

It will be a commitment, because our hearts are involved.

The emotions swirl in my head at a rapid rate. This time, I don't need Counselor Katie to sort out the facts.

Because the future lawyer in me would say there's no way this is possible. You can't meet someone, talk for hours, go on some dates, do FaceTime, and feel the way I do.

But I know without a doubt what it is.

I love him.

My head knows this is crazy. Throwing wild caution to the wind, tossing my heart out there to be broken into a thousand pieces. Going in headfirst, not telling myself to slow down, that this is infatuation at this point, and there's no way my heart can be in this place so quickly.

Yet, I don't care.

I don't need a dozen dates or to have sex with him to know what I know.

I'm in love with AJ.

The light changes, and AJ drives forward, but his eyes dart toward mine for a brief moment as he drives.

"Katie. Did I freak you out? Is this too much?" he asks, a tinge of panic running through his voice.

"No," I say, trying to hide the emotion in my own voice. I pause for a moment, trying to shove it down. "What you said … what you said was perfect."

My voice wobbles at the end, and AJ's eyes widen in surprise.

I slow my thoughts down, as my emotions are taking me by surprise, and I don't want to blurt out that I love him.

"AJ," I say slowly, my voice still shaky, "we are on the same page. I feel everything you said. I want you. But I want to build an us, in the way you described. We're on the same page."

And we have been since the day I fell into your lap, I think.

AJ exhales, and he's so adorable, I can't help but laugh.

"That was about the scariest thing I've ever had to do," he

admits. "I didn't know if you'd think I was crazy. Or if you'd be freaked out."

I reach over and slide my hand through the hair at the nape of his neck. "Not at all."

A warm smile passes over his face, one that makes my heart melt.

"You might be soon," AJ says. "After you meet my crew and my other car."

"What is so awful about this car?"

"You'll see. And you'll have every right to walk away after you see. I'll understand and let you go," AJ says, a devilish smile passing over his handsome face.

"Well, if your crew hates me like Pissy does, you'll be ending things with me tonight," I say. "I know how much you love your dogs. If they don't like me, it's the bottom of the ninth. With the other team up by ten."

AJ shakes his head. "My dogs will love you. And that cat is psycho."

"I know, she is," I declare, grateful to have someone else confirm my suspicions about Hayley's cat. "That cat is hateful. Unless your name is Hayley or Brody."

Before long, we are pulling into the parking garage of his building. AJ eases the Tesla into a spot, and as we climb out, he clears his throat.

"See this?" AJ says, rapping his hand against the window of a maroon minivan parked next to his Tesla.

"Um, yeah, it's a minivan."

AJ raises an eyebrow. "Not just any minivan. It's *my* minivan."

My mouth drops open.

"Yeah. I'm twenty-five, I have no kids, no wife. I'm a professional ballplayer, and I own a Mom car."

I burst out laughing. "I never would have guessed this."

"Want me to take you home?" AJ says as I walk around to his side.

"No," I say, sliding up next to him and slipping my arm around his waist.

AJ loops an arm around the top of my shoulders and drops a kiss on my head. "Wow. You do smell like coffee and vanilla icing. I might have to take back the no sex amendment."

I snuggle into him. "Are you kidding? I want you to take it back because the minivan is hot."

AJ chuckles. "It fits my crew. I can take all of us together in it; that's why I bought it. Let me show you."

He goes around to the back and opens the hatch. "See, I fold the third- and second-row seats down, and then they all fit."

I melt inside when I see the huge dog beds in the back. AJ loves his dogs so much that he bought a minivan to accommodate them.

Wait.

My brain cycles back to this piece of information.

He *bought* a minivan.

My pulse quickens as I digest this discovery. AJ, the man who has wanderlust, who never calls one place home, who trades out cars every two weeks so he's not bored, was able to make a commitment to a minivan.

Then I remember his Instagram while he traveled in the off season. He was all over the United States with his friends. The dogs were never pictured in a home but always outside.

"AJ, did you take the dogs with you this off-season? Is this how you traveled?" I ask, putting more information together.

"Ah, you did stalk my Insta," AJ teases. "Absolutely. We drove around the country in this van and, in certain places, my friends would fly in and hang out for a while and stay in the cabins I rented. But I couldn't leave them that long. It's hard enough because I have to during the season. I sure wasn't going to leave my Danes in the off-season."

My heart is racing.

AJ not only bought a minivan for his dogs, but he took them wherever he went, as inconvenient as it might have been, due to one thing, and one thing only.

Because of love.

Then I think of what he just told me, of his desire to build an us.

If he loves something, he can commit to it.

And when he does, his heart is all in.

Oh, my God, I'm so happy I could cry.

Law school and baseball will be challenges, but I know he has the willingness to make it work, just like I do, if we are meant to be.

AJ slams the hatch shut. "Come on, let me go introduce you to my kids."

I blink back happy tears as he takes his hand in mine.

Never in my AJ fantasy crush days could I have ever dreamed he'd be like this. Underneath the hot baseball player exterior, underneath the man who has wanderlust, the one who preferred hanging with the guys to a relationship, is this very real man with a huge and loving heart. He guards it due to his past, but the love he has for his Great Danes tells me everything.

He is open to the possibility of love with me.

AJ leads me into the industrial-style building, one in the heart of the Navy Yard district of DC. I can see why he picked it. It's modern and hip, and he could walk to the ballpark if he felt like it.

Then I see his minivan in my head, and I laugh.

AJ hits the button to the elevator, and we immediately step inside. "What?" he asks, confused.

"I'm thinking of how cool and modern this apartment building is, and then I get a visual of you wheeling into the parking garage with your minivan."

AJ backs me up against the elevator wall as it begins its ascent to the eighth floor. "Are you mocking me, Counselor?"

He slides his hands up my ribcage. I shiver in response to his touch. To the hungry look in his deep green eyes.

"I'm presenting the facts," I say, taking a moment to draw my lower lip teasingly between my teeth. "Would you like to know another fact, Andrew Joseph?"

His eyes flicker intensely. "That depends what it is. Does it involve this sexy mouth of yours?"

AJ slowly drags his thumb across my lower lip before stopping in the center. He lightly moves his thumb back and forth, setting my body spiraling into need for him.

"It does," I say. "I want you to kiss me."

AJ moves his hand to the side of my face. His mouth urgently descends on to mine, opening me, tasting me, his tongue demanding everything I can give him. His strong body pins mine to the wall, and I can feel him, his skin hot, his muscular body hard, his sensual mouth continuing to assault mine.

I move my hands to his massive back, holding on to him, kissing him harder. I love this. That kissing him makes me feel full of heat, aching with need, desperate for more.

The elevator chimes on the eighth floor. I break the kiss and frame his gorgeous face in my hands.

"I missed you," I whisper breathlessly as the doors open.

AJ takes my hand and leads me out of the elevator. He immediately stops me in the hall, drawing me into his body and reclaiming my mouth again, this time with a slow, sexy, deliberate kiss. One that is gentle, one that AJ takes his time with, but the physical reaction to him is exactly the same as before.

Need.

I want more. More of his mouth, more of his touch, more of his scent on my skin.

"I missed you, too," he whispers against my lips. "Stay here tonight, Katie. Let me kiss and touch you all night long."

I decide to let my lips tell him the answer to that one, and as I rake my fingers through his hair and my mouth sweetly discovers his again, there's no doubt as to what my answer is.

I'm going to stay and see the sun come up.

In the arms of the man I love.

CHAPTER 17

Playlist Shuffle Song of the Day:
"Cold Coffee" by Ed Sheeran

his is happiness.

I'm sitting on AJ's living room floor in one of his Washington Soaring Eagles T-shirts, sipping a cup of coffee made from his machine, and watching the sun rise in an beautiful orange and red sphere over the dome of the Capitol from the majestic floor-to-ceiling windows. I have my earbuds in, listening to "Cold Coffee" on repeat while I stroke Greta, his white Great Dane, who has her huge head in my lap.

I gaze out over DC as the city bustles to life for another day, and a feeling of utter peace and contentment fills my soul.

So many things happened last night, so many things that confirmed to my heart that falling in love with AJ is right.

First, his love for his dogs. I shift my gaze to Greta, who is content to be with me this morning, letting the sun from the window bathe her in warmth as she snuggles by my side. I met all of AJ's beloved crew last night: Greta, who took an instant shine to me; Fitzgerald, the black-and-white one with what AJ called a harlequin pattern; and Hans, who is fawn-colored. AJ rescued all of them when he moved to DC, finding his dogs through a local Great Dane rescue group. He wanted dogs that were in desperate need of a home.

I know why, even if AJ didn't say it aloud. He wanted to provide the love and security to these dogs that he never felt growing up. These dogs were all given back by their owners. Unwanted. No place to go. AJ didn't say as much, but I think he tapped into that feeling of needing a true home. It was something he could provide to these dogs, and that mattered to him.

While all three dogs are wonderful, and AJ was thrilled that I took an immediate shine to them and dog drool didn't bother me in the least, Greta is the one who stole my heart.

Greta is AJ's last rescue, and his most challenging one.

She's only a year old, and the rescue group called him with an urgent request last summer. They had a Great Dane puppy who was nine weeks old that they were trying to rescue. The dog was blind and deaf, and if they couldn't find a foster, she would be euthanized. Would AJ do it?

AJ said he was on the road but to get the dog to his dog sitter in Maryland, who would take Greta. As soon as AJ saw her, though, he knew she was meant to be his.

I run my fingers over her coat. Greta is special because she is deaf and blind. The fact that he took her, no hesitation, shows me once again what an amazing man he is.

AJ told me she really is no different than Fitzgerald, who he calls Fitzy, or Hans. She took to training easily. AJ does make a point not to move the furniture, so it doesn't confuse her. He said her sense of smell is amazing, and she loves sticking her head out the window of the minivan to pick up the scent of the world. He also said when they walk, she leans into his left side, to feel secure.

We played with the dogs, talked, and of course, kissed and

touched until the wee hours of the morning. Did some clothing come off? Yes. We were skin on skin, cuddling and caressing, exploring, but never crossing the one line we set.

And all of this makes me love him so much more.

Suddenly, I hear paws on the hardwood, and Greta lifts her head. I smile, realizing her sense of smell has detected one of her brothers.

I turn my head and see big Fitzy ambling toward me.

"Hi, Fitzy," I say, using AJ's nickname for him. He comes over and licks me, and I laugh, as he leaves a huge swath of slobber all over the side of my face.

I giggle, and Greta sits up, wagging her massive tail.

"You have kisses for me, too?" I ask Greta, even though I know she can't hear me.

I lean into her face, and she kisses me, too. I'm full of Dane love this morning.

Hans races into the living room, and as I turn around, I see AJ watching me from the hallway, his hands folded across his massive chest, his emerald green eyes shining softly at me.

"Hey. How long have you been watching me?" I ask, taking out my earbuds and raising a teasing eyebrow at him.

"Not long enough," he says gently. "You're beautiful, Katie."

Warmth fills me.

"I mean it," AJ says, moving across the sparsely decorated living room and dropping down on the floor next to me. "So many things are attractive about you, but seeing you with my dogs like this gets me."

I smile at him as Fitzy shoves his huge body across AJ's lap, as if he's a Yorkie instead of a Great Dane.

"You have incredible dogs," I say. "Have you had dogs your whole life?"

"No, I got Fitzy when I moved here," AJ says as Hans butts his hand to get his attention. "I always wanted a dog growing up, but my parents said no because it was

179

inconvenient." He's quiet for a moment. "That was their answer to a lot of things. I think Lindsay and I were a hindrance to their 'go where the wind takes them' lifestyle."

My heart wrenches for AJ, as he's just given me a glimpse of himself as a child.

"AJ, I'm so sorry you feel that way," I say, reaching for his hand. His skin is warm against mine, and I notice how the stream of sunshine hits right where our hands are entwined.

"Don't be," AJ says quickly, and his tone tells me he wants to shove the topic back into whatever drawer it sprang from. "I had a different kind of childhood, but it's nothing to complain about."

"I don't think expressing your feelings is a complaint," I tell him. "That life was hard on you. I can see it in your eyes."

AJ is silent as he shifts his attention to Fitzy, stroking him with his free hand. "I try to focus on the positives. It gave me baseball, right? Baseball gave me a place to fit in no matter what school I was at. They taught me how to roll with change. It made me more adventurous. I wouldn't be this way if I had only grown up in a few places, right?"

"You are entitled to all your feelings about your childhood, both good and bad," I say simply. "And if you ever want to talk about any of them, you can with me."

AJ shifts his gaze to me. I smile gently at him and lift my hand to his face, caressing his cheek and letting the black stubble on his face scratch against my palm.

"I'm so damn lucky you ate a bunch of crap at the ballpark that night," AJ teases.

I inwardly wince. When I fainted on AJ that night, I told him it was because I ate too much ballpark food and got hot.

Well, those points are true. I ate a bunch of garbage and had a few alcoholic beverages. It was humid and sticky that evening.

But I fainted because I was incredibly nervous about meeting my celebrity crush in person and panicked.

I bite my lip. AJ was sensitive about me being a fan at first. Although now that I see him as Andrew Joseph, and he knows that, I could tell him. I should tell him the truth about that day. In fact, he'd probably think it's funny now. I'm about to speak when AJ beats me to it.

"Idea," he says, releasing my hand so he can slide it underneath my hair. "Let's go walk the dogs and go out for breakfast. A big breakfast."

He begins winding his fingers through my curls, and the effect is drugging me. Forget the fan thing. I just want to enjoy this morning with AJ.

Suddenly, he tugs and yanks my hair.

"Ow," I laugh.

AJ winces. "Sorry, my finger is stuck in your hair again."

"Stupid Mufasa hair," I say, reaching up and unwinding my curls from his finger.

"I love your Mufasa hair," AJ says. "Even though it is dangerous to touch it. I didn't realize I'd be ensnared on a regular basis."

I laugh as I free his finger. "So, before I entrapped you, you said breakfast?"

"Not cereal. Big breakfast."

I smile happily at him. "I'm all about waffles." An idea hits me. "Have you ever been to Tryst?"

"No," AJ says, as Hans tries to wiggle his way onto AJ's lap, which is already holding Fitzy. "Come on, Hans. Can't you see Fitzy is there?"

I get up and go over to the toy basket, picking up a squeaky chicken toy.

"Come here, Hans!" I say.

But before I can blink, Hans has barreled over me in excitement. I shriek. The chicken goes flying in the air and then slams down, creating a loud squeak as it unceremoniously lands on my head. I'm flat on my back with Hans pinning me to the hardwood and a rubber chicken on my head. He's licking my face, and all I can see—and smell—is Great Dane.

"Shit, Katie! Hans! Off!" AJ says, scrambling up to help me.

I try to push myself up, but Hans has me pinned. I know I look like a cartoon character, squashed by the oversized, cartoonish dog, and I erupt into laughter.

"AJ," I say between giggles, "I'm trapped!"

"Hans! No! Get up!" AJ commands, moving Fitzy, who barks in response. He quickly gets Hans off me. "Shit, Katie, are you okay?"

I sit up and rub the back of my head. "Whoa. He's seriously strong."

AJ puts his hand on the back of my head, lightly cradling it. "Did you hit your head hard? I'm so sorry. Hans doesn't realize he's one hundred and thirty pounds of dog. Are you okay?"

"I promise I'm fine," I reassure him. "Anyway, let's get back to food." Fitzy and Greta are now circling around me. Greta once again puts her massive head in my lap, and Fitzy drops by my side. "Tryst has amazing waffles. Cornbread ones. To. Die. For."

"That really didn't bother you?" AJ says.

"What?" I ask, confused. "Waffles?"

"No. Having Hans pin you like that?" he asks. "Getting dog hair all over you? Slobbered on? You don't seem fazed at all."

I smile at him. "Hans is a gentle giant. And I got extra dog kisses. I'll take that anytime."

I see a shift in AJ's eyes.

"I'm crazy about you," he says softly. "You aren't like anyone I've ever known."

I sit very still, my heart grabbing his beautiful words and holding them close.

"I'm crazy about you, too," I say.

A silence falls between us, then AJ smiles at me.

"So, what makes these waffles so amazing? Are they served in a helmet?" he teases.

"No. But they have a patio, and we can eat outside under an umbrella. They have avocado toast and breakfast burritos and bagels and coffee and will you say yes already?"

AJ laughs. "I love how I get a choice in this."

"I asked if you would say yes, not that you had to say yes. Don't twist the facts."

"Yes, Counselor."

I grin. "Will you please have a breakfast outside with me this morning?"

AJ draws my head toward his. My breath catches in my throat as we are inches apart.

"I'll do anything with you," AJ murmurs, dropping a sweet kiss on my lips. "Let's get ready, walk the crew, and then dine."

"Will you take me in the minivan?" I tease.

AJ bursts out laughing. "No."

I decide that someday I will get him to drive me around DC in that van.

But this morning, I'll settle for walking the dogs and waffles instead.

"ARE YOU SURE IT'S SUPPOSED TO RAIN LATER?" I ASK AS I SPEAR another bite of my waffle. "Because it's beautiful out now."

AJ and I are sitting out on the patio at Tryst, enjoying breakfast under an umbrella on this sunshine-filled late June morning. We're sipping coffee, sharing our meals with each other, and being like any other couple falling in love.

I'm so happy.

AJ tugs down on the black baseball hat on his head. One that has the logo for the DC hockey team. He told me he wears this hat to try to buy himself a bit of privacy. Of course, when we were walking down the sidewalk he was stopped by a woman around my age for a picture, which I happily took for her once AJ said it was okay.

It's so weird. That girl was me less than a few weeks ago.

Except I would have been way too shy to ask AJ to pose for a picture.

"Yeah, rain is supposed to roll in tonight," AJ says, pausing to take a bite of his frittata. Then he wipes his lips with his napkin and continues. "You don't have to go tonight if you don't want to. Rain delays can be painfully long."

"Are you kidding? I don't have to work until late tomorrow, so of course I'm going. And rain doesn't bother me. I actually like a good rainstorm."

"Good. Then come back over after the game and help me put the calming shirt on Fitzy. He's terrified of storms."

"Really?" I ask.

"Yes. And fireworks. I take him out to the dog sitter in Maryland because all the fireworks over DC are too much for him. Hans stays home with Greta."

"How do you celebrate the Fourth? I'm a big Fourth of July person, so this is important," I say, grinning at him before taking another bite of my cornbread waffle.

"Well, as you know, the Eagles always play an early game that day," AJ says, taking a sip of his coffee. "Then I get together with some of the guys on the team and do a barbecue. Afterward, Chase has a party at his building. Rooftop pool with a view of the Capitol and a private cabana."

"That sounds perfect; you have a great view of the fireworks," I say. "I went to the Mall with Hayley and some Georgetown friends last year. This is my first Fourth of July celebrating it as a college graduate. Dare I say as an adult?"

"You've been an adult since you were eighteen," AJ teases,

reaching across the table and spearing another piece of my waffle.

"Technically, yes. Emotionally? No," I say, laughing. "I feel closer to it with going to law school and paying my own rent and bills and stuff like that."

I study AJ for a moment.

My feelings for you make me feel more like an adult, I think. *I didn't know how romantic love felt until I fell for you.*

"So, would you like to celebrate at an adult party this year?" AJ asks, casually leaning back in his chair.

My pulse leaps.

I decide to be clever.

"It depends. Are you inviting me to an adult party, Andrew Joseph?"

AJ grins. I can tell he loves when I call him by his full name.

"I am. Next Tuesday, on the Fourth of July, will you go to Chase McLeary's party with me?"

"I would love to," I say.

AJ reaches for my hand across the table and leans forward. "Come here."

I lean closer, mere inches from his sexy mouth, and AJ brushes his lips against mine. I inwardly sigh as I taste maple syrup and coffee on them.

What I wouldn't give to taste more of him in this moment.

"You make me happy," AJ murmurs against my lips.

Oh, I love him.

He leans back in his seat. I swear, I'm lovestruck.

"You make me happy, too," I say softly to him. "Now I have a decidedly more un-fun invitation for you."

"You're lucky I like you, because this doesn't sound promising."

I flash him a smile. "After I explain, you'll understand."

"Like Frasier, I'm listening."

I laugh. "Okay, Dr. Crane, my family has a pre-

Independence Day cookout every year. This year, it's on Sunday night. Mom does the holiday her way, and unlike the New Year's Eve party, nobody can bring their own kind of food."

"Like mini ham sandwiches with secret Katie sauce?" AJ says.

I think I just swooned because he remembered my secret sauce.

"Yes. This is Mom's healthy holiday cookout. Things on the menu include lentil burgers wrapped in swiss chard. Not that there's anything wrong with that, but on Independence Day, I want a burger. Potato salad. Beer.

"Anyway, it's for anybody who wants to come, and usually we end up having fun. Meghan and I have a tradition of going out for ice cream afterward. And I don't want you to feel like you have to say yes. Either because of the menu or if you don't want to meet my family so soon. I know it's early for that, and I promise you, AJ, I won't be hurt if you say no."

AJ stares at me. I honestly don't know which way he's going to answer from the expression on his face.

"I do have a three o'clock game that day," AJ says, adjusting the brim on his baseball hat.

"I know, so I totally understand if you say no."

"Does it matter if I show up late?"

My pulse twitches in anticipation of a yes.

"No," I say, smiling eagerly at him.

"Okay," AJ says, stroking his hand over his chin. "Then I just need to know one thing."

"What's that?"

"Your parents' address."

I am happy dancing in my head.

"I'll make sure you have that."

"Will your sister be there?"

"Yes, and probably Whitaker," I say. "Some neighbors. Cousins. But people I have known my whole life. Mom always invites Hayley, so there's a good chance Brody might come, too."

"Sounds good," AJ says. "Thank you for inviting me. That means a lot to me."

"Thank you for saying yes," I reply, reaching across the table and caressing his face with my hand.

AJ smiles the second I touch him, and love for him swells in my heart.

"What do you have planned for the day off?" AJ asks, taking another sip of his coffee with cream.

"Something very exciting," I say. "I'm going over to this used bookstore to search for vintage recipe cards."

"You do live dangerously."

"I do. I'm hoping to locate some more for my collection."

AJ studies me with his deep green eyes. "What have you made from your collection?"

I laugh. "A few things."

That sexy grin spreads across his face. "I have a challenge for us."

Us. Is there a more perfect word in the English language?

No. There's not.

"What?" I ask.

"We're going to make a meal using nothing but these recipe cards."

I think I'm going to explode with happiness. "I kept telling Hayley we should, but she said that was a terrible idea. And obviously, making frosted meatloaf for one is sad."

"Frosted meatloaf is sad for anyone," AJ teases.

"Shut up."

AJ laughs. "Let's do it. Let's make a meal with some crazy and horrifying recipe cards."

I think I just fell more in love with him. "I promise I'll pick interesting ones."

"Oh, no. I am an active participant in this. After breakfast, we'll go to this bookstore, and I get equal say in the cards."

"Wait, you'll go dig up vintage cards with me?"

"I'm in. Unless you are afraid of what I'll pick."

"Oh, this is so on," I say. "We each pick one, then one we choose together."

"Perfect," AJ says.

I stare back at him as he goes back to his frittata.

Indeed, I think happily.

CHAPTER 18

AJ was right about the rain.

A light rain began falling in the sixth inning, and they continued to play, but by the top of the seventh, it picked up in intensity, the skies breaking open and drenching the crowd. The game is officially in a rain delay and has been for a half-hour.

I'm on the concourse with Hayley now. We're both soaked, despite the fact that we had bright red Soaring Eagles ponchos on, and I can feel water squish in my socks whenever we walk.

Oy, so gross.

We're sipping bad cups of coffee, trying to warm back up. The temperature has dropped, too, and while some fans are headed for the exits, that's an idea neither Hayley nor I have even spoken of.

I smile as I warm my hands with the hot coffee. I won't leave until AJ does. Period. I'm here to support him, and if he sits through rain, so do I.

"You're thinking of AJ," Hayley says casually, taking a sip of her coffee. "Blech."

"Blech that I'm thinking of AJ?" I tease.

"No," she laughs. "This coffee is complete crap. Which begs the question, why am I drinking it?"

"Rain delay boredom," I say, taking a sip of my own cup of crap.

"Being a baseball fan, I know you are used to this, but I'm not," Hayley says.

"Bad ballpark coffee?"

"You are such a smart ass," Hayley replies. "No, I'm not used to delays going on forever like this. What if it rains for another *hour?*"

I smile, deciding not to tell her I sat through a two-and-a-half-hour one before.

And Hayley's new baseball brain probably doesn't want to know the rules regarding when a game becomes regulation. I think her head would explode. And then she would tease me for being of such a lawyer mind that, yes, I do know what the more obscure rules for the game are.

"Anyway," Hayley says, "I caught you in an AJ moment. You had that loved-up look on your face."

I blush. "When do I not think about him is the better question. Hayley, I'm so happy. I want to be with him and see where we go, and I'm not just thinking about the summer anymore."

Hayley appears thoughtful for a moment. "So, you've moved past your fear about law school impacting your relationship?"

"It will suck, and it won't be easy, but I'm embracing the idea that if we get to that point, we can work through it. I know AJ can commit to something if he wants to," I explain, thinking of how AJ treats his dogs. If he loves something, he can commit to it. I know that now. And knowing that has given me the freedom to think about moving forward with him without fear hanging over my head.

"Of course, I don't know where he will be," I say, as my other worry about AJ replaces the one I've put aside. "The

Soaring Eagles will talk to him about his contract at the end of the season."

I bite my lip. And as he continues to grow into one of the top center fielders in the league, I know he will have a huge market to test.

"You know what? If they offer him a good deal, he will stay," Hayley says, nodding in conviction. "AJ loves playing here. He likes the team and the city. And I think the biggest part of his equation will be you."

My heart leaps. "I hope so."

Hayley affectionately touches my arm. "He has had eyes for nobody but you since you fell on him, Katie. The boy is falling in love with you, if he hasn't already."

My stomach takes off like a roller coaster, exhilarated at the idea that AJ might be in love with me, too.

"I've never wanted anything more."

A man walks by with a helmet full of ice cream. I get a scent of the crisp waffle cone bowl placed inside, with that wonderful baked vanilla scent, and see he has chocolate ice cream, hot fudge, whipped cream, and sprinkles on top.

Want.

I'm about to tell Hayley I'm going to walk down to the creamery vendor near the first base side when fans start pointing to the TVs dotting the concourse, which are now tuned to the Soaring Eagles dugout. Some players have come out, despite the fact that the game is still in rain delay, and I see one of them is AJ, and another is Chase McLeary, his ginger hair giving him away upon first glance.

Intrigued, I join the crowd around the monitor, and Hayley follows me.

Brody steps out, too, and he's taken off his catcher's gear for the moment and is holding a marker and pad of paper.

"What are they doing?" Hayley asks.

"I have a feeling we are about to see rain delay shenanigans," I say.

AJ and Chase face each other, about five feet separating them. Then Chase breaks into a dance, a horrible awful, awkward dance that looks like he's a fish flopping on a dock for air. I giggle, so does Hayley, and the crowd around the TV bursts into laughter.

He stops, and Brody scribbles on his paper and holds it up. It's a score for Chase and it says:

Chaser 0

"Ha!" I laugh. "It's a dance-off!"

Chase laughs and shakes his head. Brody points his marker at AJ, giving him the signal to go.

AJ moves his hands up, holding them near his chest, and then he begins thrusting his pelvis, his body in fluid motion as he dances.

Oh. My. God.

I nearly spill my coffee as the Soaring Eagles fans scream in approval. AJ flashes a grin and holds his index finger out in a "get ready" move, and then he explodes into fancy footwork.

My jaw drops as I watch him. He's spinning and moving and flashing that sexy smile, and my throat goes dry as I watch him.

AJ is an incredible dancer.

No. Not that.

He is a *sexy* dancer.

My body responds as women in the crowd cheer in approval, my temperature rising with each move AJ makes. I hear comments floating around me like "so hot!" and "Oh, my God, did you see AJ?"

AJ spins and turns to Brody in a dramatic stop.

Chase is laughing. Brody is grinning as he scribbles and then holds up his score:

SNAKE HIPS 10

Chase shakes his head, Brody is still grinning, and AJ is laughing.

They head back into the clubhouse, and the crowd is buzzing.

I decide I don't care if the rain delay goes on for hours. I can die happy having seen my boyfriend dance like that.

As his pelvis thrust flashes through my head, I bite my lip.

I wonder if AJ would be game for moving up the line that we set for ourselves.

Because sex with him is going to be amazing if this is a preview of what the man can do with his hips.

My face burns hot. AJ might not want to move the line yet, but all I know is that when we do make love, it's going to be incredible.

And worth waiting for.

∿

FINALLY, AFTER AN HOUR-AND-A-HALF DELAY, THE RAIN LETS UP, and with towels in hand, Hayley and I head back to our seats in the WAGS section. We wipe them off and sink down.

Squish.

Ugh, everything from my socks to my underwear is still wet.

"Brody better appreciate my dedication," Hayley teases.

We resume where we left off, with the Phoenix team coming to bat at the top of the seventh. The Eagles are still up 3-2.

As Santiago Martinez, the Soaring Eagles pitcher, warms up with Brody, my phone buzzes in my purse, and I pull it out. It's my mom.

I wrinkle my nose. I know what this is about before I even

read her text. It's her annual pre-Independence Day party reminder.

"Before I answer Mom, did you and Brody RSVP for the healthy cookout?" I ask, swiping open my phone.

"We did," Hayley says. "Brody said it will be like being at home."

I grin. Brody grew up with very health-conscious parents, so eating a lentil burger with a side of celery root mock potato salad with vegan mayo is not unusual at all.

"I'm so glad Brody is coming; he can keep AJ company," I say.

"AJ," Hayley says, "is going to be fine."

The Phoenix Heat batter is announced, and I watch him take ball one. I glance down at the text Mom sent:

I just saw you on TV!

I cringe. Oh, crap. I know my hair is an unruly, matted mess right now and any makeup I had on is in the DECAY stage of life.

I look AWFUL.

Mom is typing …

You look good for sitting through a downpour. Speaking of baseball, I'm curious to meet AJ on Sunday.

I furrow my brow at her words. When I called Mom and told her I was seeing AJ, she was surprisingly neutral on the subject. I figured it was shock, that I was dating a Soaring Eagle, but now I wonder if there is something else behind it.

AJ is wonderful, Mom. You and Dad will love him, I promise.

Mom is typing …

I lift my head as the Phoenix player strikes out. Okay, two more to go and then the Eagles are up. I should be seeing AJ in the bottom of the eighth for one last at bat, unless the Eagles have a stellar bottom of the seventh, and they work their way down to his place in the lineup.

I glance down and see the text from my mom:

I hope you aren't viewing him through the lens of having a crush on him for a long time. Katie, everyone knows he was your celebrity crush, and through fate, you are dating him. I simply hope it's for the right reasons, sweetheart.

Anger begins to bubble inside of me from her words. I know it's natural for people to have their doubts given my intensity as a baseball fan, let alone AJ being my favorite player, but I hate that Mom is labeling how I feel without really talking to me. As I unpack the situation from her point of view, the anger stills. She's my mom, she loves me, and based on her facts of the situation, she's worried.

As a good mother would be.

The next Phoenix batter fouls the ball off for strike one. I quickly type a neutral response:

I understand your concern, it's a weird situation. But I promise you, Mom, I care about him because of the man I've gotten to know. I can tell you that if he worked as an architect, or on Capitol Hill, or as a chef, I would be equally intrigued.

Mom is typing …

The Phoenix batter makes contact with the ball, and the play on the field has my attention now. It's a fly ball, and I watch as AJ rushes up from center field to catch it. I stand up with Hayley as he times his dive just right, launching his body toward the ball, sliding across the wet grass, and catching the ball just before it hits the ground. Soaring Eagles fans cheer his catch, as do I, and my eyes stay riveted to him, as his uniform is now covered with wet grass stains and mud.

As a baseball fan, it's captivating to watch his sense of timing, the speed he has, the way AJ knows exactly when to launch forward, all while keeping his concentration on the ball.

As his girlfriend, I find this sexy as hell.

I keep the sexy thought to myself and cheer with the remaining crowd. Out number two, thanks to my man.

I wait for Mom's message to drop in. Hmm. This is taking a while. Now I fear the answer. Finally, it arrives:

I truly hope so, honey. I don't want you to be with a man who doesn't suit you, or who doesn't treat you the way you deserve, once your infatuation with the celebrity wears off.

I exhale. I can see the only thing that will convince her will be seeing us together for months on end before she believes my feelings for AJ are from the heart and not from a crush.

I respond:

I promise you'll see it on Sunday, Mom. Looking forward to seeing you and Dad and everyone. I promise I won't bring any ham sliders.

I insert a winking emoji at the end, hoping that will get Mom to end on a positive note. Her response immediately drops in:

Oh, Katie, I worry about what you eat when I'm not around.

And she inserts a green sick emoji at the end of her sentence.

Ha, that makes me smile. Mom would really die if she knew I used full fat mayo and butter for my awesome sandwiches.

Found off a recipe card circa 1978, but nobody but me knows that.

The next Phoenix player grounds out, so it's time for the Soaring Eagles to bat. I watch as AJ runs in from center field, toward the dugout. I wait as the large video screen gives us a look back at the spectacular plays of the evening, including AJ's sliding catch that happened a few moments ago.

I watch him in slow motion, pride filling me as I do. He's such a talent, but from the way he talks about himself, you'd never know it. He talks about working hard and where he wants to grow to.

AJ is humble about his abilities on the field.

Which makes him even sexier in my opinion.

I put my phone away as the song "Welcome to DC" blares through the ballpark. I grin, as that's Brody's at-bat song.

He's introduced as he comes to the plate, and Hayley and I both yell loudly for him, along with our core group of WAGS that has fought through the rain and stayed to cheer on the Soaring Eagles.

Brody settles in at the plate and takes ball one.

"He's such a patient hitter," I say, keeping my eye on the Phoenix pitcher as he delivers a strike across the center of the plate.

"It fits his personality," Hayley says. "Brody has infinite patience. He gets all Zen-like when he plays the game. Whereas Brady, his twin, gets into his head when he pitches. Brody says that's what's holding him back. That he has all the skills to be a great starting pitcher, but his head messes with him. But Brady's been on a good stretch lately, so maybe it's all starting to come together for him, you know?"

I nod. Brady is in the minors for the Chicago River Fox, and it's his dream to pitch on the major league stage.

Brody fouls off the third pitch.

"It's too bad Brody can't catch for him," I say, thinking about the twin connection and how Brody could really help Brady along.

"Oh, no," Hayley says, shaking her head. "Brady would hate that. He wants to prove to everyone he can do this on his own. So, it's for the best that they are on different teams."

"Is he still dating that girl?" I ask. I remember Brody and Hayley talking about them once, and how there was a new drama every week.

"Yeah, but it won't last," Hayley says as Brody fouls back another ball.

My mind drifts to Meghan and Whitaker. They don't fight, and they've been together forever, but my gut says they won't end up together, either.

Then I feel guilty for thinking it. I have no evidence for this; it's a feeling I have. That Meghan keeps talking about an engagement, and Whitaker says nothing speaks volumes to me.

That my sister, sooner or later, will be devastated.

Brody fouls off another one.

But that's the chance you take on love, I think. *You can't truly fall unless you are willing to risk being hurt.*

I know I'm risking my heart with AJ. He might not even be here in a few months. But somehow, I just know this is going to work. Even if I'm at Georgetown and he ends up playing somewhere like New York. I know it won't be easy.

But I don't want easy.

I want to be with AJ.

"Then there's Mr. Snake Hips himself," Hayley teases, as if

she was reading my mind on who I was thinking about. "The flashy outfielder who doesn't mind entertaining the crowd. Or one very special lady, I might say. Who will be seeing those hips in motion later tonight."

I laugh. "You know we haven't done that yet," I say quietly, as Hayley knows everything that is going on between me and AJ.

"Nice preview of the future then," Hayley teases.

Brody rips a ball down the right-field line, into the corner. He turns on the speed and rounds the corner for second, going into a slide that sends him flying across the dirt and his helmet sailing off for a double.

We yell for him as he retrieves his helmet, taking a moment to shake out those famous golden curls of his.

"Swoon," Hayley says, staring at her man.

I smile as my gaze shifts to the dugout, where AJ is joking around with Ryder Asbury, the right fielder, up near the railing.

Swoon indeed, I think happily.

And I can't wait to be with Mr. Snake Hips himself after the game tonight.

CHAPTER 19

"I am so sorry," AJ says, dropping a kiss on the top of my damp head as we walk toward the car in the player parking lot. "You're still soaked."

"Don't be sorry. It's merely rain. I'm wet, but I'm happy," I say.

The Soaring Eagles got Brody across the plate for an added insurance run and won the game. Finally, it's time to go home and get out of these clothes. Take a hot shower.

And make out with Mr. Snake Hips for hours on end.

"You're a trooper," AJ says, drawing me into his side.

"Careful, your clothes will get damp," I tease.

AJ stops walking and draws me into his shirt, holding me tight and squeezing me to him.

"What are you doing?" I ask, giggling. "Trying to wring me dry?"

"No. I'm hoping you get my shirt wet."

"What?" I laugh, wiggling out of his arms so I can see him. "Why would you want that?"

He slides his hand up the side of my face. "So you have a reason to take it off when we get home."

Ooh.

I raise an eyebrow at him and place my hands at his hips.

"Are you going to show me those snake hips later if I do?"

AJ grins wickedly. "Do you want me to?"

"AJ, are you changing the boundary line we set?" I ask.

His flirty expression changes. AJ cups my face in his hands, and the gentle way he's gazing at me melts my heart.

"No, but I believe in a thorough, torturous foreplay period until we do."

Then he lowers his mouth on mine, kissing me sensually, drawing my lower lip between his teeth and flicking his tongue over it in a teasing way.

I think I'm going to pass out from heat exhaustion, because my temperature just shot up to a very dangerous level.

"We need to go back to your place," I manage to say.

"Agreed."

AJ takes my hand in his and leads me back to the Tesla. We get into the car, and I stare at him as he drives out of the lot.

"Confession," I say.

"I'm listening."

I smile. I like that he's made that a bit for us.

"I want to make out with you more than I've ever even wanted to have *sex* with anyone I've dated. I can't even imagine what sex with you is going to be like."

AJ keeps his eyes on the road. "Same. I want to be with you, in any way I can. This slow burn is killing me. In the best way possible, if that makes sense. We have something, Katie, and I know when we have sex, it will cement everything for us."

My pulse leaps. He's connecting sex not only with love, but a future.

I love his heart. How he wants to protect what we have. To grow it by investing in our friendship and emotional relationship before becoming physical.

But I know AJ needs to understand exactly what he's getting if we do have this future I want so badly.

And now is the time to make sure he knows what that future will entail.

"AJ?"

"Yeah?"

I draw a breath of air for courage as he makes the super short drive back to his apartment in the Navy Yard. "I've told you how intensive law school is going to be."

"Yeah, why?"

"I need to make sure you understand what that actually means. When I'm in law school, you will have a whole lot less of me around. Or if I am, I'll have my nose buried in my laptop or book. I'll be tired. Stressed. Maybe both. Is being with me in bits and pieces and exhausted and freaked out what you really want?"

I hold my breath. My feelings for AJ are pushing me to ask the question I've been most afraid of asking.

AJ is silent for a moment. I bite my lip, anxious for his reply.

"I'd rather have bits and pieces of time with you," AJ says slowly, "than endless time with anyone else."

I start breathing again.

"Katie, I know it's going to be demanding. It's Georgetown Law; I wouldn't expect anything less. I've got this."

I blink back tears. AJ is such an exceptional man, and I feel so incredibly lucky that he cares about me, about us, enough that he will happily settle for whatever I can give while I work on my law degree.

I exhale loudly. "Thank you for reassuring me. I needed to hear that."

"Were you worried that I wouldn't understand?" AJ asks, his voice reflecting surprise.

"Yes," I whisper.

"Don't be."

He picks up my hand and laces his fingers with mine.

"It will be hard, AJ. I don't want you to go into this blindly."

"Do you think getting to play professional baseball was easy?"

"No, of course not."

"But if you were dating me in the minors, would you have done it? When I was gone all the time, playing in small towns? Maybe on the other side of the country?"

"Of course."

"Right back at you. Katie, I love that you want to be a lawyer. I love that you want to empower women and champion that cause. I want you to realize your dream like I did mine."

Emotions flood me. AJ is speaking straight from his heart. He understands sacrifice and challenge to achieve a dream.

He's telling me he will stand by my side as I chase mine.

"So, that means you want me to tell you all about my current read of how to learn to read like a lawyer?" I tease.

"Wait, you already finished the other one? About arguing?"

I love that he remembers what I was reading when we chatted on FaceTime during his road trip.

"I'm a fast reader. Quick study," I declare as he swings into the parking garage. "In fact, I'm already ahead of the book schedule I made for myself."

"And this is what you call your summer off before law school," AJ deadpans, squeezing my hand.

I laugh. "I want to show up day one as prepared as I can be."

"You're going to be at the top of your class," AJ says, easing the Tesla next to his minivan, which makes my heart melt all over again.

"I hope so. My mentor, Gemma, expects it," I say, thinking

of the powerhouse lawyer that she is. "I want to read as many of these books as I can before I have lunch with her in a few weeks."

Since I'm not interning this summer, I still want to prove to Gemma that I am taking my law school prep seriously. So, I booked a lunch with her and plan to discuss all these books I'm reading, as well as get her advice on how to handle 1L, as the first year of law school is called. I want to continue to impress her, so I can realize my dream of working for her after I graduate.

We get out of the car, and AJ takes my hand as soon as I reach his side.

"I still want a ride in the minivan," I tease.

"No."

I smile to myself. I'm so getting that ride someday.

"I want to say something before we change the topic," AJ says, glancing down at me.

I stare up at him, waiting for him to speak.

"I know Gemma matters to you because she took on your case and is a huge advocate for women's rights, but she's lucky to have someone as passionate as you are about law, someone who truly wants to be an advocate, and who will give everything she can to clients. I think Gemma should be pursuing you."

I stop walking. I reach up, lock my hands around his neck, lean up on my tiptoes, and give him a sweet kiss.

"What's that for?" AJ asks, smiling down at me.

"For being incredible," I say, kissing him a bit longer. "For believing in me. For not only wanting me to follow my dream, but to see my own worth."

I kiss him again, tasting mint on his tongue and feeling the softness of his lips as they move sensually against mine. I lift my hands to caress his face, finding his skin smooth and freshly shaven. The clean, crisp scent of his cologne seeps into me, and I drink it in as I continue to demand more with my kiss.

A groan escapes his throat, and then he laughs sexily against my mouth.

"Let's take this inside," he said, kissing me again and murmuring against my lips. "Before I have you stripping out of these wet clothes here in the parking garage."

I break the kiss and smile up at him. "Exhibitionist."

"No," he says, staring down at me. "More like I can't resist you."

I like his answer better.

As he takes my hand in his again, I can't wait to get back upstairs.

And make out with him until the sun comes up the next morning.

~

I EXHALE HAPPILY AS MY CHEEK IS PRESSED AGAINST AJ'S CHEST. I love feeling his bare skin against mine, the way the bronzed color is so beautiful, how I instantly feel warmer wrapped in his powerful arms.

AJ is playing with my curls as we lay in the dark. We've made out for hours. Laughed. Talked. Ate. Now we are snuggled together, resting against his headboard, watching *Frasier* on TV.

And I'm not only sharing the king-sized bed with AJ, but the entire crew as well. Greta is right against my side, snoring softly. Fitzy is near AJ's feet, and Hans has claimed the remaining corner of the bed.

I've never had an evening as perfect as this one.

AJ laughs at something that is said on TV, and I smile as that wonderful sound reverberates from his chest to my ear.

"I love your laugh," I say, placing a gentle kiss on his chest.

"You like my deep, sexy man chuckle?"

I burst out laughing. "You killed it with man chuckle."

AJ grins, the dimple appearing in his cheek and completely undoing me.

I love that he's so confident in himself.

"I make up for it with snake hips," AJ says, pretending to be cocky.

"Hmm," I say, pretending to think it over. "Okay, you do. Snake hips are damn hot. I had no idea you were a dancer, Andrew Joseph."

I slide my hand down to the waistband of his boxer-briefs, teasing him just a bit before trailing my fingers along his hips.

AJ groans. "You're making this boundary line hard to keep."

I kiss his chest again. "I believe you said long, torturous foreplay?"

Then I move my lips up to his neck, and I feel his body grow tighter with each kiss.

"Katie," AJ murmurs as his mouth finds mine.

I open eagerly for him, as I can never get enough of the taste of him, the warmth of his mouth, the sensual way his tongue is claiming me as his. I feel his hand snake up underneath my T-shirt, his fingertips skimming the bottom of my breast before he takes it in his hand.

I draw an excited breath as he caresses me, his kisses slowing to match the way he's touching me right now.

Heat flashes through me. I don't want him to stop caressing me. Kissing me.

AJ's hand continues to stroke me, gently, reverently. He eases me down on the bed, cradling me to him, his tongue sweeping through my mouth as he slowly moves his hand down to my stomach, trailing his fingertips over my skin, down toward the lace edging of my bikini panty, where his hand stops, and I cry out in a whimper of protest.

AJ was right.

This is long, torturous foreplay that, one, makes me want him even more if that's possible and, two, touches my heart, knowing that he wants sex just as much but wants to wait.

For love.

He breaks the kiss and draws a breath of air. I know this is his way of keeping things from crossing the boundary line.

AJ drops a series of gentle kisses over my face, starting with my forehead, then the bridge of my nose, and finally my lips.

I caress the side of his gorgeous face with my hand. "I adore you."

Which is my code for "I love you."

"I adore you, too," AJ says, lowering his mouth to mine.

I smile against his lips.

He might not have said it, but I think I understand his code, too.

I love him.

And he's falling for me.

Love fills my heart.

There is no doubt in my mind that AJ is The One for me. For now.

For always.

And I can't wait to show my family on Sunday night what a real, beautiful, wonderful relationship we are growing together.

CHAPTER 20

Playlist Shuffle Song of the Day:
"Fireflies" by Owl City

I take a sip of my rosé as the sun begins to sink into the sky. I stand on the terrace, gazing out over the deep, narrow backyard of my family home. Wisteria in full bloom tumbles over the sides of the fence, coloring the garden in deep shades of purple and green. Potted planters filled with white petunias are next to the seats. I see fireflies beginning to make their appearance as the evening is growing dark. Music filters from speakers, and right now "Fireflies" by Owl City is playing. I smile to myself. Appropriate. Soon we'll be seeing them light up the sky en masse as it grows darker.

People are milling about long after dinner has been served, sitting on one of two long sofas that flank the stone fireplace at the end of the yard. Candles flicker about, and the setting is perfect for a Georgetown evening.

An evening that AJ is about to join very soon.

It's closing in on eight thirty, and AJ has texted me that he's on his way.

I try to visualize him here, in the home that has been in my family since 1910, with the history of the McKennas to go along with it. What will he think of being in this home, one that will be mine someday? Will he be able to see himself here with me in the future?

That's a wee bit of jumping ahead now, isn't it?

I draw a breath of air to reset and let the rational side of my brain take over. I mentally place him here with these people who have been woven into my fabric. I see the next-door neighbors, Lea and Ed, who I have known since I was in preschool. They have two children I grew up with: Tom, who is a stuck-up idiot, and Larissa, who is a DC social climber. Meghan and I were, for our entire childhood, forced to play with them until we became tweens. Now we are nice at functions such as this, but I have zero in common with either of them.

Tom is talking with Whitaker, who is swirling his cocktail in his hand. Meghan, of course, is right by his side, just as she always is.

I survey the packed patio, seeing all the familiar faces of my life: aunts and uncles, cousins ranging in age from teens to early twenties, more neighbors, including some who have moved out of Georgetown but still remain close to my parents and come back for the pre-Independence Day party.

I try to picture AJ in this setting. The first man I've ever brought to this annual family event.

I'm sure he and Brody will be sought after for selfies. To talk baseball. I know this isn't ideal, but my entire family consists of huge baseball fans. Someone is always using our season tickets; not ONCE have they gone unused. I know Brody will be fine, but I worry that this will hit AJ's nerve about not being seen as Andrew Joseph but as AJ, the famous ballplayer who has his own bobblehead.

My hope is that once they get to talk baseball and have their moment, they'll let conversation go to anything but baseball, so they can get to know him as I've gotten to know him.

And then my mother can see that I truly do love him for the man he is, and not the baseball player I used to crush on.

"I just ate something totally weird," Hayley says, coming beside me and showing me her plate.

I smirk at her. "That doesn't narrow it down for me."

Hayley laughs. "This," she says, pointing to a brown square on the corner of her plate with a bite taken out of it. "It was on the dessert table. It kinda tastes like a brownie, but a hint off, if that makes sense."

I grin. "Mom told me she was testing new items this year. Do you really want to know what that is?"

Hayley appears to mull over that loaded question.

"Well, it's not bad, so go ahead," she says.

"Those have cauliflower in them."

Hayley's brown eyes widen in shock. "No way. I never would have guessed that!"

"Yeah," I say. "Did you try the chocolate chip cookies? They have lentils."

Hayley screws up her face. "Ew. I hate lentils."

"Those are bad," I say, taking another sip of wine. "I think tomorrow we need to make some legit gooey brownies to make up for it."

"Oh, yes, and I have the day off because they give us the third and the fourth off at Expanded World to the Shelf," Hayley says, referring to the non-profit where she works. "We can do those, and we can make Fruity Pebble cereal bars. We'll bring them to the game and eat them during the fireworks show."

"I can't believe I'm going to be on the infield for those," I say, "when last year I watched them from my seat as a fan. Now I get to live the dream and watch with the players and their families."

Hayley takes another bite of her cauliflower brownie.

"Katie, you're still a fan, because that is part of who you are. You just happen to be dating AJ, that's all."

I absently stare down at my cup of rosé. "I know," I say quietly.

"What's that tone for?"

"You never had this issue with Brody, because you didn't care about baseball or even know who he was. But AJ is sensitive to the fact that I was a fan *first*. I could tell it made him wary when we first had coffee."

"Katie. That night has been over for quite a while now," Hayley counters. "AJ *knows* your feelings for him. But I think he'd understand if you did get geeked out by hanging out with the team on the infield for fireworks, because that is a unique experience."

I swallow hard. "My mom doesn't think my feelings are real."

"What? Why does Justine think that?" Hayley asks, wrinkling her nose in confusion.

I smile. She's called my mom Justine or "my other mother" for as long as we have been friends.

But my smile fades as I think about what my mom texted me the other day.

"She's worried that I am applying these feelings to him because AJ was my crush first. That I want these feelings so badly that I'm falling for him with no reason."

"Are you?" Hayley asks, taking another bite of her brownie. "I have to give Justine props. Once you get the first few bites down, it's pretty good. And I'm eating a vegetable!"

"Wait," I say, irritated by Hayley's question. "How can you ask me that about AJ? You know me. You know I would never get involved with someone this close to law school if I didn't have genuine feelings."

"Exactly."

I furrow my brow.

"You know your heart. What anyone else thinks doesn't

matter. When Justine sees what a great guy AJ is, and how you are with him, she'll know it's real."

Hayley is right. It doesn't matter if anyone thinks my feelings are being influenced by my baseball-loving heart. What matters is that I know how I feel.

I know I love him.

For being Andrew Joseph.

The back door opens, and this time, Brody steps through.

But AJ isn't with him.

"Hey!" Hayley says, her eyes lighting up as he approaches her.

"Hi, Cherry Blossom," Brody says, dropping a kiss on her cheek.

"Great game tonight," Hayley tells him, as we had the game on here while we helped Mom get ready for the party. "Another run batted in for you."

"I'm in a good place at the plate," Brody says, grinning. "Hey, Katie, how are you?"

"I'm good," I say, looking for AJ to come through the door. When he doesn't, I turn back to Brody. "Where's AJ? Didn't he drive you guys here?"

Brody slides his arm around Hayley's waist. "Yeah, he's in the kitchen talking to your mom and dad."

My stomach tightens. I was hoping to introduce AJ, to be by his side when he met my parents.

And hopefully cut off any conversation about how, "Katie was your biggest fan, how strange is it that she ended up with you?"

I need to get inside.

"Um, do you need a drink?" I ask Brody, as I don't want to be rude. As I do, across the yard, I see Whitaker and Tom have spotted Brody and are oh-so-suavely pointing directly at him. I can guarantee you they'll be over introducing themselves and whipping out their iPhones in mere seconds.

"I can show him where the bar is," Hayley says. "You go find AJ."

I lean in closer to Brody and Hayley, so only they can hear me. "I'm sorry, you're going to be bombarded tonight."

Brody smiles easily. "It's all good, I promise."

I'm eternally grateful both AJ and Brody are so easy-going when dealing with fans—especially when they are at a private party where they shouldn't have to do anything but be themselves.

I head back inside the house, where people are hanging around in groups and talking in the den. Some board games have been brought out, and groups of people are laughing and playing. I take a quick look around, wondering if he had escaped that far, but no.

Oy. He's in the kitchen with Mom, I know it.

This is her command center for parties. She can easily hire a caterer, but she enjoys cooking and spreading her love of things like lentil cookies.

I cut through the room and walk down to the kitchen.

And sure enough, there is AJ, talking with my mom and dad.

My brain observes the evidence.

He's talking to my parents.

And why is he uncorking a bottle of wine?

All right. It's weird that the second he comes in, he's working the wine bottle, but that is not my biggest concern. They can't have scared him already, right? What possible conversation could they have gotten into in the span of a few minutes? They should be on the "oh, aren't we having great weather this week?" portion of chit-chat.

As I approach them, I hear what my dad is saying to AJ.

"To think I listened to Katie espouse your baseball abilities since you were in Ocean City," my father says, referring to the Soaring Eagles' Triple-A affiliate. "Along with how handsome you were."

Oy!

I immediately cut in to kill this conversation. "There you are," I say, positioning myself between AJ and my dad. "Thank you for coming."

I lean up and give him a kiss on his cheek. AJ is wonderfully freshly shaven, and his tanned skin is laced with the clean scent of his cologne.

Oh, I can't wait to snuggle up against him later tonight and kiss that handsome face all over.

"I'm glad to be here," AJ says, removing the cork. He holds the bottle in his hands, taking a moment to study me with his green eyes. AJ's gaze moves over me, drinking in how I flat-ironed my hair and pulled it into a sleek ponytail. How I'm wearing a blue, cold-shouldered sleeve blouse and a pair of pink pants for a soft, date-night look this evening.

"You look beautiful," he says, his eyes meeting mine.

I exhale. He doesn't seem to be bothered by Dad's comment.

Thank God.

"AJ brought us a bottle of wine, so of course, I insisted we try it," Mom says, smiling at me.

My heart warms. I love that he found time to get a hostess gift.

"What did you bring?" I ask.

"Organic merlot," AJ says. "I read that that has the highest concentration of resveratrol, so I figured you would approve of that, Mrs. McKenna."

"Justine, please, and yes, I do like that benefit of this wine," Mom says, appearing rather pleased that AJ went to this trouble to impress her.

"I can't believe it," my uncle Grant says, walking up to AJ as he pours wine for my mom. "AJ Williamson at a McKenna party. I'm Grant, Katie's uncle."

"Hello," AJ says, extending his hand. "AJ Williamson. Pleasure to meet you."

"Well, kiddo, you finally did it. Snagged yourself a professional ballplayer like you always told us you would," Uncle Grant says, laughing.

I glance at AJ, whose eyes betray the smile he's keeping on his face. They flicker for a moment, but that's all I need to see.

He's processing that comment.

"He's joking," I say, rolling my eyes in exaggeration to show AJ I'm not taking this conversation seriously.

"No, he's not," Eden, my cousin who is a year older than me, says. "Katie has said she was going to marry a baseball star since she was sixteen. 'A sexy ballplayer is an ideal husband,' I believe you told us."

"Yes, when I was sixteen," I counter.

"Hmm, seems like you might have the same goal as an adult," Uncle Grant teases.

I feel my face grow hot, all the way to the roots of my hair, as Eden and Uncle Grant laugh.

I glance at AJ, who stares down at me.

I see questioning in his emerald eyes.

My stomach twinges as a result.

"Oh, you two, stop it," Mom says, coming to my rescue. She passes a wine glass to me and Dad, and then pours two more for Uncle Grant and Eden. "A toast to Katie's new boyfriend. Thank you for coming tonight, AJ."

"Cheers," we all say, tapping our glasses together.

I drink the merlot, which I have to give AJ props for—it tastes of berries and spice—and eagerly swallow it down.

"I bet Katie hopes you re-sign here at the end of the season," Uncle Grant says.

"Forget Katie. All Soaring Eagles fans hope you re-sign at the end of the season," Dad says, his hazel eyes shining at AJ.

AJ smiles. "I would like to stay here, so hopefully the front office and I can find a way to make that happen."

I draw my lower lip in between my teeth. I had managed to put that thought away, of AJ being somewhere else this time next year. Now here it is, and I know it's a possibility that he might leave.

I can't picture it. Me in law school, and AJ being here through February, before he's off to spring training, and maybe relocating to a city on the other side of the country to play next season in a different uniform.

As AJ talks about the negotiation process—all in vague terms of course—I feel sick. Me in law school and AJ playing somewhere like San Francisco would make an already hard situation much worse.

But as I stand next to him, I know I would do everything in my power to figure it out. To make it work.

Because AJ is the man I love.

I stand quietly and let my dad and uncle pepper him with baseball questions, living to hear things from a true major leaguer. I'm grateful the joking about me has subsided. AJ eventually loops his arm around my waist, and pure relief fills me. I know he understands they were kidding.

I was stupid to spend time obsessing over him thinking anything otherwise.

We eventually make our way outside, meeting up with Hayley and Brody. Gah. Poor Brody, he's still cornered by Whitaker and Tom. Luckily, Meghan is keeping Hayley company, as I'm sure she's bored out of her mind with infinite baseball talk.

As soon as we approach, Whitaker and Tom welcome AJ with firm handshakes.

"This is so weird," Whitaker says, shaking his head. "AJ Williamson is dating my girlfriend's sister."

"I consider myself lucky to be dating Katie," AJ says, rubbing his large hand up and down the small of my back. My silk blouse glides against his fingertips, and the feeling is sensual. I shiver involuntarily in response.

Meghan smiles in approval of AJ's comment, and extends her hand to him.

"Hi, I'm Meghan," she says. "Katie's sister."

AJ smiles warmly at her and shakes her hand. "Hi, Meghan. I've heard a lot about you."

"Likewise," Meghan says. "Katie tells me you like old TV shows and movies like we do."

Oh, my God, I want to squeeze Meghan so hard right now. She is totally blocking the baseball talk and revealing something I told her about AJ that I liked.

And has absolutely zero to do with the game he plays.

"Babe," Whitaker says firmly, "I doubt AJ cares about your obsession with boring old shows from five thousand years ago."

I bite my tongue. There is one thing being with AJ has given me absolute clarity on: I know how a good man treats a woman. AJ respects all the things that make up my crazy, and simply knowing I enjoy these things makes him happy.

I also see with more clarity how much of an ass Whitaker is to Meghan.

"What do you like to watch?" AJ asks, turning to Meghan.

Meghan blushes. Her confidence has been rattled by Whitaker's demeaning comment.

"It's boring," she says, dismissing the subject. "I'm sure my idea of old and classic is different from yours."

"Is it *ever*," Whitaker says, rolling his eyes as he swirls his drink in his hand.

"What is it?" AJ asks, keeping his attention on Meghan.

Meghan is about to speak, but Whitaker beats her to it.

"*I Love Lucy*," he says, his deep voice laced in disapproval.

"Isn't that from the seventies?" Tom asks.

"No, the fifties," AJ answers. "It's brilliantly written. Still funny today."

I love my boyfriend.

"Yes," Meghan says, finding her voice again. "I laugh so hard at episodes I've seen a zillion times."

"Like 'Vitameatavegamin'?" AJ asks.

Meghan's eyes light up. She has found someone who speaks her Lucy language.

"Yes! Or that one where they are in that awful hotel on their way to California and the trains roll by?"

"Yep, that's another good one," AJ says, his fingertips still stroking the small of my back. "We haven't done that marathon yet, have we, Katie?"

I smile at him, and I know my face is beaming with adoration. "Nope. But we need to get one scheduled."

"Hey, Meggie, can you get me another gin and tonic?" Whitaker asks.

I see Meghan force a pinched smile on her face. "I believe you know where the bar is, love," she replies, giving him a look that says "get it yourself."

"But you got me the first one, so that is untrue, love," Whitaker says back.

Don't give in to him, I will Meghan. *Don't you dare act as his server.*

"Dude, I walked right by the bar when I came in," Brody says, smiling. "And AJ doesn't have a beer, so let's go get some."

Bahhhhhh! I love Brody.

AJ leans down and kisses my cheek. "I'll be back. In about an hour, after your uncle finishes asking about what goes on in the clubhouse," he murmurs against my ear.

I smile as he heads off with Brody, Whitaker, and Tom.

As soon as the guys are inside, I exhale loudly.

"What are you so anxious about?" Meghan asks, wrinkling her brow. "You are never anxious, unless a ballgame is in doubt."

"Meg," I say, "when AJ first walked in, everyone was teasing him about being the ballplayer I had always intended to land. It was cringe-y."

"But AJ didn't care, did he?" Hayley asks, raising an eyebrow.

"I know, you told me not to worry about this," I say, shaking my head. "But it's nagging at me."

"Katie Bug, he knows you," Meghan says. "Anyone who does understands that you want something genuine. That goes beyond his image as a baseball player. Otherwise you'd sleep with him and move on because he's boring. On second thought, if he has skills in the bedroom, keep him around a bit longer before kicking him to the curb."

We all laugh at that.

"I'm not kicking him anywhere," I say.

"Excellent plan," Hayley says, grinning at me.

We continue to talk. The sky grows darker, the fireflies begin flashing in earnest, and I wonder how long AJ and Brody are going to be held captive by my family.

"Do you think we should go rescue the guys?" I ask Hayley.

Hayley nods.

We step inside the house. I immediately spot Brody with Tom and a slew of neighbors, but I don't see AJ.

Brody sees us and says something to the group before stepping away.

"We figured you were ready to be rescued," Hayley says as Brody affectionately loops his arm over the tops of her shoulders.

"You're right," Brody teases, winking at her.

She laughs, and he drops a sweet kiss on her temple.

"Where's AJ?" I ask, looking around.

"Whitaker went to give him a tour of the house," Brody says.

"What? Why?" Meghan asks. "That's weird. It's not his house."

Something is off about this. I leave the group, headed toward the front of the house, to the first flight of stairs that lead to the second floor.

As I head up the stairs, I see Whitaker coming

down, alone.

We meet on the landing. There's a self-serving smirk on his arrogant face.

I feel the air catch in my throat.

"Where's AJ? I ask.

"He's lingering at an interesting spot on the tour," Whitaker says. "When we were all talking downstairs, naturally your obsession with baseball came up. How you were so nervous meeting your celebrity crush that you fainted on him. AJ said no, that's not true, you were sick that night."

The blood drains from my face. I place my hand on the banister for support.

"Of course, Meggie told me the truth, so I verified Eden's story," Whitaker says. "I told AJ you have had an infatuation with baseball players, and he was the strongest one yet. How he was the screensaver on your phone. How you followed him since his Ocean City days, and how all of us were impressed you landed the man you had set out to get from the time you saw him on the internet."

The room is getting dizzy. I'm fighting to think.

But all I can imagine is what AJ is thinking.

"AJ actually thought we were teasing him, so I showed him your old room," Whitaker adds, smiling. "You know, the one with all the Soaring Eagles bobbleheads collected over the years, the pictures, the cork board with AJ's picture from Ocean City on it. Oh, I know Meggie pinned that one as a joke, but I forgot to tell AJ that. Oops. Sorry."

Then he trots down the stairs, whistling as he does.

I struggle to breathe. I have to explain this to AJ. That I'm in this for him, not because I'm infatuated with getting a baseball player.

My heart is pounding as I walk down the hallway toward my room, which is at the end of it. As I step on that certain creaky board, my presence is announced.

AJ is standing in the center of my old room, the one that hasn't changed since I moved out for good last year. I see my baseball memorabilia, but other things that make up my life as well. Pictures of me and Hayley. Me and Meg. Georgetown. My bookshelf with old romantic comedies I couldn't bear to part with.

AJ slowly turns around. My heart stops beating when I see the questioning expression on his face.

"AJ, this isn't what you think," I say, desperate to explain.

"Isn't it?"

I want to touch him. But I know if I reach out for him, he'll pull away. And I can't bear that right now.

"You know me. I told you the truth that first night we walked in Georgetown. I wanted to get to know you, as Andrew Joseph. I didn't lie about that then. I'm not lying about it now."

"I don't think you're lying," AJ says, his voice soft.

"You don't?"

"I think you believe it because you want it to be true."

Oh, God. Panic surges through me.

AJ believes I'm in this for his celebrity.

"I think you want to believe you like me, but maybe you just like the idea of me because I am the role you cast in your fantasy," AJ says, his voice full of hurt. "You wanted me before you even said a word to me, Katie. Your infatuation drove this whole relationship, didn't it?"

"No," I say, shaking my head. "That's not true."

"How can it not be?" AJ cries, his voice incredulous. "You made me into what you wanted just from how I looked in the outfield. It doesn't matter what my interests are, what my thoughts are. Because of your infatuation, you'd make this work, wouldn't you? You want to believe your feelings are real. But how can they be?"

A sharp pain rips through my stomach. His words land there with a hard punch, knocking the air out of me.

Then anger takes over.

"I have shown you nothing but the real me," I say, my voice shaking with unshed, angry tears. "My interest in you, the man you are, has been genuine. The fact that my sister's idiot boyfriend, who loves to stir up trouble for his own amusement, can sway you with one conversation is eye-opening. I told you I was a fan. My room reflects that I have been a fan since I was freaking five years old. I took an interest in you as my favorite player, but I never set my sights on seducing you, which is rather egotistical of you to think. Did I get nervous meeting you? Yes. I thought I would meet my favorite player and go on with my life. You're the one who came to find me, but I guess that's irrelevant, isn't it?"

AJ blinks at that last comment.

"You know what? You can leave," I continue. "I don't want to talk to you if you believe I'm some fangirl who wants you for being a star baseball player. I fell in love with you for being you. For liking old TV shows and movies. For being passionate about amusement parks. For loving your dogs so much you drive a minivan just for them. That you were interested in my law studies and even my stupid vintage recipe cards. I loved you for all of that. But now I see a man who is doubting me for everything I've shared with him, and you have saved me from making a mistake I can't take back. And that's giving all of myself to you. You've already taken more than enough. And I've given you more than you'll ever know."

I storm out of the room, making angry strides down the hall. Tears are pooling in my eyes as I realize I told AJ I loved him as he was doubting if any of my feelings were real.

I told a man I loved him.

But the man I told those sacred words to doesn't believe in my feelings.

With that realization, I burst into tears.

CHAPTER 21

I'm no more than a few steps out the door when I hear AJ behind me, that same old floorboard that I hit groaning as he runs over it.

"Katie!" he yells after me.

I don't turn around. I'm raw. I'm hurt. The man I love thinks I'm superficial. Fake.

Nothing more than one of his legions of female fans who think he's perfect because he's a baseball player.

AJ catches up with me as I reach the top of the stairs. He puts his hand on my arm to stop me, but I angrily fling it off.

"Don't touch me. Don't speak to me," I yell as he blurs through my tears.

"Katie, we need to sort this out," AJ pleads.

"I think you already did," I say, heading down the stairs. "I'm some creepy obsessed fan who wanted to make you mine, right?"

I run down the next flight of stairs, praying that AJ gives up, but he doesn't.

He follows me right to the first landing and takes my wrist. I whirl around to face him, and I see nothing but panic in his emerald green eyes.

"Katie! Stop, just stop," AJ begs.

"Why?" I choke out, whipping my wrist back.

"Because I love you," AJ yells. "I love you, and I freaking messed up, but I want to make this right because I love you."

Now I really can't see him through my tears. I sniffle hard, trying not to snot in front of him.

Why can't I cry pretty like they do on TV?

AJ cups my face in his hands, and this time, I don't protest his touch. In fact, I feel his gentleness and protectiveness as he traces his fingertips over my skin.

"I'm sorry, I'm so sorry, I never should have doubted you," AJ whispers, his voice thick with unshed tears. "I know who you are. I can see it when you look at me."

I want to believe him. Oh, how I want this to be the truth.

"Then why did you doubt me, AJ? Why?" I whisper in anguish.

AJ's eyes grow watery. He blinks to fight back tears.

"Because I have never been enough," he admits.

"What?" I whisper back. "AJ, what do you mean?"

AJ's eyes become rimmed with red. He doesn't speak. My heart is pounding as I desperately wait for him to say something. Eventually, he clears his throat.

"I wasn't enough for my parents to ever stay in one place," he says, his voice low. "Even when I begged for them to. When I made a name in baseball, it was my ability as a player that got attention. People wanted to be my friend because of that one fragment of my life. I met girls who pretended to like things I liked so they could be with AJ. I never believed I was enough for anyone to want to be with Andrew Joseph. Until you came along."

The pain I see in his eyes, hear in his voice, tells me he believes this.

That being AJ the baseball player was all people could see.

I lift my hand to his chest, pressing it over his heart, and AJ's eyes search mine.

"I became aware of you because of baseball," I say, my voice barely audible to my ears over the pounding of my heart, "but I fell for Andrew Joseph because of this."

I take my index finger and trace the outline of a heart over his chest. "This is what made me love you. If I had to be a fan first to know who you were, to know you existed, to have the opportunity to meet you, I'd do it all over again. I fainted because I was nervous to meet you. I should have told you that. I'm so sorry I didn't. But ever since that night we had coffee, you have been Andrew Joseph to me. The man I love. I have never told a man I loved him. I know it's crazy to say those words now. My logic, fact-loving brain should fight this. Should say we need more time. More dates. More words between us. But my brain isn't fighting this because it agrees with my heart. I know the facts. And the fact is I love you."

I feel AJ's heart accelerate underneath the fabric of his shirt. His chest rises and falls as he exhales.

"I love you, too, Katie. I started to fall in love with you that first night by the canal. I fell more in love with you riding roller coasters and feeling your joy over the first loop. Seeing you play with my dogs. Hearing your passion when you talked about your law readings. It's fast, but I never doubted my feelings were right. And Katie, please forgive me for doubting yours. Please. When your entire family was telling me all those stories, I became sick with fear that who I loved was about to be taken away because I wasn't enough for you as I am."

"You as you are is all I want," I say, sliding my hands up to his face. "I love you."

"Say it again," AJ says, searching my eyes.

"I love you," I repeat, smiling up at him through my tears.

AJ's mouth finds mine. He parts my lips, slipping his tongue inside as he kisses me. But the kiss is different. It's deliberate. Claiming. The second his mouth takes from mine, I know what this kiss is.

I'm his.

He's mine.

And the boundary line is gone.

AJ's kisses become frantic. He backs me up against the banister, and I arch backwards as his mouth demands everything I can give him.

Heat grips me. I'm growing hot inside, tight, my hips longing to feel his body weight on top of me.

"Show me you love me," I pant against his mouth. "Show me, AJ. Show me."

AJ trembles against me. His body is rock hard against mine now.

He swiftly picks me up, and I wrap my legs around him as I plunge my tongue deeper into his mouth. I dig my fingers into his shoulders as he carries me up the stairs, our kisses hot and frantic. Our bodies needing to come together to express everything we are feeling inside, desperate to release everything we have denied ourselves and can't wait a single second longer to do so.

I whimper against his mouth as AJ takes me back to my room. The sounds from the party float up from downstairs, but nobody will come up here now. I feel my breasts swell and my pelvis press harder into AJ's powerful body. I want this. I want to feel his love in the most passionate way.

And it has to happen now.

AJ carries me into my old room and shuts the door behind us, flipping the lock. He presses my back against the door, and his mouth sears against mine.

I move my mouth against his, matching him in ferocity. I reach for his belt buckle. AJ slides a hand underneath my blouse.

"I've dreamed of this. Of you. Of how beautiful you are and all the ways I'm going to make love to you," AJ murmurs. He tears his lips away from mine and helps me remove my top, which we toss to the floor. He kisses my collarbones, burning a trail down the valley between my breasts, his tongue flickering between the wispy, sheer bra I have on.

"AJ," I whisper, dipping my hand down to his waist, feeling the dark hair trailing down from his navel to the waistline of his boxer briefs.

The second I touch him, he shakes violently against me.

"I don't think I can hold out," he cries desperately, his body tightening even further.

"You don't have to," I say, locking my hands around his neck. "I'm on the pill. Show me your love, AJ. Right here. I want you to love me. Love me now."

AJ reaches for my pants, undoing the button as his mouth claims mine with a heated kiss. He lets me down for a moment as we begin stripping off each other's clothing. I rip off his shirt, then his pants, and stare in amazement at the powerful body that is going to pin me against this door and love me in a way that is completely new to me.

Pure desperation, pure passion.

I stroke his hips as his mouth continues to take from mine. Then AJ moves his hands around my back, unclasping my bra, and we're finally skin on skin.

His body is hot to the touch. I stroke his huge arms, the veins, the developed chest, the body that narrows so sexily on an athletic man.

My body burns even hotter now, and the second I'm out of my pants, AJ lifts me up and pins me back against the door, his lips savage as my legs wrap around him. This time, the boundaries are gone.

AJ tears his mouth away from mine, so he can look at me.

"I love you," he gasps. "I love you, I love you."

Before I can reply, his mouth is moving against mine, in the same rhythm our bodies are about to move in together.

We're now entwined, pure heat and sweat and desperate with need for only each other.

In this moment that is going to change me, as passion is going to drive us both to a place we have never been together, only one thing is going through my mind.

I love you, too, Andrew Joseph. I love you, too.

CHAPTER 22

Playlist Shuffle Song of the Day:
"Make Me Feel" by Janelle Monáe

I stare at my reflection in AJ's bathroom mirror early on Monday morning. I have no makeup on, not even lip balm or a touch of mascara. I have dark circles under my eyes that are in desperate need of concealer to cover up lack of sleep. My flat-ironed hair is now a wonky mess, with some sections crimped, others curly, due to making love with AJ until the wee hours of the morning.

Oh, and gone is the silky blouse and classy pants. I've thrown on a red-and-white striped T-shirt with my denim shorts, and my feet are back in my white Converse kicks.

Yet I feel I'm the most beautiful I've ever been.

I see how my skin is flushed as I remember how AJ made love to me last night. The first time—the frantic, against the door, we can't wait to be together sex—was the hottest sex I've ever had. I've never felt more wanted or desired by a man in my life.

Or loved.

I notice as I relive the memories of us becoming one, my

cheeks deepen with pink. My light green eyes shine brightly. I can't stop smiling.

I also remember vividly the way AJ's skin felt against mine. The way his cologne became imprinted on my body, leaving me with the scent of him. I can still hear his voice whispering in my ear how beautiful I was. How he never wanted any woman like this. How sexy and hot it was.

And how much he loved me.

I shiver with happiness. Now I'm beaming with love.

It wasn't how I imagined my first time with AJ would be, but it was absolutely perfect for us.

Afterward, we reluctantly dressed and rejoined the party, but the whole time we were thinking of how soon we could leave and get back to his place.

And as soon as we got home, we made love again, but this time slowly and tenderly. The next time was playful. We laughed and giggled and all I could think was how glad I was that we waited for this night. To be able to layer the physical with love. That our sex could be quick and intense, loving and sweet, or goofy and fun. Our physical connection matches our emotional one, and now that we've crossed the final boundary, I know this is forever.

Which makes me practically tear up with joy.

"Hey, Counselor, are you coming?" AJ calls out from the living room.

I blink back my happy tears. "Yes, just a second!"

I take a moment to swipe some lip balm across my lips, as I need to be prepared to receive more kisses from that sexy mouth of the man I love, and go down the hall. AJ is putting a leash on Fitzy. We're going to take the crew for a walk while the sun is rising over the Navy Yard.

The second AJ sees me, his eyes widen.

I lift an eyebrow at him. "Like my sexy, out-of-control, wonky Mufasa hair now, Andrew Joseph? This is called my up-all-night sex look. So not sexy."

AJ stands up. "Wrong. It's hot. I hope to give you wonky hair every night I'm in town."

Ooh!

I have to work the afternoon shift at Scones and Such, but I get off at six. AJ, of course, has a game tonight, and afterward, we get to go down on the infield and watch the fireworks.

Hmm. I can't imagine any better fireworks than having your first time be against a door with the sexiest man alive telling you he loves you, but fireworks over the infield will be a good show nonetheless, I think with a sly smile.

AJ comes over to me, dropping a sweet kiss on my lips.

"You taste like cake," he murmurs before easing my mouth open.

I giggle. "That's cake batter lip balm."

"I like it," he says, pressing his lips gently against mine.

Hans barks.

We both laugh softly, and AJ breaks the kiss.

"I think Hans is impatient to do his business. You want to walk Greta?"

As if she senses we're talking about her, Greta comes right over to my side and leans into my leg, wagging her tail.

"I'd love to. Anything I need to know about walking a Great Dane?"

AJ hooks Greta's leash on her collar and hands it to me. "Greta will rely on you as a sense of security. She'll go to your left and lean into your leg."

I nod. Then I laugh. "It feels like I'm walking a horse."

AJ grins. "Isn't it awesome? I love that they are big, but total sweethearts."

We head out the door. And when the elevator opens, we take up every bit of space with us and the three dogs.

"Look at our crew," AJ says, punching the button for the lobby. "We take up the whole elevator."

I know there was no mistake in AJ's words. It's no longer his crew, not after last night.

It's ours.

"I love our crew," I say, allowing myself to be all mushy and sappy.

"I do, too," AJ says, staring at me as he rubs Fitzy's head.

"So where do you take our crew when you walk at this early hour of the morning?"

You would think I'd be slumped up against the elevator wall desperate for a coffee after three-and-a-half hours of sleep, but instead I feel butterflies for the man standing next to me.

"We usually take a five-minute walk over to Canal Park," AJ says. "And I grab a morning coffee at the Lot Thirty-Eight Espresso Bar. My favorite coffee place in the Navy Yard."

I begin scratching Greta's head, and her tail moves like a windshield wiper with doggie joy.

"Coffee sounds so good," I say.

A sexy smile plays on AJ's sensual lips. "Did someone keep you up late last night, Counselor?"

My cheeks grow warm. "Indeed, that is a fact. I could go *on and on* about his sexual prowess."

Which isn't a lie.

At all.

"Really? Fascinating. I'm listening."

I burst out laughing as we hit the lobby floor. "Oh, I bet you are."

He shoots me a mischievous grin, and we head outside into the sunshine.

As AJ predicted, Greta moves to my left. She's leaning into my leg, and she's so strong that I quickly realize I'm going to have to work so she doesn't accidentally tip me over. We let the dogs take care of their business and continue our walk. I think this is a wonderful start to a day. AJ and I are talking about our plans today, what we'll do tomorrow night, and joking about how people stare when they see us walking our crew down the street.

I make a vow that no matter how tired I am, no matter how late I stayed up reading, I'm not going to miss this morning walk with our crew once law school starts. I will make getting up at six with AJ a priority. And when he climbs back into bed, I'll get some coffee and grab my books and get a head start on my reading for the day.

I glance at AJ, seeing the sun glint off his jet-black hair, the stubble that is shading his jawline, and think of how complete this simple moment feels. Us. Walking the dogs. Going to get coffee and spend a little time at the park.

"So, when are we making our retro recipe cards dinner?" AJ asks. "I'm thinking my dish will be the best. Who can say no to a baked meatloaf dumpling?"

Oh, I love this man so much.

"My 'Make Your Man Happy' macaroni and cheese is not only going to make my man happy, but it's totally going to win," I say.

AJ laughs. "You took the easy route. How bad can mac and cheese ever be?"

"What about my clam puff appetizer with canned clams?" I ask as we continue to stroll through the Navy Yard, en route to the espresso bar.

I wait for his reaction. It's the same as the first time I showed him that card in the vintage bookstore. I swear he's going green in front of me.

"That sounds so gross."

"Which makes it intriguing, because if it's awesome, it's like you uncovered a hidden gem."

"I guarantee you, canned clam puffs are not a gem," AJ declares.

"Okay, so that one is a crap shoot, but your pineapple-lime Jell-O fluff is going to be great."

"Duh, it has fluff in the name. Automatic dessert greatness right there."

"AJ," I say as we come to the espresso bar, "would you mind if we shared our meal with some people?"

"Who do we hate that much?" he teases.

"No, it's more like who I love. Besides you," I say.

I watch as AJ's emerald eyes grow soft, and I know he loves hearing me say I love him.

Which makes me vow to tell him that every day for the rest of my life.

"There's no way Hayley and Brody are eating this," AJ says.

"Ha-ha, no, this isn't their kind of weird."

"So, who else is as weird as we are?" AJ asks as he draws Fitzy and Hans to a stop in front of the espresso bar. "I don't see Whitaker enjoying anything with the word gelatin in it."

I frown. Meg sent me a string of texts last night apologizing for Whitaker being a Grade-A ass. I know love is blind, but I wish Meg would see what a jerk he is.

But as Barbara lovingly pointed out to me over a big slice of sernik—polish cheesecake—and a hot cup of coffee a long time ago, Meg needs to come to her own conclusions after I voiced my initial concern. She will see what she wants to see, Barbara told me, until she values herself enough to want more.

"No. I don't love Whitaker. But I do love Barbara and Dominik. They would get a big kick out of us cooking these weird dishes. Would it be okay if I invited them to join us? I want you to get to know them, too."

AJ shifts the leashes for Fitzy and Hans to one hand, so he can touch my face with the other.

"They're important to you, aren't they?" he asks as his fingertips glide across my cheekbone.

I nod. "My paternal grandmother lives in New York, a

lifelong dream she is fulfilling after my grandfather passed away a few years ago. She's traveling with her friends, doing her own thing, and while I do love her, I rarely see her. My maternal grandmother and grandfather are not, well, maternal. It's always me giving her a kiss on the cheek, her appraising my clothing and wishing I was more like Meg in every way, because Meg is her favorite. Grandfather asks how I'm preparing for law school. That's it. Every time I see them it's the same.

"But Barbara and Dominik," I continue, "are the grandparents I have always wanted. I feel warm and loved whenever I'm with them. Dominik and I can talk baseball for hours; he's my spirit animal in that way. Barbara always has advice and a shoulder if you need it. They have the relationship I have always aspired to have. Barbara and Dominik have taken both me and Hayley under their wing, and they mean a lot to me. They are as much my grandparents as if we were related. So, it's important to me that they get to know you. As Andrew Joseph."

AJ's eyes flicker. I know he's moved that I want Barbara and Dominik to get to know him in the way I do.

"I think you have an ulterior motive," he says, the corners of his mouth turning up in a playful way.

"What?"

"If this meal goes south, which it has incredibly high odds of doing, you know Barbara will save us with her Polish home cooking."

I burst out laughing. "This is why I love you. You have a brilliant mind. So, the answer is yes?"

"It's yes," AJ says, dropping a kiss on my lips.

Hans barks.

"Okay," I say, smiling, "how about I run in and get us some coffee? What's your order?"

"Here, let me give you my card," AJ says.

"No. I'm a working woman, you know. I'll get this one.

You can pay for mine when I'm a starving law student," I joke.

"Fair enough," AJ says. "I'd like a latte, please. The sixteen-ounce size. With a shot of chocolate."

"Okay," I say, handing Greta's leash to him.

"I'm going to take these guys to the park," he says. "I have faith you'll be able to find us."

I don't even try to hide my smile. "Let's see. Insanely gorgeous guy with three dogs the size of horses. I think I'll find you. Just like I'm sure you'll spot the girl with the wonky hair from a night of passion and dark circles the color of grape jelly."

"Wrong. I'll spot the sexy woman with the wild curls, long legs, and beautiful pale green eyes, who had me the second she landed in my lap," AJ says, dropping another kiss on my lips.

Then he takes his crew and heads across the street, toward the blooming summer flowers and patches of green grass that create a bit of oasis in the Navy Yard.

Joy fills my heart. How could I have ever worried that we wouldn't work in the long run? How? I watch as AJ moves with his dogs. The man who I continue to discover and fall in love with more and more every day. The man who loves me when I'm a mess. The man who will love me when I'm buried in law school books.

I turn and enter the espresso bar, ready to get our coffees and take on the day.

One that will end with fireworks over the ballpark, but this time, I won't be watching AJ taking them in from my seat in the stands.

This time, I'll be by his side.

And I always will be.

CHAPTER 23

Playlist Shuffle Song of the Day:
"Fireworks" by the Plain White T's

As a fan of the Fourth of July, and growing up in DC, I have seen many majestic fireworks shows. Watching from the National Mall. Across the Potomac River. On a boat. Viewed on the lawn of the National Cathedral. From my seat at Eagles Field.

I didn't think anything could beat last night, sitting on the infield with AJ, gazing up at the fireworks display lighting up over park, with AJ holding me against his chest as the sky burst with colors.

But this tops it.

I'm standing on the railing of Chase's high-rise apartment building, with the city of DC spread out below, twinkling in the darkness, and the Capitol the focal point of the view as fireworks explode up over the gleaming white dome, punctuating the inky night in beautiful colors. AJ has his arms wrapped around me as we watch the sky light up in celebration of a hard-won freedom that created America as we know it.

And while we are surrounded by partygoers and other residents who live in the building, all of us gathered up here to swim, eat, drink, and now watch the fireworks, I feel as though I'm lost in another world with AJ.

Because I'm only aware of him. Of sharing this holiday with AJ, the one who is so dear to my heart, and watching the colors explode over the Capitol, the site of our first kiss.

"You aren't oohing and aahing," AJ comments, dropping a kiss on my temple.

I smile and run my hand over his strong forearms, which are wrapped protectively around my stomach.

"Is that a requirement for watching fireworks?" I tease.

AJ nuzzles the side of my face. "You're the fireworks aficionado. You did it last night from the infield. But now, in front of this huge display, you're silent. What's that about, Counselor?"

I sigh happily as I rest the back of my head against his chest. "These are the best fireworks I've ever seen. But there's a reason why I'm quiet."

There's a pause in the show, and I know the big finale is coming up next.

"Go on, I'm listening."

I wiggle around so I'm facing him. "I can't think of a better Fourth of July," I say, gazing up into his handsome face, "than to watch fireworks over the building where we had our first fireworks. Our first real kiss. That was the perfect spot for us, AJ. For our beginning."

AJ takes in my words. "That wasn't our beginning," he says, moving a hand up to my face. "Our beginning was the day we met. For you, it was the day you met your celebrity crush. For me, it was the day I met the girl I wanted to crush on forever."

The finale begins, the sky over DC filled with an array of fireworks and colors.

AJ's hands cup my face, sliding up through my post-swim

wet hair, and then he lowers his mouth to mine, kissing me as if we're the only two people on this rooftop right now.

"Happy Fourth of July," AJ murmurs sweetly against my mouth.

"Best ever," I whisper as I wind my arms around his neck.

We break the kiss as the show ends, and then I feel someone watching us. I turn and find Chase with his camera in his hand.

"I'm sorry," he says, walking up to us. "I had to get some pictures of you guys during the big finale. The composition was perfect."

"He's into photography," AJ explains.

"Ooh, can we see?" I ask, eager to look at what Chase captured.

"Sure," Chase says, moving his camera and reviewing the shots for us.

I pause as we come into view, staring at each other as if the world doesn't exist. Then my favorite shot, with AJ framing my face in his hands and fireworks exploding in vivid hues of red, white, and blue as the backdrop.

"Chase, these are fantastic," I say excitedly.

"You should see his secret Instagram," AJ says. "Tell her your side hustle."

Chase appears sheepish. "Um, I sell photography prints. Under the name M. Leary."

"Really?" I ask, intrigued.

"Yeah. I didn't want to be inundated with orders because of who I am. I wanted to see if people would buy my prints if I wasn't a baseball player."

"That is so cool," I say, eager to pull up his site later. "May I get copies of the pictures you took tonight?"

"Of course," Chase says, putting his camera down and glancing around the rooftop.

I know why. Earlier, when we first arrived with Hayley and Brody, Chase said his girlfriend, Hannah, would be here by the end of the night, after she did a lot of her coverage of Fourth of July celebrations for *DC Scene.*

I see once again how the smile doesn't meet his eyes.

My stomach tightens. I realize how Chase has been busy moving through all his guests, making sure his teammates and friends were all having fun. Laughing over drinks. Playing volleyball in the pool. Telling great stories. Talking to every single person he invited.

Meanwhile, he's missing his girlfriend, who is working. Who once again can't be here.

My stomach turns to ice.

Will this be AJ in the future? Having to go to all these events by himself if I must study?

Will he have the same sadness in his eyes that Chase is trying to hide?

I glance at AJ, who is talking with Chase, and I'm desperate to shove this fear away. I don't ever want to cause this kind of hurt for the man I love.

Hayley and Brody approach us, and I feel relief as they do. I need to put this scary thought away.

"Hey, how did Brady pitch tonight?" Chase asks, as Brody had been keeping track of his twin's game during the party.

"They won, and Brady got the win," Brody says. "Pitched until the sixth and gave up three hits, no runs, struck out eight. Since they got that new pitching coach a few weeks ago, his game has turned around."

"Brady's been hot lately," I say, as I've been following him since I met Brody.

AJ lifts an eyebrow. "Are you auditioning my replacement?"

Then he shoots me a mischievous grin, and I laugh, loving how AJ is now so comfortable with me being a fan first that he can joke about it.

"A girl never knows when she might need a backup plan,"

I tease back. "However, I prefer outfielders. But Brady is obviously in a good place with his game."

I see the pride in Brody's eyes. "Brady has fought for this. I think he has a good chance of making it up to Chicago next year, if he can keep this up."

"I think he will," Chase says, with understanding in his eyes from a pitcher's perspective. "The minor league schedule is grueling, and if he can consistently have these outings over the whole season, he will be in Chicago next year."

"Brady has great command of his fastball now," Brody says. "I think next year will be his breakout year."

As they all talk baseball, Hayley moves around next to me. She pulls me away from AJ and the guys and smiles at me.

"Very different from our Fourth on the Mall last year," she says, smiling at me.

"Right? I never could have pictured this," I say, glancing around the rooftop filled with revelers. "A year ago, I watched AJ play baseball and checked out his posts on Instagram. Now I'm in love with him."

"Whoa. In love?" Hayley asks, her eyes wide. "Did you say love?"

I nod. "I am, Hayley. AJ told me he loves me, too."

She grabs my hands and squeezes them. "The next time we are alone in the apartment, we are going to scream and jump up and down and celebrate. I'm so excited for you guys!"

"Me, too," I say, trying to focus on the excitement and happiness of being in love with a man like AJ instead of worried about hurting him or disappointing him when my life changes in a few months.

"What?" Hayley asks, her expression growing serious in an instant.

"What do you mean, 'What'?"

"Are you worried about law school again? If you are, you need to STOP."

"I hate that you know me so well," I say.

"Get out of your head, future lawyer. Are you forgetting my parents dated in law school? They are still together, more than twenty years later."

I exhale. "I don't want him to hurt like Chase."

"What? What are you talking about?"

"His girlfriend. I don't know, it just seems hard on him that she is never here for him. And AJ will have to do the same thing."

"Don't compare what you have with AJ and what Chase has with Hannah," Hayley says firmly. "We don't know what the real story is there. You *do* know the real story with you and AJ. You love each other. You'll talk about what is going to happen and adjust to make things work. But don't invent problems that aren't there, Katie. Your brain knows better. And your heart does, too."

I blink back tears. "I'm so lucky to have you as my best friend," I whisper, hugging her tight and inhaling her signature Jo Malone perfume. "I love you."

"I love you, too," Hayley says, rubbing my back. "And trust me, you and AJ are going to be fine. I know. I'm the result of a law school relationship."

I smile and release her. "You are. And you're right. From now on, I'm putting my worries away."

"Or talk to AJ about them," Hayley encourages. "Let him know you're only worried because you love him so much. I guarantee you, AJ will tell you not to worry."

"He already has," I admit. "But does he really understand what he's getting into?"

"Yes. No different than I did getting involved with Brody as a baseball player. It's not always easy, but we make it work. And I wouldn't have anyone else in my life just because it would be easier."

Hayley's words sink in. She's right.

"Okay. I'm going to let this go," I say. As if to punctuate that fact, I change the subject. "What is Addison doing tonight?"

"She said she was going to watch the fireworks from home with Willy," Hayley says.

"I think she's ready to date again. Nothing against Willy—whom I'm dying to meet, by the way—but she needs to fill up that social calendar with some hot dates. Of the non-ferret kind."

Hayley nods. "I think she's toying with online dating, but I don't think that's Addison."

"Would she let us set her up?" I say, turning around and glancing at Chase.

"No," Hayley says firmly. "Don't even think of him."

"Your mind-reading is very annoying tonight," I tease.

"Chase has a girlfriend. Even if he doesn't seem happy, he's still with her."

"Maybe because he hasn't met an amazing redhead with a passion for animals who owns a ferret."

"No. I don't get a romance vibe when I picture them together."

"You are ruining the Holly Martin novel I have going on in my head."

"Holly Martin would put her with someone else. I have someone in mind, actually. But the time isn't quite right. The logistics leave something to be desired, but I have an idea."

Ooh, now this is interesting, and as I'm about to ask her who this mystery man is that she wants to introduce Addison to, AJ and Brody come back over to us.

Crap. I really wanted to know what Hayley is plotting.

I make a note to ask her later.

As AJ draws me into his arms, my thoughts drift back to my previous worries.

I know I've made the right decision to put them away.

I believe in this.

In us.

And that no matter what the future holds, we'll face it together.

Maybe today is my own Independence Day, I think. *I will stand independent of fear. It won't rule me anymore. I will be confident in AJ being able to handle whatever the future throws at us.*

I will be confident in me, too.

Comforted by this new feeling, this freedom, I snuggle against AJ, and enjoy the best Fourth of July I've ever known.

Because it's the first one I've ever spent with a man I love.

CHAPTER 24

Playlist Shuffle Song of the Day:
"Wannabe" by the Spice Girls

By the end of July, I've learned some new things about life:

I have read more books than I thought possible about women's rights in the workplace this summer, including some on women's rights in Canada and the United Kingdom. I compiled tons of notes, all of which I'm eager to share when I have lunch with Gemma, my mentor, tomorrow.

As my time at Scones and Such ends this week, I have learned I will never, ever, no matter how many years I work in a coffee house be able to make a decent coffee-based drink.

Willy the ferret is awesome and, to my surprise, he doesn't smell bad but like grape juice. Weird, but not awful like I had believed he would smell.

Great Danes are the best dogs in the world, and I love AJ's dogs like they are mine. Which I feel like they are now.

Clam puffs made with canned clams are surprisingly good. I'll add those to the New Year's Eve party potluck for sure.

While I have kept myself busy with friends, reading, and work, I no longer like when the Soaring Eagles are on the road. I don't care if AJ looks hot in his navy road uniform. I want him home. With me.

Most of all, I've learned that my love for AJ didn't reach a max point when I told him I loved him, and when he said the words back to me. I always thought that was the highest level of love you could achieve, feeling those words, believing in them, and saying them aloud.

I was wrong.

Because I find my love growing deeper with each passing day.

I smile as my brain flips through the whole month while I wait for Hayley and Addison to meet me at a hip "vegetable only" restaurant in DC. Obviously, it was Addison's turn to pick, as Hayley and I do love us some meat. But we love Addison more, so we will happily eat vegetables tonight.

I take a sip of my water as I wait, my thoughts shifting to AJ.

I think of where we started, in April when I fainted on him, to now. We've taken advantage of the summer when he's been home, and on days when I don't work, I stay with him. We've had leisurely mornings, talking and laughing and making love before getting breakfast. We take the crew out for walks. Hang out after games with Hayley and Brody and watch movies. While I've read my books and made notes, AJ is comfortable playing video games or studying upcoming pitchers he's going to face.

I've met his sister on FaceTime, along with his parents. We've met my parents for dinner in Georgetown, and after that evening, Mom called me later and told me she was wrong. That AJ and I seemed natural together and it had nothing to do with baseball, outside of the fact that that is the reason we met—because Hayley was dating Brody and she introduced me. But the affection I have for him, she said, was because of the man he is. Mom could see that it was the man—and not the baseball player–who made me happy.

My favorite memory, though, was the one rare off day this month. And when he told me how he wanted to spend it, my heart nearly burst with joy.

He wanted to spend it getting to know Barbara and Dominik.

So, we got our dinner cards, invited them over, and spent the evening entertaining them. We laughed over our crazy meals. The meatloaf was so bad we all pushed it away, AJ conceded defeat, and Barbara saved us all with leftover pierogis.

We spent a long evening at the table, sharing food and a bottle of wine and talking for hours. I loved hearing AJ tell his journey to professional baseball to both of them, but he made sure to shift the conversation to learn about them as well. And then the moment came where I fell in love with him more deeply than I ever had before.

AJ asked them what advice they had for a long-lasting love, reaching for my hand and kissing it in front of them as he did. I was touched by his genuine interest in wanting to know their advice for a successful relationship. He wants the same future that I do, and he wants to build it right.

The whole evening summed up why I fell in love with him. AJ not only wanted to meet the people I loved but spend hours with them on his one free day, simply because they are important to me. By the end of the evening, I could tell they had become important to AJ, too.

My phone buzzes, and I smile when I see it's AJ. He's in Seattle, where it's only three thirty in the afternoon.

I read his text:

Have fun with the girls tonight. If you're up late, call me. Of course, with me being on one coast and you

being on the other, this game doesn't start until 10 your time. It will be close to 3 when we're done.

I smile and text him back:

I can be up. Only thing tomorrow is my lunch with Gemma and that's at 1.

AJ is texting ...

If you are up, call me. One more sleep until I come home, Counselor.

Happiness surges through me. Tomorrow is the end of the road trip, and AJ will be flying back after the game. I text him my exact feelings:

I can't wait until you are home. I miss you. I love you. I want our crew back together.

Then, for good measure, I insert dog and heart emojis before hitting send.

"Sorry we're late," Addison says. "I got hung up."

I look up and see Hayley and Addison sliding into the booth across from me.

"Even though I'm starving, I waited for her," Hayley says. "Because I'm nice like that."

"You are an incredible human being, Hayley Carter," Addison deadpans.

"No worries," I say. "Let me finish this text to AJ."

They start flipping open menus, and I shoot one more text to him:

Hayley and Addison are here. Gotta go. Can't wait to talk to you tonight.

As I'm about to drop my phone into my bag, AJ sends his reply:

I love you, Katie. I'm so lucky you're mine.

Happiness floats down my spine from his words. I place my phone into my purse, and when I look up, Hayley is watching me with a smile on her face.

"How's AJ?" Hayley asks.

"Ready to come home," I say, flipping open my menu. "How are you, Addison?"

"Good," she says, her eyes shining brightly at me. "Thank you for going to a vegetarian restaurant tonight. This is one of my favorite places in DC. I hope you guys enjoy it."

Addison is so earnest, so eager for us to try it, I feel guilty that Hayley and I made a pact to order an extra spicy chicken sausage pizza when we got home if we were starving from eating only vegetables.

"We're game, aren't we, Katie?" Hayley asks.

"Absolutely. Who knows, it might be so good I'll have to put some veggies in my bra for later," I joke.

We all laugh.

I take a moment to study the menu. I see a "meatloaf" made of walnuts. Hmm. With AJ's last experiment with meatloaf still fresh in my mind, I'll pass on that one. Cauliflower steak ... grilled summer squash ...

Pizza is looking like a given if this is an indication. Although my mother would be overjoyed with this place. I'll have to bring her here for lunch.

Wait. What is this? I spy a mushroom shepherd's pie, with english cheddar mashed potatoes on top. SOLD.

"I'm getting the shepherd's pie," I say, closing my menu. "What are you guys thinking?"

Before they can answer, a server approaches us. "Good evening, what can I bring you ladies to drink?" she asks as she places cocktail napkins in front of us and provides us each with a glass of water.

I think I learned my lesson from my last girls' night out. I'll stick to having a glass of wine this evening instead of ... too many.

And I'll leave my phone in my purse to ensure no more embarrassing videos are sent to AJ.

"I'll have a cabernet, please," I say, thinking that will pair well with the wild mushrooms in the shepherd's pie I've become unexpectedly excited about.

"A chardonnay for me, thank you," Hayley says.

"I'll take a chardonnay as well," Addison says.

"I'll be back with those shortly," the server says before leaving the table.

"Did you guys find something you'd be happy eating?" Addison asks, winding a lock of her straight red hair around her finger.

"You do realize," Hayley says, glancing at her, "that we came for your company first, right?"

Addison smiles. "Yes, but I want you to enjoy it and not pick something 'meh' to eat."

"I don't feel 'meh' about shepherd's pie with wild mushrooms, peas, and cheesy potatoes on top," I say, taking a sip of my water.

"Okay, good," Addison says, appearing relieved at my enthusiasm over the dish. "Hayley, did you see anything you want?"

"I'm going to have the Meyer lemon pasta with spinach and walnuts," she says. "Equally excited."

Addison exhales. "Excellent."

"What are you getting?" I ask her.

"The cauliflower steak. It's outstanding," she says, her eyes shining excitedly. "I've been craving it ever since we decided to meet here."

I nod, although the idea of eating a huge slab of cauliflower does give me a case of the "meh."

The server returns with our glasses of wine. She takes our orders, and as soon as she leaves, Addison raises her glass.

"A toast," she says. "To women friends. When I first came to DC, I was seriously lacking in the female friendship department. While I'm still searching for my dream job, I'll be forever grateful that the one I'm in now brought me to Hayley and you."

We all clink our glasses together and then take a sip.

"I think we are always guided to where we need to be," I say, thinking on Addison's words. "You were guided to Expanded World on the Shelf to meet Hayley. Hayley was guided to a random coffee house to meet Brody. I was guided to go to a game to meet AJ. Things are at work even if we don't see it."

"I hope I'm guided in a new direction soon as far as my career goes," Addison says thoughtfully. "Not that I'm miserable in my job—far from it. I love working for my boss, Mariah. And I love working with people like Hayley."

"But it's not your dream," I say. "You want to do media relations for an animal organization."

"I know, but sometimes I think I should be happy with what I have instead of fixating on what I don't. That goes with guys, too. When he comes into my life, I'll know."

"No," Hayley says, shaking her head. "Never settle. You need to go after what you want, but more than that, believe you are worth getting it."

I see the shift in Addison's eyes. I wonder if her confidence has been shaken by things in her past.

"I always write down my goals and then underneath them, what the steps I need to achieve them are," I say. "I also write down all the obstacles I see in my mind and then strategies to overcome them. I really think we come up with obstacles as roadblocks. I look for evidence to prove them wrong."

Addison's eyes widen. "I have already told you this, but I'm going to say it again. You are going to be one hell of a lawyer. When does law school start, by the way?"

A cocktail of excitement and nervousness swirls in my stomach at the words "law school." It's no longer a distant thing.

"Orientation stuff next week. Classes begin August twenty sixth," I say.

Right as the Soaring Eagles are in the middle of a heated chase with Boston for the division title, I think.

AJ and I will both be at pressure points, with AJ possibly headed toward his second postseason and me in my first full month of law school.

While I have put this worry away, every now and then, when evidence smacks me in the face, I can't help but take it out and worry about it.

"Hey," Hayley says, breaking through my thoughts, "you and AJ will handle all that crazy on your plate, okay?"

"The timing will be hard, with the Soaring Eagles chasing the postseason and me in the first month of Georgetown Law," I say, allowing myself to visualize this happening in our lives.

"What did you tell me about obstacles?" Addison says, arching an eyebrow at me. "Lack of time and stress will be present for sure, but then you'll make strategies to cope with them."

Hayley snickers. Addison grins mischievously.

"She's right, I heard that very same advice from some incredibly smart woman I know," Hayley teases.

I grin. "Thank you for reminding me of that. Time and stress are obstacles."

"And you will figure out ways to deal with them," Hayley says.

I put the worry back in the drawer. My friends are right. I'll deal with these obstacles head on.

In fact, I'm meeting with the one person who has been in my shoes tomorrow for lunch.

I think further on this while Hayley and Addison talk about work for a minute.

I'm sure Gemma will have advice on how to handle law school and a relationship. I trust Gemma. She's my mentor and someone I aspire to be like.

And I'm eager to soak up all her wisdom tomorrow to make sure AJ and I stay on the right path during this time.

Comforted by that thought, I take a sip of wine and settle in to enjoy a perfect night with my friends.

Followed by what is sure to be an insightful lunch tomorrow with Gemma.

CHAPTER 25

Playlist Shuffle Song of the Day:
"Under Pressure" by Queen and David Bowie

I fidget in my seat in the clubby-style steakhouse. The leather of the cushy chair squeaks a bit in protest, and as I see all the DC power types having lunch around me, I realize I shouldn't be wiggling around impatiently in this room.

I'm in Foggy Bottom, in a posh restaurant off Pennsylvania Avenue where I always meet Gemma for lunch. It's been months since our last one, right before I graduated from Georgetown in the spring, and I'm eager to update her on all aspects of my life. To get advice on how to handle 1L and find out how to achieve the best balance I can between my personal and school life.

I exhale as I glance around the room, at the rich wood paneling, the tables draped in pristine white linen, patrons dressed in fine suits as business is being discussed all around me. Gemma always holds our lunches here, and when she sweeps into a room, heads turn. Whenever there is a big case regarding women's rights, you can bet if Gemma isn't the lawyer handling it, she was one of the final ones considered for the case.

I mull that thought over for a moment, smoothing the fabric of the crepe navy pants I purchased at Brooks Brothers. I'm wearing the matching blazer with it and paired it with a silk navy-striped blouse. A multi-strand glass pearl necklace adorns my neck. I've not only flat-ironed my hair, but with Hayley's help, managed to pull it back into a sleek chignon at the nape of my neck.

I want to show Gemma I'm no longer an undergraduate, but a serious young woman ready to dedicate myself to law school. To become the best lawyer I can be.

One who she will want at her firm after I graduate.

I glance up and see Gemma sweeping across the room. Of course, heads turn as she moves, dressed in her signature outfit: a fit and flare dress with matching coat, no matter what the temperature is outside. Her black hair is in her short bob, not a single strand out of place, and despite the dim lighting inside the restaurant, Gemma's oversized Chanel sunglasses remain shielding her eyes.

I watch her move in awe. She's confident. Gemma knows every eye in the room is on her, and she cuts across it with purpose. She gives the air of a woman to be reckoned with.

I have known Gemma for years now, and this moment—of watching her move with confidence—is something that I never get tired of observing.

And every time I witness it, I imprint it in my brain. When I represent my clients in the future, I will walk with that confidence. Because if I don't believe in myself down to my walk, how can my clients believe in my ability to bring them the justice they deserve?

I rise as Gemma reaches our table for two in the center of the restaurant. She always reserves this table. Hell, I think it might *be* her table.

"Look at you," Gemma says, reaching forward and giving me a hug.

Her perfume—Jean Patou Joy—sweeps around me as we embrace. Gemma steps back and places her hands on my arms, giving me an affectionate squeeze.

"You already look like a lawyer," she says, smiling at me.

Her compliment makes me soar. "Thank you."

We take our seats, and the hostess places a dark napkin across Gemma's lap.

"Your server, Maxwell, will be right with you," she says.

"Thank you," Gemma says. She removes her sunglasses, slipping them into their case, and drops it into her customized Myron Glaser leather tote.

After the hostess leaves, Gemma places her iPhone on the table and smiles at me. "So, have you had a productive summer away from my firm?"

I laugh. "I have. I did an online law school bootcamp reading course. Read books about how to think and read like a law student. Then I supplemented with titles on women's rights."

I eagerly go into detail on my reading—only pausing to place our orders for iced teas and our lunch—and Gemma peppers me with questions about the books and then goes deeper: What did I think? What was my interpretation of the decision? How would I have approached it?

I love this about Gemma. She always pushes me to think. Dig in. Ask myself the hard questions. I am so blessed to have her as a mentor.

Before long, we are brought our lunches—a petite filet for me and salmon for Gemma—and I take the pause in conversation to shift topics.

"Gemma," I say, picking up my steak knife, "may I ask you for some advice regarding how to balance 1L?"

Gemma's face lights up in curiosity. "Like how to balance the reading load with outlining, study drills, things like that?"

I put down my knife. Hmm. Not exactly.

"No, my personal life," I say.

Gemma's eyebrows shoot up. "What personal life? You are going to eat, breathe, and sleep law school. That's it."

I bite the inside of my lip, and it takes Gemma a fraction of a second to see it.

"Oh, Katie, please don't tell me this is about some *man*," she says, her voice exasperated as she cuts a piece of her fish.

Defensiveness prickles my spine from her tone.

"It is," I say, watching her slice her salmon into a precisely perfect bite.

Gemma eats her bite, pauses, then stares at me. "Katie. You know better than this. Involvement with anyone right now won't last through the first semester. I know you know what the relationship curse of law school is. Don't ignore it because you don't want to believe it's true."

I see nothing but disapproval in her eyes. My stomach knots up as a result.

"Gemma, I've met someone who is exceptional. I wouldn't go through any of this if I didn't think he was the love of my life."

Gemma sighs. "At moments like this, I remember how young you are. Katie. You have incredible potential. I don't want to see that squandered on some man who won't last until Thanksgiving break. You need to be in a relationship with law school. And law school *only*."

"What if that's not what I want?" I ask.

"I thought you wanted to be a lawyer who championed women's rights in the workplace."

"Of course I want that."

"You aren't acting like it," Gemma says, attacking her fish with more surgical precision.

"Because I want to love something besides my future career?" I fight back.

Gemma's blue eyes go cold. A chill runs down my spine.

"Law school is going to take every breath you have to reach the top of your class," she says. "It would be wise to end this relationship now, so you aren't distracted by the inevitable fighting and drama that will follow when you have no time for this man."

"I was hoping you would provide me some perspective on balancing my relationship with the demands of 1L, but I can see I'm going to have to figure that out for myself," I say with determination.

Gemma lets out a huge sigh, as if I'm a child who isn't listening.

"You have fallen in love at the worst possible time in your life. Obviously, you know it too, or you wouldn't be seeking advice on how to balance it. If you knew you could, if you believed you can have a romance and law school, you wouldn't be asking me about it, would you?"

Suddenly, the drawer that Hayley helped me close springs right open, my fears now on the table along with the steak I no longer have the appetite to eat.

"I am not saying all of these things to hurt you, Katie, but to make you understand. You hear these horror stories about law school for a reason. It is hard. It's demanding. It will be some of the most challenging times in your life. You have worked incredibly hard to get to this point. Doesn't the education that will set up your career deserve your complete attention?"

"I want nothing more than to be a lawyer. You know that. But I refuse to believe I can't have love, too. Obviously, you have no encouragement or suggestions for this, and that's fine, Gemma. I will figure it out on my own. But I will not give up the man I love for law school. I won't."

Gemma is silent for a moment, and all I hear is her knife slicing through the asparagus that is on her plate.

"All right. I can see you are determined to recklessly go

down this path. But are you thinking of this man before doing this to him?"

My chest grows tight. "What do you mean by that?"

"Come on, you aren't that naïve. He might be saying all the supportive things now, but he has no idea of the world he's about to enter. Will he be happy when you have no time for him? Will he love the idea of you not responding to his texts because you are buried in hours upon hours of complicated reading? When you have to meet with your peers instead of him? When he does go out with you to a bar with your fellow first-year students, will he love the idea that all you will talk about is law school? Will your promises of 'things will be better with each passing year' be enough when he's sitting back at the apartment isolated and alone?"

One by one, her words dismantle my world. A huge lump swells in my throat.

"How is that love, Katie? I'd call that selfish. The one area you need to be selfish on, however, is your academics and your career. You know I only take the best of the best. After all these years of mentoring you, I'd hate to think you wouldn't be the best fit to join my firm for an apprenticeship, let alone a permanent position, because you didn't dedicate yourself to your education."

I gasp. "Are you implying that I won't have a chance at an apprenticeship if I'm dating AJ?"

Gemma picks up her napkin and dabs at the carefully applied nude lipstick on her lips.

"Of course not. I'm only suggesting that you do what is best for your grades. I only take the top students. No exceptions."

"No," I say, lifting up my own napkin and placing it on my plate. "You only want women to be exactly like you. Married to law school. Married to your career. I'm not you, Gemma. And right now, I feel extremely grateful for that. I will still have my friends. My family. I will find a way to carve out time for things that matter. If that makes me less in your eyes, so be it."

I retrieve my bag and stand up. Gemma's eyes lock with mine.

"You realize," she says slowly, "the wonderful opportunities I had planned for you, for all these years, will no longer be available. I hope you recognize that this man, whoever he is, will most likely disappear during the first semester—because what man is going to put up with being non-existent—and you will have thrown everything away for no reason?"

I swallow hard, so I can force the words out. "No, I don't regret this. While advocating for women in the workplace is my goal, I also have a goal to live my life. And if that means working at a different firm, I will."

She rolls her eyes. "Good luck finding that firm, Katie."

"Thank you for all the years of mentorship and the opportunities to intern at your firm," I say, my voice shaking. "I have learned so much from you, and I will always be grateful for that. Goodbye, Gemma."

With tears blurring my vision, I walk out of the restaurant and into the thick, humid air that is blanketing this late July day in DC. However, I don't feel warm or muggy. I feel shaken and cold.

Before long, I can't see outside of my tears, so I stop next to the building and lean against it, people and traffic whizzing by me.

The world, and the business of the nation, moves on.

While my world has just crumbled in front of me.

I'm sick over the fact that Gemma never saw me as a human, but rather as a woman she could mold in her image. Into the perfect employee with a personal backstory she could no doubt sell very well to the media when the time came. I was all part of her plans for her firm, and nothing more than that.

I don't care that I will never work for her. Or a firm like hers. And I don't care if that means I'll be limited because I refuse to give up my life to be a lawyer.

But she was right about one thing.

I bite down hard on my lip to hold back the torrent of tears that want to erupt.

She was right about AJ.

After years of having parents who put him *last,* after never feeling like he was enough for them to stay in a place for more than a year, what will this say to him? I will be hurting him just as much as his parents did. AJ will stay in DC, and for what? To once again be ignored like he was his whole life?

My heart pounds rapidly as I picture in my mind what will happen to him because of law school. How can I be so selfish to put him through this?

AJ says he will take bits and pieces of me, but after everything he has been through, he deserves more, so much more. What if the Soaring Eagles make it to the postseason, and I can't even go to his games? What kind of fair support is that? I won't be able to see home games, let alone a big game on the road.

His Instagram posts flip through my brain like flashcards, reminding me of the facts. How on earth could he be happy spending his entire off-season here when he drove around the country in his van for months when baseball was over last year? How could I ask him to do this, to stay here, and then I'm not even truly here for him?

Gemma is right. No matter how much we love each other, this will never work.

AJ deserves better. He deserves so much more than I can give.

The sob I tried to hold back bursts through, and I bury my face in my hands, bawling openly on Pennsylvania Avenue.

Because it's up to me to set him free so he can find it.

CHAPTER 26

Playlist Shuffle Song of the Day:
"Goodbye to You" by Michelle Branch

Since I burst into tears on Pennsylvania Avenue, I've become the world's greatest actress.

And liar.

Once I pulled myself together enough to get back to my apartment yesterday, I texted AJ and said I had a horrible migraine and I'd talk to him tomorrow when he got back from Seattle. I told him I was shutting off the phone, so I could lay in a silent, dark room and try to get rid of it.

AJ thought I was shutting out the world to get rid of the pain.

When the truth is, I was shutting out the man I loved before I'd have to tell him goodbye.

I did the same thing to Hayley, my mom, and Meghan. Told them I was sick and going offline so they didn't need to worry about me.

Once I safely tucked the world away, I cried like I'd never stop.

How could I have been so reckless, getting involved with

AJ? Fresh tears—from my never-ending supply—blur my vision as I pace outside of AJ's apartment building. I wanted love so badly that it made me selfish. I put my own wants ahead of what AJ deserves.

What AJ does deserve is a present partner. Not one exhausted by studying or stressed out by complicated reading material. He deserves more than an hour at dinner. AJ should have a woman who isn't tired. Who can be there at the biggest moments of his career. Who can travel with him when the spirit moves him.

He deserves, I think, trying to push the huge lump in my throat down, *so much more than me.*

And now I'm going to give him the freedom to find it.

My knees sway as that thought hits me. I drop down on a modern metal bench outside his building, shaking. I've come here first thing this morning to break up with the man I love. The one I know I will regret letting go, but who I'm simply saving from the pain of having to go through a horrible breakup months later.

I close my eyes, trying to shove all my emotions back in, but I can't. Tears stream down my face as I picture AJ finding someone else. Falling in love. Making love to her the way he used to do t—

I bite down so hard on my lower lip, I taste blood. That last thought, of AJ having sex with another woman, makes me want to throw up.

I bury my head in my hands. How can I do this? How can I find the strength to let him go?

Easy, a voice inside me whispers. *You will find the strength because you love him.*

I wipe my fingertips across my face, but it's a futile attempt when my cheeks are stained with tears.

"Katie? What are you doing here?"

Oh, God. I'm not ready. I can't even look in the direction of the voice, the voice of the man who tells me I'm beautiful and funny and the best thing that has ever happened to him. I want to hang on. I want to be in this world for just a few minutes longer.

AJ drops down next to me on the bench. The sun is shining brightly on this clear day, and I should feel warm.

Instead, I feel frozen.

"Katie? God, you're crying," AJ says, alarmed. "Is that why you are here? What happened?" He puts his fingertips on my chin and turns my face toward his. The second I look into his deep green eyes, when I see the love and concern in them, my soul is destroyed. I begin sobbing, and AJ dissolves in front of me in my torrent of tears.

"I w-want you to know I-I l-l-love you," I say, gasping.

AJ reaches for my hand, and his warmth, his familiar touch, sends waves of grief rippling through me.

"Of course, I know that, sweetheart. I love you, too."

A part of my heart dies with each moment he's here, caring for me. Worrying about me.

Loving me.

"Are you sick?" AJ says, his voice urgent. "Is it the migraine? I can take you to the ER."

I shake my head.

"Please, Katie, tell me what's going on," AJ pleads, dropping down on his knee in front of me, holding my clammy hands in his protectively. "Please, sweetheart. Please."

I take a moment to breathe, and then do what I have to do.

For the man I love with all my heart.

"You know how I had that lunch with Gemma yesterday," I say, forcing the words out. My voice is thick. Strangled. Foreign to my own ears.

"What happened?" AJ says, reaching up with one hand and stroking my hair.

I try to remember this moment. How good of a man AJ is. How much he cares about me.

How much he loves me.

And why he deserves more than I can give him.

"It turns out she's not the mentor I want in my life," I say. "She wants someone who is going to marry law school. Have no life outside of practicing law. That's not me. I told her our mentorship was over, and I would never apply to be a summer associate at her firm."

Shock washes over AJ's face. "Katie, I'm so sorry. I know how much you aspired to be like Gemma."

"Not anymore. I won't ever give up my life for law. I will live my life with law being a passion, but not my only one."

A crease appears in AJ's brow. "You sound at peace with this decision."

"I am," I say. I'm silent for a moment, staring down at his one hand wrapped over mine, thinking this is the last moment they'll be entwined. The last time I'll ever feel the touch of his hand. And I nearly lose my resolve.

No, I love him too much to do this. I must go forward.

I have to set him free.

"But she was right about one piece of advice she gave me." I swallow hard. "We'll never make it through law school, AJ."

AJ doesn't speak. His beautiful, soulful eyes search mine, not understanding what I said.

"AJ, we can't do this," I go on, filling the silence with my words. "You deserve so much more than I can give as a law student."

As my words wash over him, AJ goes pale. I see nothing but shock in his handsome face.

"What are you talking about?" he whispers.

"We need to break up, AJ," I say, tears slowly rolling down my face. "This can never work. And you'll hate me for it in the end."

AJ's chest begins to rise and fall at a rapid rate. His hand grips mine tighter.

"You aren't saying this."

I remain silent, the tears now dropping down on to his hand.

"You aren't making sense. You just said you don't want law to be your life, but now you are trying to shove me away because of law school?"

"You deserve better than fragments of my time during law school," I say, squeezing my eyes shut, as I'm unable to look at the devastation on his face anymore.

"Don't I get to decide that?" AJ says, his voice rising in panic. "Isn't this my choice to make? I love you. We can do this, Katie. Nobody knows what we can do except for us."

I open my eyes and shake my head. "What's the point? For you to get pissed off that I'm too tired for sex? Upset that if you are in the World Series, I can't go to the games because of my reading that is due the next day? You deserve so much more, AJ!"

"Katie. You have Gemma's version of what will happen to us. I don't care about any of those other things knowing I have you."

I remove my hands from his and violently shake my head. "Do you know how many relationships fail in law school? A ton. Do you know why so many lawyers date other lawyers? Because it's easier than continually letting down the person you love. You would resent me if we stayed together, AJ. I can't do this to you."

I rise from the bench, feeling woozy as I do. I'm saying goodbye to AJ, and it's the most gut-wrenching thing I've ever had to do.

"You can't do this to me? Or to yourself?" AJ yells at me.

I bite my lip. I see the anguish on AJ's face, and I know he's going to lash out at me now.

"I'm not afraid of what law school will bring. I love you. I'm committed to us. I know what I'm getting into. The difference is, I believe in us enough to fight for it. You don't."

"AJ, you deserve better. You deserve more that I can give," I cry.

"Quit saying that," AJ snaps. "Don't tell me what you think I deserve. Because I sure as hell don't deserve this. I love you, and you don't give a shit. You don't believe in me enough to think I can handle this. After everything I've said and done to prove my feelings, to tell you how I wanted us to be different, after giving you my freaking *heart*, you have the nerve to tell me I can't handle this?"

His words slap me as if he physically jerked his hand across my face.

"I should have known this wasn't real," AJ says, his voice shaking with anger.

"AJ, no, no. I'm doing this because I love you."

"No, you're not," he says, putting out his hand as if to put a barrier between us. "I'm not enough for you to make the struggle worthwhile. Or you don't want me interfering with your grades."

"No," I say, my heart thundering against my ribs. "It's not that. I swear that's not it!"

AJ stares at me, his face grief-stricken.

"You don't love me enough to even *try*," he whispers, his voice thick.

"AJ, oh, God, no, this is all about being what you deserve to have. Which is everything I won't be able to give you."

AJ clenches his jaw. He doesn't speak. I'm hanging on by a thread, using all the love I have for him to not throw myself into his arms and say I want to try and make this work.

I realize this is it. We're over.

"This is the greatest act of my love," I say softly, the words barely audible to my own ears. "To let you go. You'll find someone who can give you everything you deserve. I know you don't believe me, but that's the truth. But I do love you, AJ. And I always will."

"If you loved me, you'd fight for me. I'd fight for you. But you'd have to believe you were worth me fighting for for this to work."

"What?" I choke out, confused.

"You don't think you're worth it!" AJ shouts as his emotions spin out of control. "I do. I wouldn't love you if you weren't worth it. I would give up anything to be with you. You are my future. I'd never dared to think of that before. I had no problem sacrificing for you to reach your dream, because your dreams became mine, don't you see that? I don't give a damn about law school curses or statistics. I trust what we have. And I told you that. I wish you'd believe me. I wish you would believe that you are all that matters to me. You are enough. Just you."

I'm going to be sick. His words have blown through the argument I crafted and shot it all to hell.

I didn't think I was worth it.

Oh, my God, AJ is right. I stare up at him, his eyes flashing and his jaw set, and I know I've made a horrific mistake.

An unforgivable one.

I try to speak, but I can't. In fact, it's getting hard to breathe. I feel dizzy.

AJ rubs his hand over his face, and I see his eyes are rimmed with red.

I'm desperate to talk to him, but I can't. My mouth feels thick. My lips are tingling.

No, no, wait, I'm sorry, I yearn to yell.

But I can't. My panic increases as I can't get the words out. My heart is racing. I can't breathe.

"I guess this is goodbye," AJ says, his voice breaking.

I try to gasp for breath. I want to stick my hand out to reach him, to stop him as he turns around.

No! I scream inside my head as AJ leaves me. *AJ, I'm sorry, I'm sorry, I was wrong.*

Grief tears at every fiber of my heart as he walks inside the building, never looking back. A full-fledged panic attack sets in as what I have done resonates through every inch of me.

My own lack of self-worth cost me the man I love.

I'm hyperventilating. People on the sidewalk begin to approach me, asking if I'm okay, but their voices sound strange. My vision is tunneling.

And then everything goes black.

CHAPTER 27

My head is killing me.

So is my face.

But while my face has been scraped up by landing face-first onto the pavement, and I have a huge bump swelling on my forehead, it's nothing compared to the pain in my heart.

I hear the ER doctors working on a patient in the next cubicle. My doctor said she will be coming back to see me in a few minutes.

I blink back tears. This time, I couldn't wave off the ambulance after I fainted because I must be screened for a concussion. Which I'm sure I have, based on the headache and dizziness I'm feeling.

The tears begin falling again, as all I can think of is AJ. How I just made the biggest mistake of my life, thinking he needed more than I could give.

I didn't think I, in whatever way he could have me, was enough.

I force myself to dig deeper.

Why did I think that?

I wince, a combination of trying to sort this out and the

pounding in my head. I need help. I need someone who can help me sort through the mess I've made and why. And hold me while I bawl my eyes out over losing AJ.

I start to come apart as that thought echoes through my broken heart.

I've lost him.

Pictures of AJ begin flashing through my mind. The disbelief on his face as he realized I was ending things. The devastation. His frustration at my choice. How destroyed he was by my words, and then, the last image, the angry tears that rimmed his eyes as he walked away from me. When I couldn't speak to him, and I was so desperate to reach out to him—

I stifle back a sob. Then another.

As sadness is about to swallow me whole, I realize who I need. Not my mother. I made the paramedics promise me they wouldn't take me to the hospital where Dad works so they wouldn't know. Not Meghan, who would want to fix everything for me.

I need Hayley.

I need my best friend. My rock. I need to sob into her shoulder. I need her to listen to the mess I've made.

I get up off the bed—dizziness makes me sway, so I take a moment to steady myself—then I reach for my purse, which is sitting in a chair by my bed. I rifle through it, grabbing my cell phone.

I call Hayley, who doesn't even know I left the apartment this morning.

She picks up on the first ring. "Katie?"

I burst into tears, heavy sobs that leave me gasping for breath.

"Katie! Oh, my God! Where are you? What's wrong?"

I cry for a minute, with Hayley encouraging me to breathe and try to calm down. And she's right. I can't faint again.

Although at least this time, I'm in a very convenient place for a fainting spell.

Finally, I can speak. I spit out the facts like a bullet list, so I can get through it.

"I broke up with AJ. I fainted. I hit my head on the sidewalk—hard. I'm in the ER."

"What hospital? I'm on my way," Hayley says, her tone direct and efficient, which is exactly what I need right now.

I know she's going to call in sick at work for me. Now the tears fall for the love I have for my best friend. My rock. The woman who will stand by my side no matter what. Who has the strength to tell me when I'm wrong and love me through it.

I wouldn't want to go through anything in life without her, my sister of choice.

The sister of my heart.

I tell her the hospital, and she assures me she will be there as soon as possible.

And it can't be soon enough.

I STOP CRYING LONG ENOUGH TO GET THE DIAGNOSIS FROM MY doctor. My headache symptoms have dissipated, but I have a grade two concussion and abrasions on my nose and forehead. Oh, and a minor fracture of my nose, which has led to fantastic bruising around my nose and eyes. I look like someone beat the hell out of me.

After she leaves, telling me to wait for my discharge papers, I allow myself to cry again. My head hurts, my nose hurts, and the skin on my forehead and nose feel like I rubbed it with sandpaper until it was raw.

But all of this will heal.

My heart, however, won't.

As I wait for Hayley to come get me, I try to focus on what

AJ accused me of. He didn't see it as me leaving him out of love, but not loving myself enough to see my value. But how can that be? I've always been a confident woman. I know I'm strong, quirky, loyal, funny, and smart. I see the person I am, and the person I will be as a lawyer. I do see my value, so how can this be true?

I wanted to give him the world. Everything he deserved. I broke up with him because I couldn't. I couldn't bear the possibility of him resenting me in three months. Fighting with me. Wishing he was somewhere else in his van with his crew instead of trying to squeeze in an hour with me at dinner, rooted to the same city all year long because of me.

I allow my brain to go somewhere very deep into my heart. It's almost as if I hear the click of the lockbox, the lid opening, and my heart revealing its deepest fear to my brain.

I was certain I would lose AJ because I didn't think the pieces of me were enough for him to love.

I didn't see whatever I could give as worthy.

And my biggest failure was my inability to see that maybe pieces of me was all AJ needed to be happy.

I saw the tired, exhausted, stressed-out Katie that I might be as unloveable.

Might.

While AJ saw that these were all parts of the woman he loved, I saw them as undesirable parts.

Parts not worthy of his love.

When in fact, the good and the bad is what makes me exactly who he loves.

I burst into tears at this thought.

Suddenly, a curtain moves, and Hayley appears. The second she sees me, she gasps.

"Oh, my God, Katie, I got here as fast as I could!" she cries, rushing to my bedside, taking my hand in hers, and squeezing it tightly.

She doesn't ask what happened. All Hayley does is hold my hand, telling me she loves me with no words.

I stare at her through my tears. "I've messed everything up."

Hayley lets go of my hand long enough to retrieve some tissues that are behind me and press them into my hand.

"Thank you," I say, anxiously wadding them up in my fist. One, because I need something to do with my nervous energy and, two, touching my face with anything hurts beyond belief.

"Do you want to tell me what happened?"

I nod. I tell Hayley everything, starting with the lunch with Gemma, her saying the things I had feared all along. I walked away from any opportunity I ever had with Gemma but knew she was right about the inevitable with AJ. That I loved him so much and thought he deserved everything and so much more. That I broke his heart right in front of his apartment building in the Navy Yard. That he called me a hypocrite. That he wanted to fight for us, but I wouldn't. That I didn't think I was worth it. How I panicked and went into anxiety and tried to speak but couldn't. And when AJ walked away, I fainted and fell face first onto the sidewalk, woke up with strangers around me, and because I hit my head hard, ended up in the ER.

Tears well in Hayley's expressive eyes, and she squeezes my hand in hers as she listens. No words are spoken outside of the ones painfully coming from my own lips.

After I finish, a nurse comes in with discharge papers and goes over instructions for treating my concussion, broken nose, and gorgeous abrasions, and then we're ready to leave.

"I'm sorry you had to miss work," I say.

"I haven't taken all my comp time from working the gala last month. I cashed in that chip," Hayley says. "But even if I didn't, I'd take an unpaid day to be here for you, Katie."

I will myself not to cry again. "I love you."

"I love you, too," Hayley says softly. "And I'm going to help you through this."

My body goes ice cold.

Help me get through a life without AJ.

I can't bear it. I can't. I know I asked for this, but I know I've made a horrific mistake by breaking up with AJ. I was stupid. Irrational. I should have talked this over with AJ first. Instead of thinking rationally about what our life could be, I chose to focus on the messiness. The worst case scenario.

As soon as we exit the ER, walking out through the electronic doors, Hayley stops and pulls out her phone.

"Do you feel okay enough to make one stop before we go home?" she asks.

I just want to go home and die, but since that's not an option, I nod.

I mean, it's not like Hayley is going to take me out to run laps or ride a roller coaster.

Roller coaster.

AJ.

The hand-drawn Coaster Katie on a latte cup.

I shift my gaze down, wondering if the rest of my life will be filled with these memories of the man who loved me, and who I didn't trust to love all the ugly parts of my life, too.

And every single memory is like a fresh knife wound in my heart.

"Hi, Lisa, this is Hayley Carter," she says, interrupting my thoughts. "How are you? Good. May I speak to Tracey, please? Okay. Thank you."

Who is she calling? Where is she going to drag me to, in the state I'm in? When emotionally I want to die and all I want to do is bawl?

"Tracey, it's Hayley. Is Dad in?"

I gasp. She's calling her dad.

One of the top divorce lawyers in DC.

"Okay. It's very important. Tell him his daughter Katie needs him," she says.

I put my hand on Hayley's arm and shake my head no. Hayley ignores me.

"Thank you," she says after a moment. "We'll be right there."

Then Hayley ends the call and begins typing on her phone.

"What did you just do?" I cry. "Your dad is too busy for this!"

"No. He's never too busy for his family. You are a daughter to him. And you need to hear another reality outside of the one Gemma presented to you," she says without ever looking up from her typing.

Sadness crushes my soul. "But it's too late," I whisper. "AJ won't get past this. I put my hands on his heart and ripped it apart, Hayley. How could he ever trust me again?"

"Because you don't turn off love like that," Hayley says matter-of-factly as she types. She finishes and drops her phone into her bag. "It's that simple. You didn't do anything that was unforgivable because you acted from your heart. AJ will see that when he calms down. Everything you did is because you love him."

I don't speak.

"Come on. We're going to see Dad. It's time to hear what a very wise lawyer, one who has been in your shoes, has to say. There's another reality. A different future. And one that can involve AJ if you are brave enough to let him back in."

CHAPTER 28

Time seems suspended in a vacuum.

My world stopped the second AJ told me goodbye, and I will never, ever get out of that awful moment in time where I was desperate to call him back but couldn't.

But as Hayley guides me through her father's law office, I know time is moving forward. I've left the ER. I'm going to talk to her father, but I won't allow myself to hope he has the answers on how to repair what I've done to AJ.

Because if I allow myself that fragile thread, the belief that maybe I can somehow undo what I've done, and Mr. Carter suggests something I know in my heart won't work, I'll be devastated beyond repair.

I'm blocking out the stares of employees as Hayley navigates her way to her father's corner office. They probably think someone attacked me and Hayley is taking me to get her father's representation.

As soon as we reach her father's office, his executive assistant gasps when I come into view and rises from her seat.

"Oh, my God," she gasps, her hand flying to her mouth.

"I'm fine," I say numbly. "I fell. Nobody hit me."

I see doubt in the woman's eyes over that story.

"It's true. I fainted and landed head first onto the sidewalk."

Hayley looks through the large, glass windows behind the assistant's desk. I can see Mr. Carter is reading on his laptop, with a gorgeous view of DC as a backdrop.

"Tracey, can you see if Dad can talk to us now?" Hayley asks.

"I know he will," the woman says, nodding.

She turns, walks to the door, and raps lightly on it. I see Mr. Carter look up, and she announces we are here. I watch as he glances through the window, and then see the horrified look on his face when he sees me.

Within seconds, he leaps out of his chair and strides directly to me.

"I fell," I say before he can say a word. "Nobody hit me, I promise."

"Come inside. Tracey, can we get some water, please?" Mr. Carter requests.

"Of course," Tracey says.

Mr. Carter puts his hand on my back and guides me to a chair in front of his desk. Hayley takes the chair next to me and reaches for my hand.

"Katie," Mr. Carter says slowly, "what happened?"

At this point, Tracey re-enters the room and, without a word, places a box of tissues and a bottle of water in front of me.

"Thank you," I murmur. Then I glance at Hayley, needing her encouragement

"Tell him everything," Hayley urges. "Dad needs to know everything to help you."

I turn and look at Mr. Carter, the man who truly has become a second father to me, and see his face is one of deep concern.

I draw a breath of air and slowly begin talking. As I do,

it's like ripping all the stitches out over an unhealed wound, and everything that was held together falls apart again. The tears well back up as I talk about our love story. How I assured myself I could make a relationship with AJ work while in law school. How we overcame AJ's worries that I didn't love him for him, but as my baseball crush. Then I get to yesterday. I begin to unravel as I talk about Gemma. About the blinders coming off over a woman I deeply admired, to not wanting to work for her, to realizing she was right about AJ.

I get choked up as I tell the worst part of the story. I painfully explain how I broke up with AJ, the accusations he made, me not valuing what I could give him and not trusting his words when he said it was more than enough.

"I broke his heart," I whisper. "I don't see how AJ will ever forgive me for not trusting him. For ending things before law school even started."

I stare at Mr. Carter, who has patiently listened to all my romantic drama as if I have the most important problem in the world to him at this moment.

"Katie, I understand why you did what you did," he says slowly.

Surprise fills me. "You do?"

"A long time ago, I was in your shoes. I was dating Hayley's mom by that point, and I had heard how law school was going to change everything. And while it did change some things, it didn't change *us*."

The thread of hope inside of me—that tiny, fragile thread —grows a bit stronger with his words.

"Gemma gave you her idea of what 1L should be, and what your life after law school should be. In her eyes. But that's not an absolute. Nothing is in life. Your experience in law school will be yours alone."

"But what about the law school curse and all the things people talk about online?" I ask, my brain needing to argue.

While I desperately want the hope Hayley's dad is offering me, I don't want it to be a false one.

"They don't know how you organize. Plan. How fast you read. How you can use a calendar to block out your study time and approach it like a job. I never pulled all-nighters because I planned for everything. You'll distribute the work, so you won't be rushing to meet deadlines. Now this approach takes a lot of discipline, but that's you, Katie. You've wanted this ever since I've known you. You *have* the discipline to do this."

I realize I'm speaking to someone who is very successful and did it the exact opposite way of Gemma.

The thread of hope grows stronger as Mr. Carter's words sink in.

"I know you've already been doing law school boot camp according to Hayley, so you already know how to tackle your reading and outlining. You're going to work smart. If you apply the schedule with what you've already learned, you will have nights free. Believe it or not," he says, a smile lighting up his face, "not only did I have most of my nights free, and we always had dinner together, but also one full day on the weekend. I usually studied from seven o'clock in the morning to one in the afternoon on Sundays, but I kept Friday night and Saturday free for Hayley's mom and our friends. Oh, and I still managed to stay in the top ten percent of my class."

I gasp. "You did?"

"Katie. This is what I want you to take from this. You have to do you," Mr. Carter says. "Just because Gemma did it one way, and you've read about the law school curse—well, that's not doing *you*. That's projecting a truth, a certainty, onto a situation that is unique to you."

With a jolt, I realize he's right.

"You have a motivation to approach law school in this way, and that's AJ," he says. "I don't see AJ as the kind of man to sit around and wait for you to come home, Katie. He's an adult with his own interests. A man who can make his own choices. And he chose you. With your schedule. With your dreams. AJ wants *this* life."

I remain silent for a moment, forcing down the lump in my throat. "I didn't think the pieces of me I could give him were enough."

Mr. Carter studies me for a moment. "Do you get AJ all the time?"

I shake my head. "No."

"He's away for stretches at a time playing baseball, correct?"

I nod.

"And don't you just get pieces of him during that time?"

I realize what Mr. Carter is getting at.

"Yes, and I'm okay with that because I know that's his job."

"Like law school is yours," he says gently. "You were so worried about disappointing him and hurting him. And I think this is the most likely reason of all: You were so afraid of this falling apart that you pushed him out of your life because you felt it was inevitable. It was going to be a fact. And I think you did this to protect yourself as well as to protect AJ."

Tears fall from my eyes. "You're right. Oh, God, I made a big mistake."

"But this is fixable," Hayley insists, squeezing my hand. "AJ loves you, Katie. All you need to do is explain why you did what you did. You didn't break up with him because you want the relationship to end. You did it because you love him. And because you undervalue what you can give him."

"Communication is going to be key going forward," Mr. Carter says. "You need to make sure you are communicating everything that is coming up, so AJ knows when you have intense periods that might require more time studying. But Katie, people have relationships while in law school.

Marriages. Children. It can work. And I know you love AJ enough to *make* this work."

"If AJ wants to get back together," I say, realizing full well that AJ might not trust me ever again after this morning.

"Where's my future lawyer?" Mr. Carter says firmly. "You're going to give up without a fight? Without any arguments? This isn't the Katie I raised. Oh, wait."

Then he winks at me.

"You have been my second father since I've known Hayley," I say, my voice wobbly.

"Then as your second father, I want you to go to AJ and make this right," he says. "If you want this, you'll have to fight for it. But it's a case you can win, Katie. I might be a divorce lawyer, but I do believe true love will always find a way."

I rise from my seat. The sadness is replaced by fire. I messed up, but it's no different than when AJ messed up a few weeks ago. We both made mistakes out of fear. In AJ's case, of my love not being based on the man he is. In my case, I didn't believe I could be enough of what he deserves.

AJ fixed his mistake.

And now it's time to fix mine.

"I'm going to find AJ," I say determinedly.

"Now that's the daughter I know," Mr. Carter says.

He rises and comes around to where I'm standing, opening his arms to me.

I hug him, pressing my cheek against the fabric of his fine dress shirt.

"I love you," I whisper.

"I love you, too," he says, squeezing me tight. He steps back from me. "One more note, on your future career. Gemma's firm is not the only one in town. In fact, the son of one of my partners is building his own employment law firm. Very small right now, but he'll need summer associates. Of course, you would come highly recommended from a firm he trusts."

I suck in a breath. A few hours ago, my world had blown apart.

Now, this thread of hope I have is stringing it back together piece by piece.

I look from Hayley to her father, the family I've chosen, and count every blessing in the world that these people are in my life.

"I can't thank you enough for being my family," I whisper.

"And we can't thank you enough for being a part of ours," Hayley says, squeezing me to her in a side hug.

I step back from her and take a breath. I don't know what AJ will say. If he will want to talk to me yet. Maybe he needs more space to calm down. Maybe he'll shove me away. I don't know what will happen.

But I refuse to let it end the way it did, with me collapsing after he walked away, never knowing the words that were in my heart.

And hopefully my apology, with a promise of a new me in the future, will be enough to bring us back together again.

CHAPTER 29

By the time we get back to our apartment building, I'm desperate to talk to AJ. I need to go to him as soon as possible and tell him everything that is in my heart. I asked Hayley to take me straight back to his place, but she urged me to come home first and rest for a bit as that is what my discharge papers say I'm supposed to be doing.

I protested. But since she was the one driving, I really didn't have much say in the matter.

She's on her phone while we ride up the elevator.

"You know I'm going to call an Uber if you don't take me to see AJ," I say firmly.

"Then why didn't you set that up already if you are? You could have had one waiting for you downstairs if you had."

Dammit.

This concussion is making me slow.

"You need to give him time to calm down," Hayley says gently, repeating herself for the one thousandth time since we left her father's office.

I sigh in exasperation. "No, I don't. I don't want him to continue thinking my last words to him were nothing. He doesn't know that I regret everything. That I want him back, and if I'm lucky enough that he will say yes, I'll never let him go. That I'm going to do law school my way, and he's going to be a part of it. Don't you see I have to do this now? Now, Hayley!"

I start unraveling at the end, panic creeping its way back in.

"Hey," Hayley says firmly, putting her hand on my wrist, "AJ will see you and understand the delay. And do you honestly think you have one big fight and that's it, strikeout? This is like a swing and a miss. You missed the mark, but you are still at the plate, Katie. You are still in this game; you've just stepped out of the batter's box for a moment to collect yourself."

I stare at her in shock. Not only is Hayley right, but she described it in perfect baseball terms.

"I'm absorbing more than you think I am," she says, raising her eyebrows at me. "And I know you. I know AJ. I know this is going to be okay."

The elevator opens on our floor.

"We need to see Barbara and Dominik first," Hayley continues. "I've been texting them updates on your condition. I knew they would want to know."

I feel fresh tears pool in my eyes. Barbara and Dominik are the other members of the family of my heart.

"I want to see them," I say, thinking of burying myself into Barbara's shoulder and crying as she comforts me. I imagine Dominik sitting down in his chair and giving me the straight-up advice I need to hear and telling me to go get on with it.

We immediately head to their apartment. Hayley raps on the door.

"Barbara? Dominik? It's Hayley and Katie, we're back from the ER," she says.

I hear Barbara and Dominik's muted voices behind the door. I know the second I see Barbara, I'll burst into tears again.

Barbara opens the door, and her hand flies to her mouth the moment she sees me.

"Katie!" she cries, horrified by my appearance. "Oh, my God!"

Before I can even take more than a step in, I'm wrapped in her arms, her rose scent and paper-thin skin enveloping me into a huge hug.

I close my eyes and breathe in her comfort. Draw from her warmth. Feel her love.

I feel her hand protectively stroke my hair, and AJ flashes through my mind. How he always loved my curls, how they were so foreign to him and so unique to me in his mind. I bite down hard on my lower lip to keep from bawling for him.

I squeeze my eyes in a desperate attempt to force the tears away, then I open them.

And I see AJ standing in Barbara's living room.

I gasp in shock, taking a step back from Barbara, my hands covering my mouth as a sob chokes out.

AJ is here.

Waiting for me.

"AJ," I say, forcing his name out.

Before I can say another word, AJ strides across the room in an instant and lifts his hands to my hair, as if he's afraid he will hurt me more if he touches my battered face.

"My God," he whispers, his voice thick as his green eyes, the ones still rimmed with red, search my own. "Katie, I'm so sorry. I had no idea you were going to faint. I never would have left you if I'd known. I'm so sorry I wasn't there to stop this. Are you sure you're okay? Maybe you should see the Soaring Eagles doctor about your concussion. In fact, I will make that happen. Let me call someone."

"No," I say shaking my head. "I don't need that. I just need you."

I hear voices and then the door open and close, but I'm only paying attention to the man standing in front of me.

The man I love.

"My body will be fine," I assure him, "but my heart is broken."

AJ's eyes fill with tears. I force myself to keep talking.

"I made a huge mistake, AJ. The biggest one of my life in thinking I was giving you more by letting you go. I should have talked to you about my fears. About the law school relationship curse. When Gemma spoke about that, I thought I was being selfish trying to keep you. I saw her words as truth, not as her own experience. You always told me the pieces of me would be enough, but I couldn't believe that."

"Katie," AJ says, his voice thick as his fingers cautiously run through my hair, "I swear to you, right here, right now, that I can deal with whatever law school throws at us. I can live with you being stressed out. Studying while I watch TV. I swear to God, I can. What I can't do is live without you," he finishes, his voice catching on the last word.

My tears fall as I watch AJ struggle with his emotions. He pauses, swallows, and after a moment, continues.

"I never should have walked away," he whispers. "Never. I should have fought for us. For you. You wouldn't have fainted if I had."

"No," I say, sliding a hand up to his face, "you were blindsided and hurt. This is all my fault. All of it. As soon as you told me it was me, my own doubts about being enough that were destroying us, it was like the truth reached up and shook me out of my fear. But I started having a panic attack, and I couldn't speak when I needed to."

AJ's eyes flash with recognition. "You mean … you wanted to stop me?"

I nod furiously. "In my head, I was screaming at you to stay. So you could hear me say I was sorry and this was a mistake."

AJ lets out an anguished breath. "Oh God, Katie."

"AJ," I say, "I had a long talk with Hayley's dad. A

successful lawyer. And I realize now that I had taken all the experiences of people I had read about online, and Gemma's, and made them into a truth. But that's not my truth. It's not going to be *our* truth."

"It's not?" he asks.

"No. I'm going to treat this like my job. I'll have work hours and non-work hours. I'm going to work strategically and methodically so we have our time together. We'll have a day on the weekends together where it's just for us. Our relationship isn't going to take second place; it will be a priority along with both our careers. I need to be with you as much as I need to be a lawyer."

AJ swallows hard, as if he's trying to hold all his emotions together. I continue with what I have to say.

"AJ, if you will take me back, I promise it won't matter where you end up playing baseball; I will make this work. You are the man I love. You are the only man I'll love, even if you are across the country. I will take you in pieces rather than live without you."

AJ wrinkles his nose. "What are you talking about?"

"If you end up signing with another team," I say.

He shakes his head. "I'm not going anywhere."

"But earlier you said you didn't know where you'd end up," I say. "I know Los Angeles and Seattle want you. They will give you more money."

"I told my agent to get the deal with Washington done," AJ says, his fingers caressing my hair. "The money doesn't matter. Being with you does."

I gasp at his admission. "When did you tell him this?"

"After we went to Thrill Kingdom."

My heart is pounding.

"I knew after that night you were The One," AJ continues in a whisper. "I have money, Katie. I don't care how much more I can get. I will take less to stay here. To stay with the team I love. More importantly, to stay with the woman I love."

I can't speak. I can't.

"Katie, you're it. You are. With you, I don't feel the need to travel for months on end. Moving was all I knew. But then I met you, and now I know I want a home. With you. With the crew. I want these roots, ones I never wanted before. That was before I fell in love with you."

"I want that more than anything," I whisper.

AJ slides his hands to my waist, drawing me into his body. He places the gentlest of kisses on my lips, one full of tenderness.

Of love.

AJ lifts his head. "I love you."

"I love you so much more. And no matter what comes our way, I'm not shoving you away. Never again, I promise."

"I'm going to hold you to that, Counselor."

I smile as I put my hands over his heart.

"That's yours, Katie. I have never given my heart to anyone. I had to find you to find love," he whispers.

"I love you, Andrew Joseph," I say again.

"I know you do," he says. "Dominik pointed out that all of your actions were driven by a deep love for me, even if they were wrong."

"How did you end up here, anyway?" I ask, gazing up at him.

AJ stares down at me. "I called Dominik after I calmed down. I told him I knew you loved him like a grandfather, that he knew you as well as you knew yourself, and I asked him how I could convince you that our love could get through law school because I wasn't going to share my life with anyone else."

My heart is in my throat as I process his words.

AJ wanted me back as soon as he walked away.

I begin crying again. "I'm so lucky to have you."

"Dominik told me anything you did was because you were scared. That you were stubborn, but you also loved me. And that love would win in the end because we were meant to be together. Then he told me to trust him because he knows what's up," AJ says, smiling.

I smile through my tears. "He does."

"While we were talking, Hayley texted Barbara, and that's when I found out about the accident," AJ says, the smile evaporating and his face going pale. "It was all I could do not to rush over there, but Hayley told Barbara that you were already being discharged and to come here to wait for you."

I have a flashback to Hayley being on her phone in the ER, and now I know what she was doing. And why she wanted to come straight back here instead of taking me to the Navy Yard.

"These were the longest hours of my life," AJ says. "I was so worried about you, sweetheart. You have no idea the thoughts that went through my head. And I vowed I'd fight with everything I had to make you see that we need to be together. I don't care if the world says we are going to fail; I know we won't."

"We aren't," I promise him. "This is it."

"I'm going to marry you," AJ promises. "And we'll have a kid crew in addition to the dog crew."

My heart—which was in pieces just before I walked in the door—now has more joy than I have ever known.

"Our own baseball team?" I ask, grinning at him.

AJ winks at me. "At least three."

"I'm good with three."

"We'll need to practice a lot once you are better. So when that time comes, we know exactly what to do," AJ suggests with a devilish, sexy smile.

"Shall I draw up a contract?" I offer.

AJ laughs. "Yes, Counselor. You may put that in the contract. Binding. Unbreakable. And forever."

As he lowers his lips to mine for another gentle kiss, I let that last word linger in my head.

We'll have bad days and good days and days when I might not be where I want to be because of school, but AJ will have those same days because of baseball. Our schedules will be crazy, but they make up the people we are. I wouldn't want AJ any other way, just as I know he wants me the way I am, too.

Forever.

And that is one contract I'll happily sign on the dotted line.

EPILOGUE

November 27th
Washington DC

I bend over the vintage recipe printout, following the directions to finish the pumpkin pie I'm making for Thanksgiving tomorrow.

Thanksgiving. I can't believe it's already here.

I pause for a moment, looking around the colonial row house that is my home now. On this blustery, cold autumn day, I have pumpkin-scented candles lit around the living room and the kitchen. I have put fall-themed pillows on our sofa, and filled white ceramic pitchers with vibrant branches with colored leaves. I have throws draped over the back of the couch, in easy reach for when I'm reading or snuggling on the sofa. Our dog crew is sleeping happily in front of the roaring fire.

This home is perfect, I think, taking in the view. But not for all the reasons I listed.

This home is perfect because it's the one I share with AJ.

I smile as I fold the Cool Whip into the pumpkin mixture,

perfecting my 1970s pie filling before spooning it into the crust.

The day we got back together was the day that cemented our forever. AJ didn't hesitate to ask me if I wanted to live with him. I never hesitated in my answer. He suggested we rent a place near Georgetown, as it would be convenient for me to get to campus—and to maximize our time together.

We spent August scouring for places and found this corner townhouse, one built in 1900. Our little house is on a cobblestone street lined with trees and is steps away from Georgetown. As soon as we entered this house, all pristine white and updated with stainless appliances, hardwood floors, exquisite molding and a fireplace in the living room, we didn't waste a second to sign the lease. I don't think I've had a happier moment in my life than when AJ took the keys to our new place, opened the door, and carried me inside as if we had gotten married.

It's our home. All eighteen-hundred square feet shared with our Great Dane crew.

It worked out perfectly, because Brody was able to break his lease and move in with Hayley, so they are living together, too.

As I think of my best friend, I remember the conversation Hayley's father had with me that horrible July day when I broke up with AJ. His advice was right. Just as Hayley's father predicted, I found I *can* manage the workload. In the beginning, I was getting a handle on law school, and the Soaring Eagles were headed for the end of the season and the playoffs. AJ and I communicated about our pressures and stresses and what we each needed. We worked together to balance baseball and law school the best we could.

The Soaring Eagles were eliminated in the postseason, which crushed not only AJ but me, too. I could see the team cracking under the pressure, and as I sat in the stands with Hayley, holding out hope they could somehow pull this out, we watched them lose at home for their final game of the year.

As soon as the season was over, AJ was rewarded with a massive multi-year contract that made my jaw drop. Our financial future was always bright, but now we'll never have to worry about anything. AJ, through his foundation, has already handed over big checks to Great Dane rescue organizations, non-profit veterinary services, and baseball programs for underprivileged children in celebration of his new deal.

After the season ended, AJ didn't find himself alone in DC. Brody stayed to be with Hayley. Chase McLeary opted to remain as well. They work out together in the mornings and often grab lunch afterward. Or hang out and play video games, go to movies, go fishing, etc. I love that AJ has his closest friends in town, and while I'm at school and Hayley is working, the guys have their own time together.

I open the refrigerator, retrieve my pie off the counter, and slip it inside so it can chill. I bite my lip as I shut the door. Hannah dumped Chase right after the season—and after she had loads of selfies of her being a Soaring Eagles girlfriend slapped all over Instagram. According to AJ, Chase was devastated, but decided to stay in DC despite the fact that he could easily go back to Arizona, where he's from. I think the three of them are determined to work together during the offseason with the focus of making it to the championship next year.

Because I treat law school like a job, I still carve out time for Hayley and Addison. We'll meet up for dinner or coffee. Get pedicures. Go shopping. I make sure we do this at least once a month, and of course, we always have our group chat on WhatsApp, so I talk to them daily.

Now Barbara and Dominik, on the other hand, I see every Tuesday. They come over in the morning, and while Dominik and AJ take the dogs for a walk, Barbara makes us prepared meals for the week, cooking in our kitchen. When I come home for lunch, I'm always treated to something amazing that day, and we all sit down and eat together. It's the biggest gift she could give me, doing the cooking like this to save me time, which Barbara says she loves.

So Barbara asks us what we'd like to eat, gives us a shopping list, and we have everything ready for her when she comes over. Then she takes over, which we are both grateful for.

The future I was afraid of—not having any spare time, driving AJ away, not seeing my family and friends—hasn't happened. I'm working harder than I ever have, reading and studying and outlining the most complex material I've ever had to digest, but I'm happy.

And all those fears I had of AJ getting bored? Those never materialized either. Between his friends and his dogs and his own interests, AJ has acclimated just fine to having a home here in DC.

With me, I think happily.

Meg is still with stupid Whitaker, both in their final year of school. After that crap he pulled at the Fourth of July party, I have had to fight every urge not to grab Meg, shake her by the arms, and scream YOU DESERVE BETTER at the top of my lungs. When I vented this to AJ one night as we lay in bed, he stroked my hair and told me to fight that urge, that his gut told him they weren't going to last. He knew I wanted to be there for Meg when that happened, and thought if I interfered now, it would simply drive a wedge between us when there didn't need to be.

Well, Meg hasn't woken up to what a jerk Whitaker is yet, but I know AJ's right. And I'll be there to help her pick up the pieces when she does.

As far as our families go, my parents adore AJ and quickly saw that our love is real. That we are a team, that we are the best versions of ourselves because of each other. AJ's family flew in for the playoffs, and I sat with them at two games. They are nice people who embraced me completely, as did his sister, Lindsay. I have a break over Christmas, so we are going to spend it with them in Ohio, where they are living now.

I have so much to be thankful for this Thanksgiving, I think.

I hear the key turn in the front door, and I know AJ is back from the errand he said he had to run. The dogs run to the door, barking, and I smile, as the crew is always just as eager to see him come home as I am.

"Counselor, I'm home," AJ calls out good-naturedly.

I smile at the sound of his voice. "In the kitchen making pie with Cool Whip!"

I hear that low-throated chuckle of his, and my heart dances happily inside my chest.

I hear the dogs and AJ coming down the hall, and I see him walking toward me, carrying a box in his hands.

"I thought you were running out to get wine tonight for our Friendsgiving," I say.

"I got sidetracked, but I promise I'll go out and get it before Brody and Hayley come over for dinner."

"So where have you been?" I ask, eyeing him suspiciously.

"Getting something for you," AJ says, handing me the box. "Careful, it's kind of heavy."

I take the wrapped white box with a large red bow on it. It *is* heavy. I immediately set it on the granite countertop.

"You brought me a present?" I ask, touched by this sweet, unexpected gesture.

"It's almost Thanksgiving. It's to show you how thankful I am for you," AJ says, his green eyes burning brightly at me.

"You are already the only gift I need," I say, touching his face with my hand. AJ hasn't shaved, and his stubble feels wonderfully rough against my hand.

"While I love that sentiment," AJ says, taking my hand and pressing a kiss onto my open palm, "I think you'll love this gift."

"May I open it?"

"Yes, I want you to."

I eagerly untie the bow, then carefully unwrap the paper. I gasp as I see what AJ has given me.

"AJ! A collection of vintage recipe cards!" I cry happily.

I lift the clear top off, my fingertips eagerly scanning the indexes of these recipes from the seventies.

"This is so exciting. A complete set?"

"A complete set. With a bonus."

I stop flicking cards. "What bonus?"

"Go to the last index."

I glance down at the last index tab in the box. There's no label on it. I see a card and pull it up. There's a picture of ice cream in a Soaring Eagles helmet, and at the top it reads:

Reception Menu for the Wedding of Katie McKenna and Andrew Joseph Williamson

I stare it in confusion. Wait. What?

Reception?

Wedding.

I stare up at AJ as my hand begins shaking.

"I took the liberty to come up with a suggested menu on the back," AJ says.

I flip the card over:

First Course: Cinnamon rolls, scones, coffee with cream

Second Course: Ice cream sundae as big as your head

Third Course: Empanadas

Fourth Course: Frittata and waffles

Fifth Course: Clam puffs, meatloaf dumplings, perogies

Sixth Course: Wedding cake

I'm trembling all over. These are all meals we shared when we first started dating. I drop the card in shock.

"Katie," AJ says, taking my hand in his, "I knew by the second course you were the woman I'd marry someday."

Oh. My. God.

Everything feels surreal as AJ retrieves a box from his coat pocket. He drops down on one knee in front of me. AJ opens the velvet box and shows me a gorgeous oval emerald ring, set in diamonds.

"Katie McKenna," AJ says softly, "the thing I am most grateful for this Thanksgiving is you. I love you. You are my home. Will you be my wife? Will you marry me?"

An excited squeal escapes my throat, and AJ laughs.

"You're not going to faint, are you?"

I shake my head. "No. And the answer is yes. YES. Yes, I will marry you!"

AJ grins and slips the ring on my finger. It's breathtakingly unique and reminds me of the color of his eyes.

AJ rises, and I jump into his arms, wrapping my arms and legs around him as we both laugh. My lips find his, kissing him over and over and over.

AJ sets me down. I put my hands on his black overcoat, staring at my ring in shock.

We're engaged.

"Katie. I know law school is your priority, and you don't need the distraction of planning a wedding. We will get married when you're done."

I nod. "I like that idea."

"When I asked your dad for your hand, I assured him that was the priority," AJ says firmly. "I will keep my word on that not only to him, but to you."

I fight back tears at his thoughtfulness, not only toward me, but also toward my parents.

"I know I should have waited to propose," AJ says, "but Katie, I was looking at you on the couch a few weeks ago and you were reading. It was us and the dogs and I've never felt such a peace. Secure. Grounded. You didn't even lift your eyes from the page, but you reached over and began playing with my hair, as if to say, 'I'm here and I love you.'"

He pauses, and I see he's getting choked up.

"I was home," AJ says, his voice thick. "You were my home. I wanted you to know that. To have this ring and know you have my heart."

My heart swells with emotion as I hear his words. I begin to get choked up, too.

"You are my home, AJ," I say. "I love you, Andrew Joseph."

His eyes glimmer with unshed tears when he hears his name.

"I'm glad I was the player on your bulletin board," he whispers.

I smile. "Me too."

As AJ kisses me, I know I'm safe at home.

For the rest of my life.

THE END

Wondering what happens with Addison? Look for her to find her own love story in *A Complete Game*, coming Autumn 2019.

ALSO BY AVEN ELLIS

If you enjoyed this book, you might enjoy my other romantic comedies:

Connectivity

Surviving The Rachel

Chronicles of a Lincoln Park Fashionista

Waiting For Prince Harry (Dallas Demons #1)

The Definition of Icing (Dallas Demons #2)

Breakout (Dallas Demons #3)

On Thin Ice (Dallas Demons #4)

Playing Defense (Dallas Demons #5)

The Aubrey Rules (Chicago on Ice #1)

Trivial Pursuits (Chicago on Ice #2)

Save the Date (Chicago on Ice #3)

The Bottom Line (Chicago on Ice #4)

Hold the Lift (Rinkside in the Rockies Novella)

Sugar and Ice (Rinkside in the Rockies #1)

Reality Blurred (Rinkside in the Rockies #2)

A Royal Shade of Blue (Modern Royals Series #1)